The Front Nine

The Front Nine

By

Tate Volino

Cover photo by Tate Volino.

ISBN 13: 978-0615952765
ISBN 10: 0615952763

ALCHEMY BOOK, LLC

This book is dedicated to the game of golf. Thank you for all of the joy and pain.

Special thanks to:

Ken and Tricia Eales
Dick Angelotti

Also by Tate Volino

Gold Albatross
Pull the Pin
Ilium Way #11

The Front Nine
A Collection of Stories

1. The Greens Reaper

"Quiet down! Quiet down! I'm bringing the meeting to order. Quiet!" Phil Delome bellowed. Finally the murmurs ran dry. "Now listen, we have a lot to talk about and a lot of different opinions. Everybody should have a voice, but we need to do it in an orderly fashion. If people start interjecting or arguing when it's not their turn I will use my authorized power and oust you from the meeting. Clear?"

There was a slight return of low voices, but when Phil glared around the room it ceased instantly. He looked upon the faces of his fellow members and friends. He saw a variety of expressions, though most were some combination of fear and anger. The Peninsula Club had been their common bond for decades. They had full control and could run it as they pleased. Now, like many other clubs, they were being forced to adapt to new realities in the marketplace. Other old line clubs had accumulated war chests over the past few years and were plowing the dollars into their courses and facilities. At the other end of the spectrum were brand new, high-end clubs that were attracting the nouveau riche from the city. Helipads were now a required amenity. The Peninsula Club's members had money, but were afraid to put those dollars into a sinking ship. They were facing a catch twenty-two where they needed new blood in order to upgrade, but had to upgrade in order to entice new blood.

"I have a number of proposals to present tonight. However, as you all know, we simply can't afford to do everything at once. What we need to do first is set our priorities. Therefore, based upon the input from other board members I've broken our choices into four main categories: greens, fairways, clubhouse/landscaping, and expansion into sports such as tennis. I've asked board subcommittees to prepare a ten minute summary on each one, which they'll now present. It will include the cost, timeframe, and scope of the various projects. Once they've finished I will take a preliminary vote to see where support lies. If possible we'll winnow the list down further and reexamine the surviving choices in greater depth. Any questions?"

He was floored that there weren't any. "Alright, being none, I'll go ahead and turn the floor over to our vice president who will start with the clubhouse report."

Phil was glad to hand things off for the moment and stepped down from the dais to get some fresh air. He walked out a nearby door and was greeted by the cool, spring breeze. The first thought he had was: *I should just leave now. How did I get stuck right in the middle of this storm swirling around the club?* He knew he couldn't leave, however, there were too many people relying on him to guide them out of this valley. He leaned on the railing and peered west across the Long Island Sound at the lights of New York City. The gleam of the distant buildings reached out across the dark water toward him. Out of a city of millions all he needed was fifty good, new members. That would give him an infusion of cash and all of the breathing room he would need for the remainder of his term. After that someone else could deal with the headaches. Maybe that would happen soon, but tonight all he had were the members currently filling the room behind him.

He heard the door open and his wife appeared. She stepped up next to him and put her arm around him. Staring out toward the Sound she said, "You're doing a great job in there. They all believe in you and everyone knows this is going to work out."

"I'm not so sure, Sandra. We're in serious trouble. We've been cutting back on expenses year after year and now all of sudden it has come back to bite us. The course has suffered and now we are being forced to be reactive instead of proactive. Current members and potential new ones can sense that. We're not fighting from a position of strength."

"I understand, dear. Just do the best you can. That's all anyone can ask of you."

"Thanks," he said, taking hold of her hand.

They remained there in silence for another ten minutes before heading back into the meeting room.

Phil returned to his chair and waited patiently until the final report concluded.

"Alright, thank you, gentlemen, for handling those topics. What I'm going to do is ask for a show of hands to see where we stand. Who is in favor of starting with the clubhouse?"

Only a few hands appeared.

"Fairways?"

Again, only a couple of votes.

"Expansion?"

Only one vote. That gentleman looked around and, seeing he was alone, quickly withdrew his hand.

Phil felt emboldened. He was fully in favor of focusing on the greens and had been lobbying hard to persuade others. Now it appeared that they might have a consensus.

"And finally," Phil said with faux anticipation. "Greens?"

A forest of arms sprung up across the room. It was at least ninety percent. The members looked at each other and seemed very pleased. Someone started a low chant. "Greens, greens, greens," and it quickly built. Soon the others who had voted for the optional projects also raised their hands. "Greens, greens, greens."

"Enough," Phil said, holding up his hands to quell the uprising. "I think it is safe to say we have a mandate. I must say that it gives me a warm feeling inside to see a level of unity like I haven't seen in a while here at The Peninsula Club. More than anything else, that is what we need to return to greatness.

From here we can move forward with haste and determination. We will fine tune the proposals for renovating the greens and select the best contractor as soon as possible. We will keep you posted on our progress and look forward to showing you our results. Thank you and good night. I move to adjourn the meeting."

"Seconded!" blurted a number of the board members in unison. They all knew better than to throw away the goodwill that was surging through the room. If they were to allow any questions it could trigger a shift in the mood and suddenly the environment could turn hostile.

On his way out, Phil received more congratulatory handshakes and pats on the back than ever before in his tenure. He moved steadily toward his car, again hoping to avoid being dragged into any detailed discussions about what was going to happen. He made it safely to his car where Sandra was already waiting in the driver's seat.

"Was I supposed to pick you up in the getaway car in front?" she joked.

"No, this is fine. Now drive!" he said with mock urgency.

She meandered out of the parking lot at idle speed, waving to friends as they went. It was a slow motion escape. Once they were back on the main road she asked, "Are you excited, Phil?"

"Yes, and scared to death. I hope this will work. I really think it will, but there are so many variables to consider. So many things that could go wrong."

Two weeks later, Phil was still riding his wave of support. He was at the club everyday even if he wasn't playing golf. In fact, he had been so busy he normally only had time for nine-hole rounds. There was a sense of optimism and enthusiasm that was lifting the members and staff. Phil, however, was a realist and knew the next few months was his swiftly closing window of opportunity.

It was a crisp Friday morning and Phil stretched as he climbed out of his Cadillac parked in the reserved spot near the clubhouse entrance. Phil was a big, burly man. At his peak he'd been six feet four inches, though age was starting to scale back that height a little with each year that passed. He maintained a full head of hair that had transformed from a youthful, sandy blond to a mature, snow white.

From behind his silver rimmed glasses, he scanned the front of the clubhouse as he always did, noting lots of little imperfections that needed attention. Overall it was still a marvelous Georgian-style structure, but regular coats of paint could only do so much. Nonetheless, he knew his attention needed to be elsewhere right now.

Today was an important day. They had quickly narrowed down the companies they were considering and were down to the final two. A team from the club led by Phil would be meeting with each of the finalists this morning and then hopefully signing a contract by day's end. It was a major first step and it would ensure that dirt on the course would start moving before the end of the month.

While ascending the broad front steps, Phil saw the doors fly open and the club's general manager, Mitch Evans, emerged in a frenzy. Mitch was stocky with curly, gray hair. He was very energetic and talked with his hands, even when he wasn't actually speaking.

"Phil, we've got a big problem."

Phil stopped and tried to determine what might be coming. He kept a calm demeanor on the outside as his internal nervous system prepared for a jolt.

"And what might that be?"

"Clyde isn't here. We can't locate him anywhere. There's no answer on his phone. We called his wife and she said he left as he normally does this morning. I've even had a couple of the guys backtrack the routes toward his house to see if there was a car accident or something. What should we do? Agronomy Concepts will be here in an hour."

Phil considered the situation silently. This was odd as Clyde Jarrett, Peninsula's superintendent, was the most reliable member of the staff. He had arrived at the club six days a week at five a.m. sharp for years. Phil had started referring to him as "the magician" because he had been able to consistently do more with less, due to a regularly shrinking budget. *Where in the world could he be?* One idea that quickly popped into Phil's head was the fact that Clyde hadn't had a raise in years. Perhaps he was upset that new funds would be going to outside firms while he was forced to stay at the same pay level. Still, skipping today's meeting just didn't seem like a tactic that Clyde would employ.

"Alright, let's go inside and see what we can figure out. Hopefully it's nothing serious and either he'll make it here or maybe join us by phone."

Inside the conference room Phil found two of the other team members paralyzed by fear. They both were belittled by the vast, walnut table before them.

"What do we do, Phil?" asked Marge Stapleton as soon as he entered. Her tone sounded as though the sky was preparing to fall.

"Yes, what do we do?" echoed Joe Marist, sounding just as certain of their imminent demise.

"Relax," Phil said reassuringly. He knew he was going to have to be the voice of reason today.

"But Clyde *has* to be here for these meetings," Marge continued. "He knows all of the technical information regarding the grasses and chemicals and drainage..."

"Look, Marge, we're now all pretty well versed in those things as well. We won't be flying blind. We can still make a well informed decision if we have to."

"I don't feel comfortable making a choice this important without him," Joe said. Phil could tell that Joe was already seeking to cover his ass. Joe didn't want to be on the hook for making the call without Clyde if something ended up going wrong.

"Don't worry yourself, Joe," Phil said condescendingly. "I'll take the heat if necessary."

Joe crossed his arms and sat back in his seat looking hurt.

"What do you want to do, Mitch?" Phil asked, turning to the one team member he thought he could rely on.

"I don't know, Phil," Mitch said pensively. "There's a lot riding on this – potentially the survival of the club. And Clyde is a big part of that. I'm fully in support of you and will do everything I can if you still want to make a final decision today."

Phil evaluated the circumstances he was facing. He didn't want his desire to show strength clouding his ability to make a good decision. He was confident in his level of knowledge, but knew that Clyde was the expert. If something unusual came up it could lead to bigger problems down the road. He scanned the wall and was struck by all of the framed pictures of holes on the course taken at a time when the greens looked magnificent.

"What about this? Let's see if we can get both companies to give us a few more days. That should be a reasonable request. We'll simply tell them that we need a little more time to prepare."

"That's a wonderful idea," said a relieved Marge.

Both Mitch and Joe nodded their heads in agreement.

"Alright, Mitch, let's get them on the phone so they can save the trip out here."

Phil was pleased that both companies were willing to give them an additional week. He now had until next Friday to locate Clyde and stay on track.

***

It quickly became apparent that seven days might not be enough. Clyde had simply vanished from the face of the Earth. Last Friday, he had pulled his truck out of his garage in the dark and now there was no trace of the man or the vehicle. Clyde's wife had contacted the police who began a routine missing persons investigation. Phil and several members had called in to express the urgency of the case, but finding a middle-aged man that had driven off somewhere was not a priority. They didn't issue "Amber Alerts" for people like Clyde.

Phil and Mitch did their best to form a volunteer search party. Clyde's house was only fifteen miles from The Peninsula Club and there were only a few routes he could have taken. They searched the roads for any sign of a vehicle driving off the side and inquired at local businesses along the way. They found nothing. One member recruited his grandson who dove in lakes for golf balls. However, the map only showed a few small lakes in the area that a truck could feasibly reach and they wouldn't even know where to begin.

The news had of course spread like wildfire through the membership with the conspiracy theory fringe sending a slew of emails guessing at Clyde's whereabouts. Phil could sense the animosity building as Friday approached. On Thursday night Phil and Mitch made the decision to move forward. They simply couldn't wait any longer. They would do the best they could with the support of Clyde's far less experienced staff.

***

The team was once again gathered in the conference room on Friday morning waiting for the first company to arrive when Mitch's cell phone rang.

"Hello?"

"Mitch, this is Dale Camden from Agronomy Concepts calling," said the voice.

"Let me put you on speaker," Mitch said, tapping the screen and setting his phone on the table as the others gathered nearer.

"It sounds like you are all there already," Camden said.

"Yes, we are. Are you still coming?"

"Well, I've got some bad news unfortunately. We're going to have to withdraw from your bidding," Camden answered, stunning everyone in the room. "We've been working on a bid for another club and they engaged us yesterday. As you know, we are a smaller player so we simply can't start two jobs this size at the same time. All I can tell you is that if you do put it off for a few months we hope you'd still consider us. I do apologize."

There was a moment of silence as the team members traded glances.

Phil finally spoke, "We understand, Dale. It's our fault for not closing the deal last week. No hard feelings. We liked what you had to offer and will come back to you if things change. Take care."

Mitch hung up and they sat staring at the table without a word. Finally, Phil stood up from his chair and put his hands forcefully on the table top.

"Hey, guys. The good news is that really makes our decision a lot easier. I'm going out to the range to hit some golf balls. I'll see you all back here right after lunch," he said and then walked out.

***

That afternoon Phil was feeling more relaxed knowing the weight of the decision had been lifted. Their plan was to meet with TurfTec and then move forward as if nothing else had changed.

The meeting went well and at the end Phil asked TurfTec's representative, Larry Odom, for their commitment sheet.

"There is one issue on here that we do need to talk about," Odom said casually.

"What's that?" Phil inquired.

"We had to make some adjustments to our pricing structure."

"Adjustments?"

"Let me show you. There are a couple of line item changes, but basically it boils down to a fifteen percent price increase."

"Fifteen percent higher?" Phil said, worried that his eyeballs had just bulged out against his glasses.

"Yes, unfortunately we've had some supplier price increases announced this week so we have to pass those along."

"Okay. Anything else?" Phil asked.

"Nope. That's it. Let us know if you have any other questions. Otherwise you can sign the commitment and fax or image it over. As you know, everything is locked in for five business days."

"Thanks, Larry. We'll let you know one way or the other before that."

The group stood up and shook hands before the TurfTec contingent departed. The Peninsula team remained in the conference room.

"Shit! What do we do?" Marge asked, surprising the others with her profanity.

"I'm not sure we have a choice now," Mitch concluded.

"You're right," Phil said. "If we start going back out to other companies we are going to lose weeks of work time. Mitch, do you think they knew about Agronomy Concepts and that's why they up-priced us?"

"Pretty likely. I'm almost certain that Agronomy Concepts is working with Burlington Country Club. It's a small enough industry that they find out quickly what everyone else is doing. They probably knew that they had us on the ropes and could squeeze a little more out of us. Besides, TurfTec is a much larger entity and can be more selective about their jobs. They've got some new course construction work so our deal isn't as big of a project."

"I'm not happy about it, but here we are. I say we do it," Phil said, looking at the others.

"Okay," said Marge.

"I approve," added Joe.

"Let's do it," said Mitch. "Do you want to go ahead and sign and send it out now?"

Phil thought for a moment.

"We probably should. But let's wait until Monday. We've got five days and I don't want them to think we are too desperate."

"Sounds good," Mitch said, appreciating Phil's strategy.

***

Sunday mornings were normally quiet at the club, with many members attending church and then playing in the afternoon. Phil decided it would be a good time to sneak in a round without too great of a chance of conflict.

The night before he'd sent out a broadcast email message to the membership indicating that they were going to select TurfTec for the greens renovation. He decided to be fully transparent with the members and informed them of the higher than anticipated pricing. It was still within their approved budget and he warned that waiting any longer could lead to even higher costs.

Phil had just joined up with a friend on the third hole when he noticed another cart racing toward them. It certainly didn't look like someone who wanted to join them to play.

As the cart came closer, Phil could see that the driver was Jimmy Debrano. He was an acquaintance, but not a close friend.

"Good morning, Jimmy."

"Hey, Phil. Sorry to interrupt your round, but I have something really important to tell you."

Phil immediately thought the worst and worried what this could be about.

"No problem. We're just hacking it around out here. What is it?"

"I talked to a buddy of mine and he knows a guy that can help us with our greens. He says this guy has worked at some top courses and done really well. My pal mentioned The Peninsula Club and the guy said he could fix our greens and do it for less. I saw your email yesterday and was hoping we could still talk to this guy first."

"Well, I appreciate the offer, but we're really past that stage now, Jimmy."

"It wouldn't hurt just to talk to him though. Maybe he has some ideas that could save us some money elsewhere."

Phil had resigned himself to the fact that they would be moving forward with TurfTec. However, their price increase at the end was still bothering him. The other issue was that they still likely needed a new superintendent. Perhaps this gentleman would be interested in that role.

"I'll tell you what, Jimmy. Give me his name and number and I'll call him tomorrow and hear his story."

"Great, thanks, Phil. Here you go," Jimmy said, handing Phil a scrap of paper from his pocket.

Phil examined it and saw the name, Gryphen Reed.

"Play well," Jimmy said and then drove off.

***

The decision team was gathered around the fax machine in the main office and Phil ceremoniously hit the "send" button. They watched as the machine swallowed the commitment letter that Phil and Joe, the club's secretary, had freshly signed and dated.

"We're on our way," Phil said proudly.

The group dispersed and Phil followed Mitch back to his office. He closed the door and both men sat down.

"So this is the guy I wanted to talk to you about," Phil said, handing the paper with the name and the number on it to Mitch. "Ever heard of him?"

Mitch read it and thought for a few seconds.

"Gryphen Reed? Nope, doesn't ring any bells. I'd remember a name like that."

"I didn't want to say anything to the others, but I thought we could give him a call. I don't see him fixing our greens alone, but we can at least see if he could be an interim superintendent."

"Sure, we might as well," Mitch said, hitting the speakerphone and dialing the number.

"Yes?"

"Hi, is this Gryphen Reed?"

"Speaking."

"This is Mitch Evans and Phil Delome calling from The Peninsula Club."

"What can I do for you gentleman?"

10

Phil replied, "One of our members, Jimmy Debrano, had given me your contact information and asked that I give you a call. We're preparing to rebuild our greens and have engaged a contractor to begin that work. We may be in need of an interim superintendent. Is that something you might be interested in?"

"I can help you with your greens. Greens are my specialty."

"Do you think you can work with an outside contractor?"

"If you go with my approach you won't need them," Reed said confidently.

Phil and Mitch exchanged quizzical glances.

"What do you mean?" Phil asked.

"I can fix your greens and do it better and faster. Perhaps I could come by this afternoon to meet you in person and give you my proposal and references?"

Phil again looked to Mitch and raised his eyebrows.

Mitch mouthed the words, "I'll be here."

"Well, okay, maybe three o'clock," Phil suggested.

"I look forward to meeting you."

Mitch hung up and held up his hands.

"That was kind of strange."

"I'd say so," Phil agreed. "But I can't wait to meet him."

***

Mitch was standing by his window peering out over the eighteenth green when Phil entered the office shortly before three o'clock. Phil walked over and joined him.

"I think that's him," Mitch said, pointing at the lone man pacing around the edge of the green. Gryphen Reed was average in size, but looked physically strong. His thick arms and broad chest were the result of manual labor rather than hours spent in the gym. His tanned skin almost seemed to glow in the afternoon sun.

They watched intently as the man examined the putting surface from different angles. Randomly he would bend down and run his fingers across the grass. He tugged at it in a few spots and then appeared to put some in his mouth.

"Did he just eat some grass?" Phil asked.

"I think he did. I'm not sure that's safe for human consumption. We put a lot of chemicals on there."

As he was speaking, the man turned and looked up toward their window. Phil stepped back uncomfortably.

"Don't worry, he can't see us. It's bright out and there's too much tint on the windows."

Phil wasn't so sure. The man seemed to nod at them before walking toward the clubhouse.

"Here he comes."

The receptionist ushered Mr. Reed into Mitch's office and they shook hands before taking seats at a small conference table in the corner.

"Thank you for coming in Mr. Reed," Phil said. "Let me preface this by saying I'm not sure we actually have a job available. We have been very involved with the process of selecting a firm for our greens and then about a week ago our superintendent went missing."

"That's unfortunate," Gryphen said, appearing unconcerned.

"What we're trying to accomplish is to begin rejuvenating our club and course by starting with the greens. What we may need is someone with turf expertise to help us manage the process. It's been so hectic that you are the first person we've been able to talk to. I'm sure you know we'll have to interview other candidates as well."

"I honestly don't think you'll need to do that."

"Sorry?" Phil said, somewhat surprised at Gryphen's remark.

"I'll make this easy, gentleman. I understand your *process* and I can easily see the situation you are in. I'm confident that I can solve your problems. I can do it faster, with less down time, and for less than TurfTec is going to charge you." He handed them a one page timeline and budget summary with a bold figure at the bottom. It was less than half of what they were going to pay TurfTec and the job would be completed in a shorter time period. "Here is my resume and some references. I have proprietary methods and products and, therefore, prefer to work alone."

Phil was again caught off guard by the mention of TurfTec. They hadn't told him who they'd chosen. *How did he know that? Maybe Jimmy had told him.*

"I applaud your confidence; however, we've just engaged TurfTec today. So that's not going to change," Phil stated.

"You can rescind that."

"We can?"

"Sure, you've got seventy-two hours to unilaterally exit the agreement."

Phil and Mitch were suddenly considering something that they almost couldn't believe. They didn't know what to say to Gryphen's proposal. They flipped through his resume and references. The few courses that Mitch did recognize were ultra-exclusive.

"It looks like you move around quite a bit," Mitch observed.

"I like to travel and see different areas. It's a challenge to work in varying climates and conditions."

Mitch tilted his head to acknowledge that it seemed logical.

"I'm sure you gentlemen have a lot on your plates so I'll let you get back to it," Gryphen said, standing up to leave. "I'm flexible in terms of time, but can start right away. You're real deadline is the seventy-two hours on your commitment. Contact me if you'd like to move forward." He shook their hands and departed.

They waited for a moment and then discussed what had transpired.

"Wow! That was interesting," Mitch said, still in disbelief.

"I know! I've never had an interview like that before."

"So what are you thinking, Phil?"

"I don't know what to think. I hate to admit it, but I'm actually giving him some serious thought. Look at that price and timeline. Do you think it's legitimate?"

"Who knows? If it is I don't know how we couldn't give it real consideration."

"Maybe they know," Phil said, pointing to the reference list sitting on the table in front of them.

"Let's find out," Mitch said. He grabbed the page and hustled over to his desk. He dialed the first number for a course located in Colorado.

"Hi, is this, Rick Covey? This is Mitch Evans calling from The Peninsula Club out on Long Island, New York."

"What can I do for you?"

"I'm calling about a gentleman we are considering for a position here at the course. His name is Gryphen Reed."

"Oh, Gryphen. Really? He's all the way out there?"

"Yes, he said he likes to travel."

"I guess."

"So what do you think of him?"

"Hire him."

"You didn't have to think about that very long," Mitch noted.

"Nope. If he came back here today I'd fire my current guy and replace him with Gryphen. He's an odd bird and I never really trusted him, but his results were incredible. We've never been able to get our greens as nice as when he was here."

"Did you do renovation or just repair?"

"That was one of the most shocking things. He reconstructed a number of the greens and had the grass fully grown in just a few weeks. The members were in awe."

"Why did he leave?"

"He came in one day and said it was time to go. That was it."

Well at least he told you before leaving, Phil thought in regard to Clyde's disappearance.

"We've hired a company to do the greens, but he told us that they're unnecessary."

"I don't know what kind of shape your greens are in now, but my guess is that he's telling you the truth. He exceeded every expectation we ever had. People around here called him *The Grass Whisperer* – like he had some kind of mystical connection with the greens. He let our other guys handle the tees and fairways, which was fine because those tend to be the easy part. It's the greens that are important."

"Don't we know it," Phil interjected.

"Well, thank you for your time, Rick. You've been very enlightening."

"My pleasure. I hope it all works out for you."

"The plot thickens!" Mitch said after hanging up. He was almost giddy; as though meeting with Gryphen today was like finding lost treasure.

"Call the next guy," Phil directed, sharing Mitch's excitement.

The next number was for a course in Wisconsin.

"This is Rob Perry."

"Rob, this is Mitch Evans calling from The Peninsula Club in New York. I'm calling about a gentleman named, Gryphen Reed. He provided you as a reference."

"Ha! I'm surprised he even remembered my name," Perry said with a laugh.

"Why's that?"

"He always seemed to be in his own world. Always did things his own way."

"Yes, he is quite different. What about the quality of his work?"

"Second to none."

"That's what we're hearing," Mitch replied.

"Now, like I said, your HR person is going to hate you if you hire him. I always tolerated him because his work on the greens made my life a lot easier. The members didn't mind him, but he ruffled plenty of feathers with the staff. His mannerisms could really put people off. It was mostly verbal, but there was one incident."

"Oh, what was that?"

"We had a young smart-ass cutting grass and he wasn't following Gryphen's orders to the letter. He cut a green too short and Gryphen went off on him. The guys who saw it go down said the kid took a few swings at Gryphen first. Then Gryphen beat the hell out of the kid. I was afraid we might get sued, but the kid was so embarrassed that he quit and left town. The funny thing was that green should have fried, but Gryphen brought it right back into shape."

"We'll have to consider that aspect," Mitch noted.

"And did anyone tell you about the koala bears?"

"Koala bears?"

"That's a great story. I heard it from a guy who worked at a course with Gryphen down in Florida. They had a big eucalyptus tree next to one of the greens and the fallen leaves were always making a mess. Gryphen had decided to cut it down, but the general manager heard about it and told him to hold off. Sure enough, a couple of the members raised a ruckus and they got the Board to block the tree removal. So what do you think Gryphen did? He finds two koala bears somewhere and brings them out to the course. He puts them on leashes anchored to the ground near the trees, but just far enough away so they can't climb up the tree to get fresh leaves. Instead they lumber around the green picking up the leaves as they fall. Problem solved."

"You're kidding?" laughed Phil, imaging the bears crisscrossing the green.

"It may have been embellished over time, but I think it was based on some level of fact. I mentioned it one time to Gryphen when he seemed to be in a good mood and he muttered: 'Damn lazy bears. Couldn't keep up.' Then he walked away."

"And the members didn't have a problem with the bears being chained to their course?"

"Apparently not. They were cute and functional. They're timid, so when golfers would approach the green they'd scamper out of the way. It went alright for a few weeks and they kind of became mascots for the course. Then one of them got taken out by a blazing approach shot; bound to happen I suppose. The other one soldiered on for another week or two. One day the first group through found nothing but a few clumps of fur and a bloody collar. They were pretty sure that one was eaten by a gator."

"That's insane," Mitch said in disbelief.

"No, that's Florida. The heat down there cooks the golfers' brains. Bottom line, as long as he doesn't suggest that you buy some marsupials or goats for course maintenance I'd let him work his magic there at Peninsula."

"Thanks for the heads up, Rob."

"My pleasure."

After concluding the call, Phil and Mitch were even more in shock.

"I'm not sure if I can handle any more of these calls," Mitch said with a sigh.

"Come on, this is great. And we have to conduct our due diligence."

They made two more calls and heard more of the same. What had started the day as a complete long shot was now looking like a highly viable option.

"So what should we do?" Mitch asked.

"Right now there's nothing I'd like to do more than call TurfTec and tell them to stick their fifteen percent increase right up their ass. I'm just worried that it's clouding my judgment. If this guy can do what he says at this price we'd be fools not to hire him. Think of what else we could do with the extra money."

"I agree. Why don't we get Marge and Joe involved and see what they have to say."

"I know what they are going to say. Unfortunately we don't have time for that. If we're going to take a chance on Reed it's going to have to be a *decision*, not a *discussion*," Phil said before pausing to think. "If something does go wrong we need to minimize the damage. I'll make the call and I'll take the heat. I can't put your job at risk by having you involved in this decision."

"Phil, I appreciate your courage, but if things go wrong I'll be losing my job anyway. I'm in. You're going to need support and together we can sway Marge and Joe."

"Thanks for the vote of confidence, Mitch. I can't believe I'm saying this, but let's hire Reed. Hell, if this thing works out we'll end up being heroes."

"I'll settle for being employed."

***

As expected, Phil ran into resistance with Joe who had to sign the rescission letter and the new agreement with Gryphen. Phil was relentless and assured Joe that he would be protected from any backlash. Once all of the paperwork was complete, Phil knew that he'd have to inform the membership of their new direction. He warned his wife and sent out a lengthy email. He would have liked to have had a meet and greet session with Gryphen and the members, but he suspected that would be the wrong approach given Gryphen's quirks. Instead, he asked that they give Gryphen room and let him do his job without interference. Phil made the bold move of asking everyone to direct their comments and concerns directly to him, which they probably would have done anyway.

The first two weeks were surprisingly smooth. The members were told of selected closures and played temporary greens when necessary. Gryphen chose several of the current maintenance employees to be part of his team. Most of the work was taking place early in the morning and later in the day so Phil and Mitch had limited interaction with Gryphen. They were content for now to take a hands-off approach and hope that his references had not over-exaggerated his abilities. They joked with each other that they were giving the "koala" room to roam freely across Peninsula's greens.

Then came the ambush. Phil was walking across an open area near the driving range when a cart drove over from the course and pulled in front of him, blocking his path. A second cart, containing the other two members of the foursome, veered in and cut off the side route.

"Good morning, Phil," Eddie Butler began in a friendly tone. "Do you have a moment?"

Phil looked side to side at the golf carts pinning him in place. "I guess I do."

"Look, Phil, you know we're all in this project together and we don't want to create any dissention. But a lot of us are really getting worried. Have you seen the mess out on number thirteen?"

"Eddie, you knew that we were going to have to put up with some headaches during this phase. It would be a lot worse if we were implementing TurfTec's proposal. We're only two weeks in so we have a long way to go yet."

"We know, Phil. We just don't want to get to the end of that road and find out that we've been had. Remember El Capitano? Their contractor took them for one point two million dollars and left the course in ruins when they walked. Now it's a public goat track. I can't afford the time or cost of starting over at a new club. I'm married to Peninsula. No one knows what this guy is doing. I've seen renovations before and they don't look like this. Number thirteen is a disaster. He's killing off the good grass that was supposed to be retained."

"I know. I've been out there. We need to have a little faith and give it time to play out."

"Have you seen the weather forecast, Phil?" Wyatt Smith said, piling on. "A week of record heat is coming. I don't care how much you water that damn thing; if he kills it off any further it will never come back. It'll have to be scraped and reseeded – that will take months. We don't have money in that budget for sodding two thousand square foot greens."

Phil's response was interrupted by the rumble of a massive front end loader approaching. The men all watched as it drove straight toward them. It came so close to the first golf cart that when it did stop the enormous steel bucket was hanging over Eddie's head. They were paralyzed as Gryphen emerged from the driver's seat and climbed down. He pulled off his heavy leather gloves and leaned against the support post for the roof of Wyatt's cart.

"Good morning, gentlemen," Gryphen said with a friendly grin.

It was the first time Phil had seen Gryphen smile.

The members didn't know what to say and looked at each other nervously. There was an overwhelming feeling that Gryphen knew what they were talking about.

"Hello, Gryphen," Phil said, glad that Gryphen had arrived to rescue him. "What's on the agenda for today?"

"I'm heading out to do some work on lucky thirteen."

"What a coincidence, we were just talking about that one," Phil replied.

"Yes, we were a bit concerned about your approach. Phil was assuring us that you had it under control," Eddie chimed in.

"Then you'd do well to listen to Mr. Delome. What he's saying is accurate."

"It's just that..." Eddie started to say.

"Complete the phrase, Mr. Butler – What doesn't kill you..."

"Makes you stronger," Eddie mumbled, not appreciating the lecture.

"Simple as that. There are some areas that I can save, but I need to push them to the edge so that they'll be as strong as the new grass. It may sound like tough love, but it's the only way to get the consistency that I demand."

The foursome had pinned down Phil giving him no place to go; however, Gryphen was able to turn the tables with only a few pointed sentences. Now the group wanted to depart as quickly as possible.

"Do you fellas have questions about anything else I'm doing?" Gryphen added.

"Nope. Can't wait to see your final product," Eddie said. The cart let out a high-pitched beep as he threw it into reverse and jerked it backwards. The other cart followed closely behind leaving Phil and Gryphen alone.

"I thought I was the one that was supposed to be protecting *you* from angry members," Phil said.

"No worries. It wasn't very fair since you were the only one that didn't have a vehicle."

"Thanks for intervening."

"Are you catching a lot of hell, Phil?" Gryphen asked, watching the members drive off into the distance.

"It's been eerily quiet. That was one of the first signs of some anxiety among the membership. Knowing how things work around here, it's probably the tip of the iceberg. If someone's worried about something they don't keep it to themselves. It's even worse now that all of these guys use email."

"I see it everywhere. It's no surprise to me. That's why I won't dance around it. You have to take it head on."

"You have to remember though, Gryphen, I'm a politician. I have to keep my constituents content."

"I always think it's funny when they say a club president has "won" the election. Don't you feel like a winner getting the most thankless job around?"

"It's not completely thankless. It can be brutal at times. A club has to have leadership, though. Projects always take longer than they should and issues are more difficult than they should be. The payoff is when you see things get done. I'm not trying to put the pressure on you, but the work you're doing is beyond important for me, my constituents, and this club."

"Pressure doesn't bother me. I simply need time and patience. I've made good on my promises before and I'll do it again here."

"I believe you, Gryphen."

"Well, I better get back to work and move this tractor before somebody yells at you about that."

As Reed walked away, Phil asked a question that had been on his mind since the day they'd first met. "Gryphen, why The Peninsula Club?"

"What do you mean, Mr. Delome?"

"I mean why did you choose us?"

"You offered me the job and I took it."

"If you're who you say you are there would be plenty of jobs at more significant places than this. Why did you come here?"

"It seemed like a challenge. That's what I like," Gryphen said before climbing on and firing up the engine.

Phil waved and headed back to the clubhouse. He was quickly warming up to Gryphen. Even if this wasn't going to be a long-term commitment, Phil hoped it would last long enough for Peninsula to turn the corner and return to prominence.

***

Despite the forecasts, two days later it started raining at The Peninsula Club. The general area was getting scattered showers, however, for some reason Peninsula was getting more rain than anywhere else around. For two days it poured and the course remained closed.

The following weekend Phil was playing a round and was stunned when he arrived at the thirteenth hole. They were still employing a temporary green, but the regular putting surface had turned a bright, emerald green. He walked over to the edge of the green and bent down to examine the lush new growth. He tugged at a few blades. They were strong and well rooted. Phil stood back up and walked toward the back, right side of the green where it was being expanded. There the grass was lower and not quite as mature. Still, it was way beyond what he would have expected to see based on how it looked a week ago. *I think this is going to work*, he thought, as a portion of the weight he'd been feeling started to lift.

He rejoined his two playing companions back at the temporary green who were patiently letting him enjoy his inspection.

"So what do you think, Phil?" one of his buddies asked.

"Look at it. Amazing. Simply amazing."

"It looks great, Phil. I think you made the right call."

"We'll see. It's way too soon to claim victory. We were lucky to get all that rain. It's probably going to be hotter and drier in the next few weeks. With our limits on irrigation water we might be asking too much."

"Nothing else we can do other than see how it plays out. Come on, Phil, let's putt," the other player said.

Phil missed his short putt on the temporary green and then picked up. They were playing a two putt maximum given the situation. As they headed to the next hole, Phil found himself turning his head several times to catch another glimpse of Gryphen's marvelous work.

Following the round, Phil couldn't wait to hurry into the clubhouse to find Mitch. He barged into Mitch's office where he found him on the phone. Phil paced around the office impatiently waiting for Mitch to finish his call.

"Let me guess, Phil. You just saw thirteen?" Mitch said, beaming as he hung up the phone.

"Have you been out there?" Phil asked excitedly.

"Yeah, I was driving around early this morning and headed out that way. I was blown away when I saw it."

"It's hard not to be excited, but behind that I've got a nagging sense of worry."

"About what?"

"If it seems too good to be true..."

"...It probably is. I know, Phil. But results are results."

"He talked about using his 'proprietary' products. Do you think he's using any illegal chemicals or fertilizer?"

"When I see number thirteen I'm not sure I care," Mitch joked. "It's possible. For whatever reason, he doesn't strike me as the kind of person who would take that approach."

"Yeah, you're right. I'm trying to concoct things to worry about."

"Stick to our plan, Phil. No reason to change now. You do your best to keep the members content and I'll keep an eye on Gryphen."

***

The month of June was one of the hottest and driest on record for Long Island. Travelers arriving to New York by plane could easily make out the golf courses by the long, brown rows of land laid end to end. Every golf course on the island was suffering as grass was drained of life and shriveled. Every course except for one: The

Peninsula Club. Word had quickly spread that Peninsula not only had living grass on their greens, but that most of them were now in perfect condition.

Mitch was fielding new inquiries every day from members of neighboring clubs that wanted to play at Peninsula. Once they played, many of them were also inquiring about memberships. He couldn't believe how quickly their standing was improving.

Several high end clubs had been forced to halt play to prevent further damage to their greens until the summer rains arrived. Needless to say, the millionaire and billionaire members were not happy being told they were not allowed to play *their* course. Many of them demanded that the general managers and pros find them a place to play. In the area there was now only one option: Peninsula.

Mitch had been afraid that all of the extra traffic would take a toll on what was still a work in progress. So far that didn't seem to be the case. Each day the greens looked better and stronger.

He consulted regularly with Gryphen who assured him that their new surfaces could take the abuse. He even approved of Mitch's idea of extending tee times by two hours to accommodate all of the demand. Besides all of the positive word of mouth, the massive flow of additional rounds also provided a financial windfall for the club's coffers. Things were going far beyond what he and Phil had thought possible just a few months ago.

Mitch walked out of the clubhouse near dusk one evening after another long day in the office. He had worked with the marketing officer to sign up three new full members today. Before departing he headed toward the maintenance facilities to see if Gryphen was still around. He wanted to thank Gryphen and let him know how well things were going. Gryphen put in an unbelievable number of hours at the club and Mitch knew that he even slept over many nights.

When he turned the corner he saw Gryphen walking toward his office. Mitch stopped quickly and pulled back when he noticed that Gryphen had a companion. Mitch couldn't make out any details from that distance; however, it looked like an attractive young woman. He watched as Gryphen held the door open and let her into his office.

He wanted to sneak closer and see if he could peer inside. He decided that was a bad idea. Gryphen had been working like a dog and if this was how he fulfilled his personal needs Mitch had no problem with that. He turned and walked to his car, ready to head home and eat dinner.

***

The rain finally arrived in July. It was too late for several courses that had completely lost their greens. The buzz at The Peninsula Club was still growing, however. They now found that Gryphen's greens drained better than every other course on the island. They seemed able to take any amount of rain and were playable as soon as it stopped.

Peninsula's annual Fourth of July tournament had been a raging success with every spot spoken for. Instead of a course on the brink, they now possessed a valuable commodity that others wanted a piece of. The existing membership was now starting to develop a bit of an attitude. They were also beginning to resent the new members who were gobbling up tee times and slowing down the normal pace of play.

Things came to a head on a Friday afternoon. A group anchored by a new member was putting on the twelfth hole. On the tee waiting and watching was a group of long-time Peninsula Club members. They had grown increasingly aggravated as the group ahead played slower and slower. The golfers in the lead group were lining up two foot putts, constantly making side bets, and generally playing and behaving poorly.

One of the new member's guests was Bryce Dexter, a high profile hedge fund manager. He had examined a short putt from every side and when he finally made his stroke the ball slid by without even touching the hole. He now had a putt of equal length from the other side. His buddies had a good laugh and asked if he wanted to go double or nothing on the comeback. He accepted without thinking twice. Once again he started his lengthy pre-putt routine.

The members on the tee were beyond flustered.

Tom Wilder, who was eighty-years old, blurted out, "Come on, before I get any older!" It was loud enough for the golfers on the green to hear.

Dexter put his hands on his hips and glared back at Wilder. He tried to refocus and finally addressed the ball. This time he had the right line. However, he forgot to hit it hard enough and it crawled toward the cup before stopping on the edge. His playing companions high fived each other and had another good laugh at Dexter's expense. Bryce stood staring at the ball, hoping it might somehow move forward.

"It isn't dropping, Bryce," one of the other players said with glee.

Dexter responded by spewing profanity that echoed through the trees. He then smashed his putter into his ball and the ground, collapsing the hole.

His friends stopped instantly and stared. That was crossing the line.

Apparently he still had more to go. He jumped around in a circle and pounded his putter head into the green tearing deep, dirty gashes. He looked like a crazed monkey slamming the ground with a bone.

His display of anger lit the fuse of Wilder's group. They were in their carts making a bee-line toward the green.

Dexter was getting ready to finally walk off when the Peninsula members confronted him.

"You're going to pay to repair that you son of a bitch!" scolded Wilder, flaming like a father protecting his child.

"Hell, I'll just buy this whole dump and kick you out old man. Now get out of my way. Go back and play your front tees, geezer," he said, before walking rudely past Wilder.

Wilder was livid, "I'm not done with you punk."

Dexter stopped and turned. He pointed his putter at Wilder and said, "I'm about to do to your face what I did to that green."

"Excuse me," said a voice that scared everyone there. There was a loud *clang* as a flash of black, serrated steel knocked the putter from Dexter's hand. "You're not demonstrating what we consider proper etiquette here at The Peninsula Club."

Both groups stood petrified as Gryphen ran his dirty fingers down the blade of the massive machete he was holding.

"See those sand containers on your cart, Mr. Dexter?" he continued. "You are going to go over and get both of them and fill the holes you just made so these gentlemen can attempt to play this hole.

Dexter was afraid to move.

"You're going to do that *now*," Gryphen reiterated, raising the point of the machete to Dexter's chest.

Dexter backed away nervously and then ran to the cart. He grabbed the sand and ran back up to the putting surface where he scurried around pouring out the green-tinted sand.

"Be sure to smooth them all out, too," Gryphen called. "We don't want any bumpy spots."

Dexter got down on all fours and brushed the filled divots with his hands. He kept looking up anxiously at Gryphen.

His buddies were enthralled seeing Dexter humiliated this way. But none of them dared to even crack a smile.

"Okay, that looks alright. Come here," Gryphen commanded.

Dexter did as he was told.

"Now you're going to apologize to Mr. Wilder and then you will be leaving The Peninsula Club...and not returning. Your friends are welcome to play on if they choose. Is that clear?"

Dexter nodded. "I'm sorry," he mumbled to Wilder, who still felt like a deity being worshipped.

"Would you like me to drive you in?" Gryphen offered.

"No, that's okay," said one of Dexter's friends. "We're all going to head in now. Sorry about all of this," he added, ushering the group toward their carts. They all jumped in and tore off as fast as they could.

Gryphen started to walk away as though nothing had happened.

"Thank you, Mr. Reed," Wilder said gratefully.

"No problem. Enjoy the rest of your round, Mr. Wilder. I'll get that green fixed up right away."

The legend of Gryphen Reed was growing quickly at Peninsula.

Wilder and his group continued their round feeling like they were on cloud nine. Every few minutes they would recount the story among themselves of what had just happened. They couldn't believe how lucky they'd been to get someone as skilled as Gryphen to work at Peninsula. The fact that he was also apparently a bad-ass significantly increased their enthusiasm. It was like having Clint Eastwood with a green thumb.

On the seventeenth green Wilder was lining up a putt when something caught his eye.

"Is that somebody's ball mark?" he asked the group, not remembering anyone's shot being in that spot.

They all shrugged and shook their heads.

Wilder walked over and grabbed the shiny material. He held it up to the light to study it closer. He was struck by its heavy weight relative to its small size.

"What is it?" asked one of his partners.

"I think it's a gold nugget," Wilder said, walking toward the others.

"I don't think that's a nugget, Tom. It kind of looks like a dental filling," one of the others noted.

"Yeah, I guess you're right," said a puzzled Wilder. "I wonder how that got there."

"Maybe Gryphen punched somebody in the mouth for not fixing their ball mark and knocked it out," joked one of Wilder's friends.

"That's weird. I guess I'll drop it off in the pro shop in case anyone is looking for it."

***

Mitch was at the bar in the grill room enjoying lunch and watching the morning groups finish on number eighteen. It was the marquee green, visible from wall-to-wall, full length windows that encased the dining rooms. It looked better than Mitch had ever seen it look before. The August sun was shining bright and all of the golfers had beaming smiles.

It was clear that the renovations would be finished before month end. That was two months sooner than TurfTec had quoted. They were now using the excess funds in the budget to move forward with other improvements.

In a meeting with Phil the day before, both men discussed how relieved they were that their gamble was paying off. The new worry that both of the men were confronting was when Gryphen might decide to leave. Based on his resume it looked like he normally stayed around for at least eighteen months to two years. However, with Gryphen there was absolutely no way of knowing when he might depart. Therefore, Phil and Mitch resolved to have a sense of urgency to keep the momentum going.

A member stopped and shook hands with Mitch on his way to lunch.

"The course is in great shape and getting better every day, Mitch. Nice work."

"Thanks, I appreciate that."

"Did you see the story about that hedge fund guy today?"

"No. Who are you talking about?"

"The jerk that went nuts out on number twelve before Gryphen kicked him out."

"Oh, that guy," Mitch said, having already heard the story repeated what seemed like several hundred times.

"It was in the *Wall Street Journal* and I saw a piece on CNBC this morning. Apparently the guy has disappeared. Wall Street is nervous because his funds are interconnected to all kinds of companies and entities. They're afraid that there might be some kind of fraud or accounting irregularities and that's why he decided to go AWOL."

"I'll have to check it out when I get back to my office."

"Couldn't happen to a nicer guy," the member said sarcastically, before walking off.

Mitch was quite intrigued by what he had just heard and quickly finished his lunch and dashed back to his office. He easily located the story online and skimmed the details. There were lots of facts and figures about the funds. In terms of Bryce Dexter, however, the only news was that he was gone. His wife reported that he left for the office early the prior morning and no one had seen or heard from him since. His subordinates were scrambling to reassure investors that nothing was wrong with the investments.

Mitch leaned back in his chair and pondered the article. When he read the few lines about Dexter he couldn't help but think about Clyde. It was sad, but in the excitement of the past few months he had almost been forgotten. The last thing Mitch had heard was the police still had zero leads in the investigation.

Turning to the credenza behind him, Mitch pulled out a drawer and found the paper he wanted. He picked up the phone and called the number for Rick Covey.

"Hello, this is Rick Covey."

"Hi, Rick, I don't know if you remember me, but we spoke a few months ago about Gryphen Reed."

"Oh, sure. How's that going?"

"Beyond expectations. We can advertise the best greens on Long Island and it's the undisputed truth. Gryphen has been amazing."

"Glad to hear it. What can I do for you?"

"I have kind of a strange question and it relates to Gryphen. Do you recall if there were any unexplained disappearances at the course or in the area back when Gryphen was there?"

"Like an alien abduction or something?"

"No, nothing crazy. Perhaps someone involved with the course just leaving without any notice or maybe missing without a trace."

"It's been a few years, but let me think about it for a minute. Out here it actually happens more than you'd expect. There are a lot of empty spaces for people to fade into. Most of the time hikers stumble upon the body or someone finds the remains after winter thaw. Now there was a guy who died out on the back nine a while ago."

"How did he die?"

"Well, we assume that he fell over the cliff that borders several holes. It's a magnificent stretch back there. If you get a chance to play out here you should really try to see it," Covey said, taking more pride in his course than interest in Mitch's inquiry.

"What do you mean *assume*?"

"His cart was parked out there with his clubs. He was gone. There's a swiftly moving river at the bottom so he probably went over and was swept away. He was playing alone so no one saw it."

"They never found a body?"

"Nope."

"And that was when Gryphen was there?"

"Yeah, definitely. That was a time when the greens were at their best."

"What about employees?"

"You know how they are. It's definitely not uncommon for them to just stop coming to work. Especially grounds crew guys. Who wants to get up at five o'clock in the morning when you are hung over?"

"Anyone in particular that you can remember?"

About the time the guy went over the cliff there were two young guys that left. Like you said, no notice or anything, just didn't come to work anymore."

"What kind of workers were they?"

"Oh, they were both terrible. They did lousy work and we knew they would sneak off into the woods together to get high. That's why nobody cared. It saved us the hassle of firing them."

"Did you ever try to find them to send a final paycheck or anything?"

"Nah. Again, not worth that hassle."

"Thanks for the information. I appreciate it."

"So why are you asking, Mitch? Did Gryphen do something wrong?"

"I don't think so. I'm trying to do a little detective work on our superintendent who was here right before Gryphen arrived. No one knows what happened to him."

"Well, good luck, let me know if I can help."

Mitch hung up and leaned back in his chair. Maybe something was amiss in Colorado, but it could just be a coincidence. It was certainly nothing concrete. He held up the reference page and considered whether or not to call the next name. *Maybe I'm watching too much TV? This is crazy.* He set the paper down and turned back to his computer. The little voice in his head bounced back and forth. Finally, he picked up the list again and dialed the number in Wisconsin.

After exchanging pleasantries, Mitch asked Rob Perry the same question. Perry didn't hesitate to answer.

"Sure, he would have been here when Richey vanished. This is a pretty quiet town so that's one of our most notorious cases. But I doubt Gryphen had anything to do with that whole affair."

"Why is that?"

"The usual clichéd story. Richey had a young, trophy wife who stood to benefit nicely if her husband died. What was so interesting was that the lack of a body caused two problems. On the one hand, the police, who were sure she did it, couldn't prove he'd been murdered. On the other side, the insurance company wouldn't pay out on a huge policy if she couldn't prove he was dead."

"What happened?"

"It went in circles for about two years. Finally, she was tired of the hassle and being in the local limelight so she left town. There were plenty of joint assets that she controlled so she did okay – just not the big score. The rumor was that it was a five million dollar policy. As far as I know the police still have their case open, but it's not active."

"Any employees?"

"I can think of two guys. The older one had some real mental issues so that was no surprise. He was moody and volatile. We were glad to have him out of here. The younger guy seemed to have potential. He wanted to learn all about agronomy and was excited to have an expert like Gryphen around. He was always shadowing Gryphen to see what he could learn. The kid had some kind of online romance with a girl out west so our guess was that he heard the call of love and followed it."

Mitch thanked Perry, hung up, and went back into thought. Prior to Clyde, Peninsula had several employees who decided to stop coming to work; however, there was always some kind of trace with those people. Especially nowadays, there was normally a cell phone number and an e-mail address at a minimum.

As for these "problem employees" – could Gryphen be helping courses with more than their greens? Mitch wondered.

Things had been going so well the last few months that Mitch didn't even want to consider that Gryphen was involved in these disappearances. Still, he was worried that if he let it go and something even worse happened it would be on his conscience.

The next person he thought about calling was Phil. Phil had also been on an emotional high recently and Mitch didn't want to bother him with potentially unfounded allegations. He considered his options and decided the best route might be doing some investigative work on his own.

***

That night Mitch worked late and waited to make sure all of the staff had departed. He watched the parking lot near the maintenance buildings, keeping a close eye on Gryphen's truck. It was close to seven thirty and he was working on his computer when he looked up to see the taillights of the truck moving toward the exit road. Mitch quickly shut everything down and left the clubhouse.

It was a beautiful warm night outside. It was darker than usual as a bank of clouds had blocked out the falling sun near the horizon. Mitch felt a rush of excitement as he moved across the putting green. His steps were silent as he walked briskly across the firm, lush grass.

Mitch approached Gryphen's office and scanned around in every direction. He was confident that he was now alone and the only sounds he heard were chirping evening insects and the faint rumble of cars on the highway in the distance.

He climbed the metal stairs and tried the door. It was locked, which he'd expected. He pulled out the extra key that he'd brought and carefully opened the door, somehow worried that it might be booby-trapped. His heart was thumping along at a brisk pace.

The office had windows that faced east, so it was completely dark when he entered. He immediately wished that he'd brought a flashlight. Instead he fondled around and found the light switch. The fluorescent tubes came to life with a flicker and hum.

He had no idea what he might be looking for so he started by examining Gryphen's desk. There was almost nothing on or in it and everything was neatly organized. Mitch moved on and began going through the cabinets that lined the walls. Rows of supplies and small equipment filled each one in an orderly fashion.

In the corner was a well-worn, brown couch and easy chair. Mitch assumed that this was where Gryphen slept when he spent nights at the course. Next to the couch was a wooden rack filled with golf maintenance magazines and journals. Mitch was already questioning why he was even here.

There was a door at the back that led to a second room. Mitch tried it and found it was open. He once again located a switch and illuminated the space. With cinderblock walls and a concrete floor everything was soaked in dull gray. This room had an industrial feel with larger equipment and tools. On one side there were hoses and large tubs. Hanging from the ceiling were chains and hooks mounted on tracks, which were used to lift and move heavy items such as engines. The air was thick with the smell of petroleum products. Mitch walked around and ran his hands along the swinging chains as he went. At the far end of the room was a large sliding door that led to the tractor shed. Mitch gave it a tug and it wouldn't budge. He walked back and stopped near the tubs. Here there were several fifty-five gallon drums and a number of bags of powdery material. The bags indicated quicklime, phosphorous, magnesium, and salt among other things.

Ah, this must be the proprietary products. Mitch thought. *I wonder if he has his recipes written down or if they're all in his head?*

He turned his attention to the drums. They were marked with a hand stamped logo that said SoilNT.

Hmm. I wonder what SoilNT is?

Mitch tapped on one of the drums and it sounded full. He looked at the lid and saw that it was locked down with a levered handle. He tried to force it open, but failed. He searched around and quickly located a small crow bar. He wedged the end into the handle and popped the clasp. The lid shot off and fell hard on the floor with a metallic clatter. The loud noise in the acoustically challenged space rattled Mitch.

He approached the container and saw that it was filled with a dark, syrupy liquid. There was something that looked like a clump of weeds floating at the top. He poked it tentatively with the bar.

"Shit!" he yelled as the mass spun around and revealed the mangled face of a man.

Was this Dexter?

The surface moved again and a hand, severed at the forearm, rose from the fluid.

"Oh my God! Shit! Shit! Shit!"

He wanted to run, but his feet were frozen. He wanted to put the lid back on, but he couldn't get any closer to the vat of human brew. Finally, his heavy feet began to turn toward the door. He didn't think he could see anything worse tonight. He was wrong.

"Oh shit..."

31

"Good evening, Mitch," Gryphen said with a sinister smile. He looked truly happy to see Mitch here in his realm. In his hand was the large, black machete. "I tried to make it clear that my methods are *proprietary*. You should have accepted that. But to answer your question, *yes*, SoilNT is people!"

"How can you do this?" Mitch asked, shaking with fear.

"How can I not? You've seen the results. Mother Nature is a strange lady."

"But...people?...I don't understand."

"You mean how I learned my techniques? Good story," Gryphen said, now sounding chatty *and* menacing. "Purely by accident. At my first course we had a guy request that his ashes be scattered on a green where he'd hit his only hole-in-one. Almost instantly the green looked better than every other one on the course. Players were making macabre jokes about it. Me? I was intrigued. My brother happened to be taking a gross anatomy class at the time and was willing to lend me a hand...and a leg...and part of a torso." He paused for a moment to see if Mitch had a reaction.

Mitch stood expressionless.

"Oh, come on. That was funny. *Lend me a hand.* Anyway, I experimented with different samples and added ingredients. It was like a slightly gruesome science fair project. One variable that was clear: fresher was better. So finally, when the first opportunity presented itself, I made the jump from spare parts to the real deal."

"Let me guess – a lackluster maintenance employee?"

"Yep. Hey, if the guy had bothered to work a little harder he'd probably still be alive. So there you have it – mix my love of agronomy with my long-standing homicidal tendencies and it leads to a flourishing career."

Mitch shook his head in amazement of what he was listening to.

"Why Clyde? He was a great employee."

"Yeah, maybe so. Sometimes opportunities present themselves and sometimes you have to create them yourself. I had been scouting out courses around here and Peninsula looked like the best option for practicing my craft. Despite what you think of me and my methods you simply can't argue with the impact my grass has had here."

Sadly, Mitch could not.

"What are you going to do now?" he asked.

"Well I was in pretty good shape in terms of supply. Now, however, I can do even more. I think you're going to help me with the

32

changes I was considering on number six," Gryphen said, walking forward while dragging his machete across the chains hanging from the ceiling. "I'm sure The Peninsula Club will appreciate the sacrifice you're making for the club, Mitch."

***

Phil sat in the clubhouse reading the want ad he had placed in one of the golf industry journals.

Seeking General Manager for growing club featuring the best greens on Long Island.

2. Most Dangerous Round

"I now pronounce you husband and wife, you may kiss the bride."

The gathered guests cheered as Brandon Newsome leaned in and kissed his new wife, Ashley. The two looked like the perfect couple and everyone in attendance was certain they would one day produce the world's most beautiful children. Brandon was tall and handsome and looked like a red carpet actor in his tuxedo. His masculine features and pushed back, brown hair had landed him occasional modeling jobs during college. The new Mrs. Newsome was athletic and had attended college on a golf scholarship, although she also found time to compete for her school's swim team. She had wavy chestnut hair that flowed down onto her white dress and emerald green eyes. Brandon liked to tell her that she had the best greens he'd ever seen.

The two had first met on a golf course three years earlier. Brandon was making the turn while playing with three friends and saw Ashley practicing at the driving range. She was absolutely gorgeous and had an incredible golf swing. When he told his friends that he had to meet her they laughed at him and told him to hit his tee shot. He didn't. Brandon was too afraid that she might not be around when they finished the back nine. He took his clubs off the cart and told them to play on without him. He walked over to the range, set his clubs down next to Ashley, and began hitting balls. His friends were completely stunned by his show of bravado.

Ashley had seen what he'd done, but acted as though he wasn't even there. After hitting a few shots he declared that he was ready to play and asked Ashley if she would join him for nine holes. She saw that he was very handsome and clearly a good golfer so she accepted his offer. They had a great round and had been together ever since.

The happy couple held hands and walked down the aisle toward the church entrance. They took a quick detour to a small side room and then waited for the guests to move outside and prepare for the next phase of the ceremony. Brandon had hoped they could skip the small projectile gauntlet; however, Ashley's mother had insisted that it be done. Now that he was married, it was the first of many concessions that Brandon would be making over the coming years.

The best man notified them that the hurlers were ready and Brandon and Ashley dashed out the front doors toward the waiting car. Over the span of just under fifty yards they came under heavy fire from siblings, aunts, uncles, college teammates, and several people who didn't seem to be connected to either the bride or groom. They were pelted with handfuls of birdseed that came like shotgun blasts from every direction. Brandon threw Ashley into the back seat and dove in after her. The door slammed and he knew they were now safe. He spit out small seeds and picked kernels out of his ears. He then turned his attention to his wife and groomed her as best as he could. There was a small trail of seeds resting in her cleavage and Brandon thrust his mouth down to try and retrieve the debris. Ashley screamed with surprise. They laughed and kissed the rest of the way to the reception.

The couple knew they had to share the rest of today with family and friends, but first thing tomorrow they would be on their way to Costa Rica for their honeymoon.

***

The plane landed at the San Jose airport and the Newsomes disembarked and retrieved their luggage. They made their way outside the terminal and were able to locate the shuttle bus that would take them and other arriving guests out to the Vida Serena Resort and Spa. The facility had just opened the year before and had received rave reviews. The golf course on the property had already been rated as the best in all of Central America. A close friend of Brandon's worked for the parent corporation that managed the resort and was able to get the couple a highly discounted rate for their week-long stay.

San Jose was a modern city, but as soon as they passed through the suburbs the road became rough and undulating. The local driver showed no fear as he navigated the jungle highway. The passengers steadily tightened their grip on the armrests. After a thrilling half hour, the wild ride finally eased to an end. They returned to smooth pavement and drove up the entrance road to the resort. It was still a tropical setting, however, the chaos of the jungle had been replaced by well groomed lawns and perfectly aligned trees. They pulled into the canopied area in front of the main building and were immediately greeted by resort staff. Personal concierges escorted them through check in and made sure all of the guests' needs and wants were being addressed. Everyone there was smiling and everything seemed to be moving in perfect sync. It was like a vacation factory. Ashley noted that it reminded her of the old television show, *Fantasy Island*.

After the long journey, they spent the remainder of their first day relaxing by the massive pool and drinking at the swim-up bar.

"I can't believe we are here already," Ashley said, taking in the lush, tropical surroundings. "The last few days have just been a crazy blur."

"I agree, Mrs. Newsome. But hopefully now we'll have some time to slow down and unwind. This place is absolutely incredible."

"We'll have to get Dave a nice thank you gift for helping to get us in here for such a great price. I'm really looking forward to seeing the golf course tomorrow. Based on the rest of this place the pictures probably don't even do it justice."

"Yeah, the golf should be nice, but I'm looking forward to something else before that," Brandon said suggestively as he floated even closer to his new bride and kissed her passionately while his hands wandered below the water's surface.

***

The couple's first tee time wasn't until ten o'clock so they were able to sleep in and then grab some breakfast. Ashley had purchased several new golf outfits just for the trip and modeled her favorite one before they left the room. Brandon had not gone so far as to make any new acquisitions, but still brought some of his nicer attire. Together they looked like a pair of serious golfers, which in reality they were.

The golf facility was a short walk from the main resort building and the couple checked in at the pro shop.

"Good morning, we are the Newsomes," Brandon said proudly. Calling his wife by *his* last name was a fun new novelty. When he looked at her standing next to him at the counter he felt like he'd made a great acquisition.

"Ah, welcome to Vida Serena, Mr. and Mrs. Newsome," the man at the counter said.

Brandon felt another surge of delight. He liked it just as much when someone else noted that she was now his wife.

"We have your clubs all loaded up and ready to go. Give me a moment to check you in and we'll have you on your way," the man continued. He looked at his monitor and made a few clicks on the mouse. "I see this is the first of three rounds we have you scheduled for this week."

"That's correct," Brandon replied.

"What other plans do you have during your visit?" the clerk asked as he finished running the transaction.

"We are signed up for a rafting trip, an eco-tour, and also a day of zip-lining," Ashley said enthusiastically.

"The zip-lines are one of my favorite things here at the resort," the clerk noted. "As employees we get to do them occasionally on our days off. I brought my wife one time and she screamed with fear and delight the whole time. She was so loud that I think she scared away much of the wildlife for several days."

"Mrs. Newsome here thinks she is pretty tough, so we'll see whether or not she frightens off any animals," Brandon teased.

"And you're sure you don't want to bring a caddie with you for the round today?" the clerk asked.

"No, I think we'll be okay," Brandon replied. They preferred to play on their own and read their own putts. They were also trying to keep their budget within reason.

"Okay, just please be sure to watch where you are going out there. It is beautiful, but there is some treacherous terrain. Regardless of where your golf ball decides to go make sure that you stay on the course at all times."

"We are pretty good players so hopefully we won't stray too far from the fairways," Ashley assured him.

"Here you go. You're all set," the clerk said handing them a slip of paper. "Just head down the path out the back and you'll find the cart waiting near the bottom. Enjoy you round and remember: stay on the course."

"We will," Brandon replied as they hustled out the door.

When they found their cart Brandon saw a red sign on the dashboard that said: STAY ON THE COURSE AT ALL TIMES. As he drove toward the range, Brandon swerved wildly and mocked, "Oh no, I might not be able to stay on the course!"

Ashley laughed and held on for the ride.

***

The first tee was breathtaking. They had to park the cart below and walk up a series of switch backs to get to the elevated tee box that was essentially built on a cliff.

38

"Wow! This is ridiculous," Ashley said, not even thinking about hitting her shot yet.

"I'll let you have the honors, Mrs. Newsome," Brandon said, equally impressed with the vista.

Ashley hit her ball off into the sky in front of her and it seemed to carry forever before finally hitting and bounding down the broad fairway. Brandon followed with an excellent opening drive and they drove down to hit their next shots. They found the fairway and green to be perfect. It didn't look like the new course was seeing much play so far.

The second tee was equally impressive. This one was placed inside a natural alcove in the side of a towering rock wall. There was a steady drip of beads of water across the opening and it felt like hitting from the mouth of a cave. The couple was immediately turned off by the fact that the "grass" was actually synthetic turf, however, upon investigation and after a few practice swings they found it to be the most realistic fake grass they'd ever seen. It was a very unique location, but clearly not conducive for growing a natural grass teeing area.

The next few holes had more modest teeing areas, but the fairways and greens of the rolling par fours took on more of the emphasis.

By the time the couple reached the sixth hole they still hadn't seen any other golfers either ahead of them or behind. It was a remote and peaceful wonderland of golf. Brandon was enjoying the round, but also found the secluded and alluring setting to be very stimulating. After hitting their tee shots he moved up behind Ashley as she was sliding her driver back into the bag. He ran one hand up her chest and the other down between her legs.

"Stop," she said, only partially resisting.

"Come on. There's nobody around. Tarzan wants a little bit of Jane out here in the jungle."

She giggled and squirmed under his grasp.

"We can do more of this later after golf."

"Yes, that is already on the agenda," he said. "But right now we have some time for a little break. I can't help myself; you look way too sexy in this new outfit."

"Okay," she said, shifting her hands behind her and pulling him in close. His compliment had been the right thing to say at the right time. "But just a quickie. It needs to be a short par three, not a long par five. Deal?"

"I'm already teed up and ready to hit," he assured her, grinding himself against her tight cheeks.

Brandon saw a small clearing just off the edge of the fairway and headed that way. He parked the cart and quickly had his shorts around his ankles. He forcefully grabbed Ashley and pulled her onto his lap.

"Hang on a second," she protested. "I need to go to the bathroom first."

"Okay."

She dashed over toward the boundary of the area and squatted down. Brandon was watching her with amusement.

"Turn around!" she ordered.

"We're married now. I'm going to see this and a lot more."

"Well, I can't go here with you watching."

"Alright."

He turned slightly and then looked back.

"I saw that," she said.

He shifted around in the cart, but she was still uncomfortable. Ashley was close to a wide bush and decided to go around behind it for more privacy. She found an open spot and wiggled her clothes down onto one foot before squatting down. When she was half way finished something moved quickly in the leaves near her feet and she jumped up in a panic. She tried to run, but after her first step she tripped over her skirt. She screamed and fell forward onto another bed of leaves. Her momentum carried her further and suddenly she was sliding downhill. Ashley had not realized how steep the slope was and tumbled down while brush and saplings tore at her arms and legs.

Brandon heard her screams and leaped from the cart. He too tripped on his shorts and landed on his face. He got up and ran to the edge of the clearing with his clothes dragging along.

"Ashley!" he yelled. "Where are you?"

"I'm down here," she replied. Her voice sounded very distant.

"Let me get dressed and I'll be right down."

"Maybe you should go and get help, I'll wait here."

"No, I'm coming down to get you," he said firmly. His new wife was in trouble so his masculine side was clouding his decision making. Going to find someone to help them would have been the smart choice. "I'll be right back, Ashley."

Brandon hurried back to the cart and got dressed. He ran to the course where he'd seen a length of green, nylon rope strung along the fairway. Racing back to the forest, Brandon passed the cart where there were several full bottles of water. He also didn't bother to grab anything from his bag such as a towel, bug spray, or a club that might come in handy down below.

There was a sturdy looking tree at the top of the hill and Brandon tied the rope around its trunk. He knew the rope wouldn't reach all the way down, but went ahead and began his descent hoping that he would get close enough to Ashley before letting gravity do the rest of the work.

"I'm coming!" he yelled gallantly, as he repelled down the rugged slope.

"Okay. Be careful, honey."

He bounced back and forth and lost his footing several times. The falls had left him with scrapes all over his legs. He looked down at the blood dripping from several wounds and realized that he should have put on the rain pants he had in his golf bag. Also, his hands were now on fire as the coarse nylon rope dug into his skin and created a friction burn. He cursed himself for not putting golf gloves on before starting down.

When he reached the end of his rope he still could not see Ashley below, but could hear her voice more clearly.

"I'm going to slide the rest of the way," he called to her.

"Alright, I think I can see you now," she said.

Brandon turned around and eased down onto his butt. He was going to try to go down feet first so he crossed his legs and let go of the rope. Initially his pace was moderate, but after about twenty feet he accelerated quickly. His foot caught on some kind of vine and it sent him spinning. He ping-ponged off several trees and rocks before he was able to stabilize his movement. Finally, he sailed through a patch of brush and flopped to a stop on an open area where the ground was level.

He looked up and saw Ashley standing above him. She was naked from the waist down. Normally Brandon would have found this very arousing. Right now, however, the pain all over his body was overloading his brain circuits.

"Uhh, that really hurt," he moaned.

"Tell me about it," she concurred.

"Where's your skirt?" he asked.

"I lost it on the way down."

"Sorry, I didn't see it; otherwise I would have grabbed it."

He forced himself to his feet and took off his shorts and handed them to her.

"Here put these on," he said.

"Thanks," she said gratefully, admiring him standing in his boxer briefs.

Brandon was now looking around and trying to devise some kind of plan. He had hoped they would be able to climb back up, but the bottom of the hill was far steeper than he'd realized. From this vantage point it felt like the course was now miles away. The area where they had landed appeared to be part of a rough animal trail. Brandon glanced in both directions and weighed their options. Following the route that ran parallel to the course back toward the clubhouse seemed like the wise choice. The path looked more promising in the other direction though, as it was more open and appeared to ascend along the hillside.

"What do you think?" Ashley asked.

"I think we have to head up. At least get to where we can yell for help if need be. Let's go," he said decisively, taking her hand and leading her up the path.

The route was very primitive and their progress was slow. Ashley was still scared, but she was now glad that Brandon had decided to come down for her. The jungle was full of bugs and there were strange noises coming from every direction. After a half hour on the move, the heat and humidity were already starting to take a toll. Surrounded by thick vegetation there was absolutely no breeze in the valley.

"I need to take a break," Ashley said. She was extremely thirsty already.

"Okay, we can rest for a few minutes."

"Why didn't you bring some water with you?" Ashley asked

"Hey, I was in a hurry to save your cute ass," he said, slapping her butt. "We wouldn't be down here in the first place if you had just peed next to the cart."

"You shouldn't have been looking," she countered. "And *you* were the one that had to leave the golf course."

"Yeah, well next time maybe you should wear a baggy sweatshirt and pants so I'm not completely distracted from the game."

Although playful, it was their first fight as a married couple. Brandon couldn't wait until they got the chance to have makeup sex.

They both needed a rest; however, stopping gave the insects even more time to feast on them so they were quickly back on the move. They soon came to a more open section of the trail, which lifted their spirits. The couple could finally stand up straight and walk normally. A break in the tree line gave them a chance to look out over the beautiful vista below them. Brandon was enjoying the view, but he also noticed that the forest had now become very quiet.

Ashley was startled when something soft hit her in the side of the head. She initially thought Brandon was messing with her.

"Stop it!" she said.

"It wasn't me," Brandon replied.

Ashley touched her hair and discovered that it was something brown and foul smelling.

"Gross!"

"Was it a bird?" Brandon asked, looking up cautiously.

"I don't know."

A moment later another projectile arrived and landed near their feet. The next one hit Brandon in the arm. The silence was instantly shattered when several monkeys in the canopy above burst into frenzied laughter. It preceded the arrival of more flying feces.

"Let's get out of here. I think we're being ambushed," he said, pushing her forward.

They moved as quickly as they could while branches and fronds slapped them from every direction. Brandon could hear the monkeys on the move as well. Their screams seemed to be getting louder and more numerous. He looked up and could see the sinister, dark bodies swinging effortlessly through the treetops above.

"Help!" Brandon yelled as he fell and hit the ground. His vision had been impaired and there was a burning pain around his eyes. One of the monkeys had landed on his head and was gouging at his eyes with jagged claws.

Ashley screamed and stood paralyzed while Brandon rolled around on the ground trying to remove his unwanted primate hat. He finally pried its hands from his face and flung it down hard on the ground. Instinctively he threw his body on top of the creature and tried to crush it in anger. It was howling like a hyena and squirming franticly.

Ashley screamed again, even louder. She spun around in place and Brandon could see that a monkey had now landed on her back. The animal was gripping her ponytail and riding his gyrating wife. The monkey looked like a crazed little jockey.

Brandon got up and lunged toward his wife. He grabbed the furry passenger and tried to get the monkey off her back. The creature had a death grip on her hair and would not let go. Ashley wailed in pain as her head was snapped back.

Brandon was distracted from his task by the realization that the first monkey had now latched onto his lower leg. As soon as he looked down he saw the monkey sink its fangs into his calf muscle.

"Son of a bitch!" he yelled.

Anger was now superseding Brandon's pain. He stomped his foot down in an attempt to once again dislodge the demon. It simply would not let go. He dragged his heavy leg over to a nearby rock and kicked it as hard as he could, sandwiching the monkey against it. The second impact crushed the animal's spine and caused it to finally drop. It hit the ground twitching and shrieking. Brandon grabbed a downed branch nearby and clubbed the monkey in the head. The branch was too flexible, however, and kept bending against the primate's skull. He now wished he'd brought one of his golf clubs down with him. The stick was sharp at one end so Brandon leaned his weight against it and impaled the monkey's torso against the ground.

He turned and saw that Ashley was down on all fours crying. The rodeo monkey was still in the saddle. Brandon walked over and grabbed the monkey's head with both hands. He made a violent twist and snapped the animal's neck. He threw it down in disgust just in time for another attacker to land on his back. Brandon didn't even hesitate before slamming himself backwards against a tree. The monkey sent a blood curdling scream right into Brandon's ear. It dropped to the ground and Brandon stomped it with both feet.

There were now two more monkeys on a rock near Ashley preparing to attack. It was a violent, gory battle and a cacophony of sound overwhelmed the jungle. Brandon moved towards the new arrivals and one of them bounded away. The second one was enveloped in a flash of tan as a spurt of blood flew toward Ashley, who was still on her knees. A second later Brandon saw that the monkey had been snatched by a much larger predator. It was the biggest wild cat Brandon had ever seen outside of a zoo. He knew immediately that it was a jaguar.

The cat pinned the monkey down and locked its deadly jaws into the prone primate. The jaguar looked at Brandon and Ashley as if to say: *that's how you do it!* It then walked off silently into the jungle with its kill.

The forest's volume dropped as the monkey army was now in full retreat.

The Newsomes were bruised and bloodied, but could only laugh when they looked at each other.

"Talk about giving you a honeymoon to remember," Brandon said.

"Other than our injuries, no one is ever going to believe this story," Ashley said, shaking her head.

Not wanting to wait for any other visitors to arrive, they wiped themselves off the best they could and returned to their trek.

***

From where they were there was still no real sign of the golf course and they hadn't heard any golfers since leaving the property. Brandon felt like they were paralleling the holes above and gradually moving higher, but still worried that they might be moving away from it. He figured they had a couple of hours of daylight left. He was trying his best to remain confident, but knew they would really be in trouble if they were trapped down in the jungle when night fell.

A short distance later, the path was intersected by a small stream trickling from above. The couple stopped and looked at it intently.

"Oh, I'm so thirsty, Brandon," Ashley bemoaned.

"I know. Me too."

"The water looks so clear. Do you think it's okay to drink?"

"You can't go by how it looks. The things that will make us very sick are too small to see. My other concern is that this could be flowing down from the course and could be filled with pesticides and chemicals."

"I knew you were going to have some logical reason why I shouldn't drink it. Just a sip is all I need."

"Just a sip is all it takes to get sick. We're both thirsty, but we can't risk it yet. We'll be okay for at least a day or two."

"A day or two?" Ashley said in surprise.

"That's worst case, just hypothetical. Most likely we'll be out of here in a few hours and be back sipping drinks by the pool and laughing about monkeys tonight."

"I sure hope so," Ashley said, leaning down to examine the stream more closely. She ran her fingers through the cool water. "Oh, that feels so good." She gathered a handful and poured it over her neck.

"Careful," Brandon warned. "You also don't want to get it in any open wounds."

"Are you my husband or my mother," Ashley mocked, gathering another scoop of the liquid.

"Okay, you deserve a break," Brandon conceded, joining her on the ground. His wrists didn't appear too bad so he dipped them in. He took off his shoes and eased his feet into the coolness. "Wow, that is nice. I feel reinvigorated already."

"The bacteria are very soothing, aren't they?"

"Very funny. I'm just trying to make good use of all of those hours I've spent in front of the television watching those survival guys. They always warn you about the water. Urine is a-okay in their book, but don't ever drink the water."

"They don't know everything. I'm thirsty and there's a clear stream right in front of me. I'm throwing caution to the wind," she said defiantly, filling her hand and drawing it toward her mouth.

"No!" Brandon yelled as he lunged toward her and swatted her arm.

"You are serious about following the rules," she said, laughing at him. "I was only testing you. I wasn't really going to drink it."

He gave her his angriest look, but she was unfazed. Then he noticed something on her arm.

"What is that?" he asked, pointing toward her elbow.

She pulled her arm back and saw the small, colorful creature latched onto her skin. "Eww, it looks like a frog." She tried to flick it off, but it held tight. She grabbed it with her other hand and had to pull hard to dislodge it. It left a red welt where it had been attached and was now stuck to her thumb. "Get off me," she commanded, flinging her hand back and forth.

"There's another one," Brandon said.

She looked and saw that another one was parked on the back of her arm near the triceps.

Brandon grabbed a nearby leaf and used it like a napkin to grab the second frog. Ashley felt the tug on her skin as Brandon yanked it off. She used a stick to scrape the one off her thumb.

"Now you've got one," Ashley said. She found a leaf and groomed her husband.

Neither one of them could see the frogs jumping or feel them landing on their bodies, yet the amphibians continued to appear out of nowhere. Ashley wedged another one off Brandon's leg. It left a red spot right next to the bite wound from the monkey.

"Let's get away from the stream," Brandon said, picking up his shoes and helping Ashley to her feet. They shuffled away quickly, looking up and down their appendages in a panic. When they stopped further along the path they finally appeared to be frog-free.

"They must only like being near the water," Brandon said, bending down to put his shoes back on. When he went to stand back up he wobbled a bit. "Whoa."

"I know," she said, watching him. "Something's wrong."

He stood still and looked about. The air seemed to be pulsating around his head. The chaos of the jungle's sounds started to sound almost melodious. "I knew it! Poisonous frogs!"

"What did the survivor guys say to do?"

"I don't know. I must have missed that episode," Brandon admitted.

"Are we going to die?" Ashley asked, although at this point she already didn't care. The jungle was becoming so much more pleasant by the second.

"Don't know," he replied indifferently. He was ultra focused on a bee buzzing nearby. Everything seemed to be buzzing, particularly Brandon and Ashley.

Ashley giggled. "It kind of feels like that time I took way too many Xanax pills before going to my family reunion. I couldn't stop laughing at my great aunt, Gretchen. She looked like a frog. I expected her to start snagging flies out of the air with her tongue." The memory brought on a new burst of laughter.

"I'm thinking about that time I came out from under anesthesia when I had surgery on my knee. That was a great buzz. They had a bunch of little cereal boxes there to choose from." He was thinking about Tony the Tiger on the Frosted Flakes package. Tony had taken the place of the jaguar rocketing out of the vegetation a few hours ago. He envisioned Tony chewing on the monkey and saying: "Mmm. Monkeys! Theeey're great!"

Ashley spun around and hummed along with jungle's song. "Damn, Brandon, this is way better than golf."

"Yes, it is," he said, rocking back and forth. He made an effort to focus on the fact that they needed to get out of the jungle, but failed. He seemed to have the attention span of the insects that were circling around his head. Suddenly before his eyes the Cheerios honey bee was dancing the Macarena. A moment later he was sure he saw Lucky the Leprechaun scamper through the bushes in search of his Lucky Charms. His attention finally locked onto Ashley.

"We should really get going," he said, ogling her with desire.

She noticed his stare and gazed back at him. "Oh no you don't, mister. That's how we ended up down here in the first place."

"Oh yes," he said, moving straight toward her.

She turned and ran down the path screaming. He ran after her, laughing maniacally. The couple bounced off brush and stumbled over debris. They felt like two kids playing tag.

"I'm right behind you, Mrs. Newsome. Here comes, Brandon!" he snarled.

She made a decent run, but soon succumbed to his superior speed. He tackled her gently and they fell down on the path, unable to control their laughter.

"Stop," she protested half-heartedly as he fondled her.

He wrapped his arms around her and rolled onto his back, pulling her on top of him.

"Stop. No, please don't," he squealed in a feminine voice, wriggling underneath while he held her in place.

She kept laughing and looked at his eyes.

His hand slid down her spine and grasped onto her firm cheek. He wedged her legs apart with his knee and pulled their groins together tightly. With his other hand he palmed the back of her head and forced their lips into a hard embrace.

She quickly gave into the ways of the jungle and rocked her hips up and down on his.

He pushed her away and said, "I want my shorts back. Now!"

Ashley stood up and did what she was told, unbuckling the belt and kicking them off to the side. She bent over, yanked his underwear down to his ankles, and positioned herself on top of him. She was now attached to him as firmly as the frogs had been latched onto her skin.

Brandon looked up at Ashley. Her beautiful face was stationary, but everything around her was spinning. He closed his eyes and they pounded each other to the sound of the jungle beat. They rolled around on the ground and writhed in pleasure. Somewhere in the back of Brandon's mind a tiny little voice said: *I hope none of these plants are poisonous.* Brandon's libido promptly smashed the little voice against a rock.

At one point Brandon opened his eyes and spotted a Wheaties box nearby. The pre-plastic surgery face of Bruce Jenner came to life and started cheering him on. "That's it, Brandon. Go, Brandon, go!" Brandon closed his eyes and shook his head trying to remove the troubling vision. *Maybe we are going to die?*

Ashley was now totally lost; the frogs were talking to her. The noises coming out of her were a combination of laughs and moans. Brandon forced her onto her back and locked his arms behind her knees. Her legs were up in the air and she looked like a frog on its back making a futile attempt to leap. She started yelling, "Ribbit! Ribbit! Ribbit!" It was bizarre, but Brandon found it to be a total turn-on.

Where the frog-induced high ended and sleep took over was unclear. Ashley woke up and saw Brandon lying next to her. Her head seemed clearer, but it still took a minute to get her bearings. She poked Brandon and he slowly opened his eyes and looked around cautiously.

"Are you okay?" Ashley asked.

"I think so," he said sitting up. "I actually feel pretty good."

"Me too. No hangover. What time is it?"

"Almost four o'clock. Luckily we weren't out too long. I guess the frog poison ran its course."

"That was completely crazy."

"We may have to get some of those as pets and keep them in an aquarium at the house," he suggested.

"I think we need to leave them here by their little stream."

The couple got dressed and walked onward.

***

An hour later their shadows were growing and the jungle was becoming noticeably cooler. The noises were also beginning to change as the daytime creatures headed for shelter and the nocturnal ones prepared to take over the rain forest.

They were moving steadily higher toward a ridge that Brandon hoped was a reachable part of the course. He was optimistic that they could get there in an hour of two. At this point he also began to feel like they were being watched. He would catch a glimpse of movement just outside of his field of vision and hear noises that sounded more like humans than animals. It was clearly something different than the monkeys.

The couple was exhausted, but marched on in silence. Ashley would pause periodically and lean on her knees, but she refused to sit down. After what had already happened today she had no intention of stopping now.

Brandon grabbed her suddenly and halted her progress.

49

"Did you hear that?" he whispered.

"What?"

"It almost sounded like voices."

Brandon waited, hoping to hear the sound again in order to be able to place where it was emanating from. He hoped that it might be someone calling from the course above, but it sounded more like it was in the trees around them. The seconds ticked by and the noise didn't return.

Brandon shrugged and they moved on. A few minutes later he heard it again.

"I did hear it that time," Ashley confirmed quietly.

"Do you think we should yell for help and see if they respond?"

"I don't know. What if it is somebody stalking us?"

"Who else would be down here?" Zack asked.

"Considering what has happened already, I'm not sure I want to know."

"Let's just get up to that point and if it's not the course then we can yell and our voices should carry a lot further."

"Sounds good."

The shot of adrenaline from fear helped them pick up their pace. Brandon's heart skipped a beat the next time he heard the voice. It was clearly in the jungle and it was getting closer.

The next noise was something whizzing past their heads. The object hit a tree ahead and Brandon could see that it was a rock with some kind of string attached to it. It was definitely manmade and it had been intended to hit them.

"Run!" he said.

They slashed through the forest tenaciously. Brandon wanted to be between his wife and whatever it was that was now chasing them, but he took the lead to batter through the undergrowth faster.

Brandon saw the path becoming more open and it was turning upward directly toward their intended destination. He reached for Ashley's hand and pulled her along.

"Come on. This is our way out," he said, panting hard.

They were now running at a full sprint.

Brandon looked over his shoulder quickly and finally saw their pursuer. A thin, dark skinned man wearing only a loin cloth had emerged onto the path about a hundred yards behind them. He was jogging, not running, and Brandon sensed that they were going to be able to outrun him to the top.

"We're almost there. We can beat this guy," Brandon encouraged.

Ashley didn't want to look back, but couldn't help herself. She glanced down the path toward the man and then stumbled, screaming as she went down. Brandon hoisted her back up and pushed her ahead. She raced up the trail and then stopped dead in her tracks. Brandon slammed into her.

"What?" he yelled.

She pointed up ahead without a word. There, blocking their path, were three more similar looking men. Two of them had spears and the third had another rock on a string that he was spinning like a lasso.

"What do they want," Ashley asked, her voice trembling.

"I don't know."

Brandon looked back and saw that there were now two other men on the path behind them. The natives were all walking toward the couple at a measured pace.

"Should we try to fight them?" Ashley said.

"With what? I don't think that is our first option."

Brandon and Ashley were both taller than any of the men, but it was six versus two and the natives obviously had the home course advantage.

"Maybe they are scared of us. We're probably on their land. Maybe we can get them to understand that we just want to get back up to the course," Ashley said.

When the men had closed to within twenty feet, one of them began barking instructions at the Newsomes. It wasn't anything that resembled English so the couple just stood in place with their hands up in the air.

The man said it again and pointed his finger toward the ground.

"I think he wants us to get down on our knees," Ashley said.

"Okay, just kneel down slowly."

The natives got even closer holding their spears drawn.

"Hello," Brandon said as if he were addressing a group of aliens. "We are from the resort and just want to get back up there," he added, pointing toward the course.

The men looked at each other and started talking among themselves. A few of them smiled and then laughed. The man who appeared to be their leader said something else and then rubbed himself through his loin cloth.

He advanced slowly toward Ashley as the tension mounted. He stopped in front of her and looked her up and down.

Brandon sensed the situation was not headed in the right direction.

The chief then thrust his hand down and grabbed Ashley's breast through her tight shirt. She screamed and swatted at him. Brandon lunged at the man, but didn't quite reach him. The men were small, but very quick. Three of them were instantly upon Brandon and pinned him to the ground with spears at his neck.

Two other men had already grabbed Ashley and were holding her down on her back. She screamed and fought, but was too weak at this point to put up enough of a defense. The men were sweaty and had overpowering body odor.

The chief walked above her with a sinister look on his face. He then produced a small pouch from his belt. It contained a cream that he rubbed on his penis. In a matter of seconds the man's member had grown to a full erection.

Brandon was watching sideways from the ground nearby. He was terrified about what was happening, but couldn't help but be impressed by whatever magic potion the chief had just used. Brandon felt certain he could make millions of dollars marketing whatever it was on the Golf Channel.

The chief now squatted down above Ashley and pulled her shirt up. He tugged at her nipples and rolled them harshly between his thumb and index finger. He slapped and squeezed her breasts to the delight of his men. They were all now in a frenzy and were making some kind of cheering noise.

He turned and began shoving the shorts down her legs. She tried to resist, but the baggy garment came off easily and she was now exposed to all of the admiring natives.

The men made ooos and ahhs as the chief rubbed the freshly shaven area between her legs. The men pried her legs apart and the chief laughed with delight and placed himself in between. Before entering the chief turned and stared directly at Brandon. He was clearly looking for a reaction.

Brandon felt an anger like he'd never felt before and glared back at the man who was preparing to share his new wife.

The chief smiled proudly and then turned to take care of his business.

Brandon watched as the chief's smile quickly disappeared. In fact, the man's entire head had just disappeared in a flash of black.

Ashley let out the loudest scream of the day as the decapitated attacker flopped down upon her naked body and spewed blood from the gaping wound at the top of the torso.

Brandon wondered if he was experiencing a second wave of dementia caused by the frog poison. He couldn't believe the information entering his eyes at the moment. Now standing above his wife was a man wearing a blue jump suit with the course logo and wielding a massive, black machete. The rest of the natives had already disappeared and Brandon found that he could sit up.

"Are you folks all right?" the stranger asked as he rolled the corpse off Ashley.

"I guess so," Brandon said, rubbing his neck, in part to be sure his head was still attached.

Ashley could not answer as she was still sobbing and trying to regain her composure. The man handed her the shorts and turned away while she redressed.

"Who were those guys?" Brandon asked.

"They are part of a local tribe that lives down here in the forest. Interestingly, they don't consider the property that the course is built on to be part of their territory so we never had an issue with them during construction. Most of the staff didn't even know they were down here. As you can see, it is a much different story when you enter their realm."

"How did you find us?"

"A little while ago I came across your abandoned cart. I looked around and saw the slide marks going down the hill. What were you doing way back there? Did one of you hit a really bad slice?"

"No, just a potty break gone wrong," Brandon admitted.

"Well, I assumed that you would find this path and head east. It's a good thing you came this way. Had you gone the other way it would have taken you right toward their village. If you two had strolled in there we might never have seen you again."

"I can't believe you have a resort right next to these savages," Ashley whimpered.

"That is the sacrifice you make for building a golf course in a third-world paradise. That is also why we continuously warn all of our visitors to never leave the course."

"But this is a serious danger," Brandon said, motioning toward the jungle.

"The world is a dangerous place," the man said frankly. "Speaking of which, we need to get moving. They scare pretty easily, but if we wait around too long they might come back with some reinforcements."

"Are they going to want revenge for what you did?" Brandon asked, looking down at the chief's head lying on the ground nearby.

"Based on his appearance, this guy wasn't a senior member of the tribe. Just a platoon leader. His men will pick a new leader and forget all about him. I think they also know if they start any real trouble with us we could have them wiped out very quickly. Eventually it might happen anyway if we decide to add another eighteen holes as a valley course."

"Thank you so much for your help, Mr.?" Ashley said.

"Reed. Gryphen Reed. I'm on the greens staff here at Vida Serena."

"I really appreciate it," Brandon said, shaking Reed's hand.

"No problem. I'm glad I was able to help. Follow me," he said, starting up the path.

Gryphen quickly led them up and out of the valley. Brandon and Ashley were exhausted, but after what had just happened they had more than enough inspiration to keep them moving.

When they reached the top of the hill Brandon and Ashley were overjoyed to see the course. The group all climbed into Gryphen's maintenance vehicle and he drove them back to the cart on the sixth hole.

"Do you need me to run in and get you some other clothes?" Gryphen offered.

"No, we'll be okay. We have rain gear in our bags that we can use," Brandon replied.

"I don't suppose you are going to finish your round?"

"Definitely not," Ashley answered immediately.

"Would you like me to escort you back to the clubhouse?"

"Thanks, but we'll be alright now. And you can be quite certain that we won't be exiting the course along the way."

"You folks take care and I'll call the pro shop to let them know you're on your way in."

Brandon and Ashley drove back across the opening holes as fast as they could. When Brandon parked the cart near the clubhouse, the clerk who'd checked them in that morning raced out to see how they were doing.

"Are you alright, Mr. and Mrs. Newsome?"

"We're fine now," Brandon said wearily.

"I was worried when Gryphen called in to say that he'd found your abandoned cart. I'm so glad he was able to locate you quickly."

"We were in trouble, but he saved us. He's a hero," Ashley said.

"He's also a top-notch greens keeper," the clerk noted. "I'm sorry you didn't get to finish your round. The back nine is even more spectacular than the front. I will go ahead and credit today's greens fees back to your account," he assured them.

"That's okay. You told us not to leave the course and we didn't listen. Lesson learned," Brandon said.

The couple unloaded their clubs and trudged up to their room. That night they had room service brought in for dinner and first thing the next morning they re-packed their luggage and changed their flight out of Costa Rica.

***

After dropping off the Newsomes, Gryphen Reed drove back out to the trail where he'd found the couple. He unloaded a large bag from the back of his cart and retraced the route down to the native's body. It was still in the path right where he'd left it and flies were starting to buzz around.

"Can't let this go to waste!" Gryphen said before tossing the severed head in the bag and then shoving the body in after it.

3. Hazard in the Hazard

"So you've really never had anyone dive these lakes before?"

"Never."

"These ponds must be loaded. It's pretty rare to find virgin water anymore."

"Come on, hop in the cart and I'll take you around on a tour so you can see the layout for yourself."

"Sounds good, I can't wait to see what you have out here."

Carlos Santiago, the general manager at Pine Hollow Golf Club, drove off toward the first hole. His passenger today was Riley Hess, a professional diver who scoured the bottom of golf course lakes to retrieve the lost possessions of unfortunate golfers. Riley had started out his underwater career in the Navy and remained an active recreational diver after leaving the service. Six years earlier a diving buddy had hired Riley to assist him in his golf ball retrieval business. His friend subsequently experienced heart problems and had to give up diving. Riley took over the existing relationships and over the past two years had steadily been adding new courses to his book of business.

Riley had been referred to Carlos by the superintendent at another course where he already made regular dives. He had heard of Pine Hollow, but didn't know much about it other than it was a successful private club. That normally meant high quality golf balls and lots of them. It was outside of Riley's current territory, but he dove at the opportunity to move into a new area.

As they followed the winding cart path below tall slash pines, Riley immediately liked what he saw.

"This is a beautiful course," he said, noting the rolling, emerald fairways and the pristine, well-placed lakes on the first few holes.

"Thanks. Like every course, Pine Hollow has had its ups and downs. Right now we are really hitting our stride in terms of conditions and membership. Among private clubs we have more rounds played than anyone around," Carlos replied.

Riley was glad to hear that as more golfers equated to more lost balls.

"How long have you been here?"

"Seven years. I was hired during the last down turn to help revive the club. It took a few years, but with improvements to the course and the proper type of targeted marketing we've boosted membership four years in a row. Also, the residential developments in the area are growing again and bringing us new golfers."

"If you've never had retrieval services out here before why are you considering it now? I know sometimes members get bent out of shape about having people out here in *their* lakes."

"That's a good question. I discussed the idea of hiring you with the Board and they gave a very tepid go ahead. Revenue is quite strong and there are plenty of rounds being played. I reminded them that when times are good everyone becomes complacent. Then, when the tide turns, you have to be reactionary. I argued that I wanted to be proactive and came up with a list of options to consider, including ball retrieval. Based on your proposal, it looks like ball harvesting can provide added revenue with little or no expense. I'll take that every day of the week."

"And now that I'm seeing the place first hand I think my projections are on the conservative side," Riley said.

"From a demographic standpoint we have upper to high net worth golfers. The typical member uses new, brand name balls. The pro shop only sells top end golf balls and we move a lot of inventory. We have a solid base of low handicappers, but there are plenty of hackers, too. I've seen people put three and four balls into just one lake out here. And even the good golfers can dunk a few balls during a round if the wind comes up. Heck, just look at TPC Sawgrass up the road. It's amazing how many balls the pros hit into the lake on number seventeen during the Players Tournament."

"It looks like the fourteenth out here isn't an island green, but it's close," Riley said, referencing the course map and satellite photos he'd printed out.

"We'll be there in a minute. It's a gorgeous hole and I think you will really like the water hazard."

They cruised around a curve beyond the thirteenth green and arrived at the course's signature hole. Riley was already excited about the opportunity at Pine Hollow and when he saw number fourteen he could hardly contain his enthusiasm.

"Look at that!" he said, staring out at the symmetrical, oval green perched on the far edge of the lake. The shelf of land sloped down from the ridge behind and projected out into the lake. There were no bunkers, but the front and sides of the green sloped aggressively downward.

For Riley, the highlight was the water lapping menacingly at the base on the green.

"Pretty impressive, eh? Everyone around here calls it 'Beauty and the Beast'. It's great to look at, but it can really punish a score card."

"Does that slope continue down into the water?" Riley asked.

"Yes, it stays rather steep. We encourage golfers not to even attempt rescue missions along the edges. A number of clubs have reportedly been lost along there and at least one lawn mower."

"I can imagine," Riley chuckled. "Was the green constructed of fill?"

"Actually, no. The interesting thing about this one is that the peninsula was already there. In fact, the holes on this part of the course were all built around that little outcropping. Legend has it that when Marvin Kennedy first saw this spot on the property he absolutely insisted that it would be the green for a par three. He would not even consider having it as part of a par four or five.

The lake is also unique. It is the only one that is completely natural. The others were all either dredged or reshaped. It is not the biggest one on the property, but it is the deepest."

When they arrived at the turnout by the green, Riley jumped up from the cart and trotted quickly to the front edge. He looked down and could see nothing but darkness after the first few feet. There was no vegetation visible and the water appeared to be quite clear. It was optimal for the accumulation of golf balls. The only potential down side was the depth. If it was too deep and had thick sediment on the bottom Riley would have a challenge. Pulling balls out of muck in deep water would quickly cloud Riley's view and he would have to take lots of breaks to allow the sediment to settle.

"I can sense your excitement," Carlos said from behind.

"Yep, this looks like the mother lode."

"There are some other good ones, but I figured this one would get your attention."

"I wish I could jump in there right now."

"You take your job seriously."

"It's like a treasure hunt. There's white gold down there," Riley said, staring into the water.

On the trip in they also spent some time taking a look at the long, par five sixteenth hole, which had a lake running parallel to the fairway down its entire length. Riley noted the particular spots where most of the wayward shots would likely collect.

It was a Wednesday afternoon so they had encountered only a few groups of golfers on the course. When they made it to the sixteenth green Riley saw a worker spraying a liquid across the grass surface. As with most fertilizers, it smelled ghastly.

Carlos pulled over and waved to the employee.

"Come on, Riley. I'll introduce you to our head greens keeper."

They walked out and met the man at the edge of the green.

"Gryphen this is Riley Hess. Riley this is Gryphen Reed, an irreplaceable part of our team hear at Pine Hollow. We thought we had gotten our greens in pretty good shape and then we hired this guy. He's taken them to a new level this past year. Look at that surface," Carlos said, squatting down to admire the perfectly uniform vegetation.

"Very impressive," Riley acknowledged.

"Thanks. Just doing my job and trying to keep it."

"Riley is out here to take a look at our lakes. We are discussing the possibility of having him dive the lakes to retrieve golf balls," Carlos said.

"That sounds like a good idea. Watching some of these guys play it's a wonder that the water in the lakes hasn't already been displaced."

"Our golfers aren't *that* bad," Carlos countered.

Gryphen shrugged. "It was nice to meet you; I'll see you around. Good luck and be careful. You never know what you might find down there."

"Nice to meet you, too. Take care."

Carlos drove the rest of the way back to the clubhouse and invited Riley up to his office. The hallway inside was lined with pictures highlighting the club's history. Carlos stopped to point out several particular images.

"Here's a shot of our founding family, the Kennedys."

"Are they all still involved in the club?"

"Just Tobias. Marvin Kennedy, his father, passed away shortly after the club was completed. He put all of the energy of his final years into getting this place built. As for Curt, the other son, my understanding is that he had a disagreement with Tobias and left. Apparently there had always been a strong sibling rivalry and they couldn't manage the course together.

Tobias took the reins and the club got off to a strong start. Then, as is often the case in Florida, a recession hit and times turned lean. There have been a couple of swoons over the years, but Tobias has been able to hang on and bring Pine Hollow back every time. He's in his seventies now so I don't know how many more cycles he is going to navigate through. He has been hinting for a while that he is ready to start divesting his ownership. In the time that I have been here he has already handed off a lot of his former responsibilities. Right now he is up in Canada and his summer vacations have been getting longer and longer each year."

"Does the family still own the club?" Riley asked.

"It is set up as a partnership and Tobias is the majority interest holder. The members all own minority interests. He has earned a lot of confidence over the years so the club has avoided any real battles and everyone has been content with the arrangement. But with things going well right now I sense that he wants to leave while the club is at a peak. His family also owns a lot of the surrounding land that is being developed."

"Family ownership is now the exception. Most of the courses I'm dealing with now are owned by corporations or being run by a management company."

"That's definitely the trend in the industry. The members and the board are starting to kick around some options of how they will move forward. They want to preserve the character of Pine Hollow, but a lot of them want to play golf and not handle administration of a club. They would rather pay a third party to do the dirty work."

"It's hard to argue with that."

They proceeded to Carlos's office and sat down to discuss business.

"I think I know the answer to this question already, but what do you think about diving Pine Hollow?" Carlos asked.

"It is a great looking course and I think it is a tremendous opportunity. I have no doubt we can both make money harvesting the balls down there."

"Excellent. I looked over your proposal and ran it past our finance committee and everyone was fine with your terms. All of your references spoke very highly of you so I think we are ready to move forward.

As I mentioned, we are planning to be closed for maintenance in two weeks. That would give you a four day window to be out here with no golfers raining down on your head. Will that work for you?"

"I will be here first thing on that Monday morning," Riley said, consulting the calendar on his phone. The final day overlapped with another job he had scheduled, but Pine Hollow had far greater potential so he planned to move the other dive.

"We are looking forward to working with you, Riley," Carlos said, shaking hands.

"I can't wait to see what's beneath Pine Hollow," Riley replied.

***

Riley sat on the shore of the third hole at Pine Hollow checking his equipment and preparing for his first dive. He was a burly man – not fat, just thick – who filled his wet suit to capacity. After he began to lose his hair in his late twenties, Riley cut the remaining growth progressively shorter. Finally, he went all in and started shaving his head. That was around the time of his divorce so it seemed like a good way to make a new start. When he emerged from a lake and pulled back the neoprene hood, his head looked like a light bulb perched on top of the black shoulders.

It was a warm, steamy morning, but the skies were clear and the forecast for the rest of the week had unseasonably low chances for rain. The lakes on the course were relatively large with good natural cleaning. The balls would be spread across a wider area, but the water was clearer than in smaller ponds. Another positive factor was the lack of any significant vegetation along the edges. This allowed more balls to roll down to the first shelf, made entry and exit easier, and limited the natural hiding spots for wildlife. At this point in the year, alligator mating season was over. Most of the beasts were content to lounge in the sun and bask in the afterglow.

After reviewing the maps, Riley had developed a game plan for his four days on the course. He decided to start with a few of the easier holes, like number three, in order to get some of the low hanging fruit and show quick results for Carlos. Number fourteen was more daunting and Riley knew that he should wait until tomorrow to head out there. Nonetheless, he was hoping to squeeze in a quick dive later today.

By mid morning he had two dozen large mesh sacks lining the shore of his first lake. They looked like piles of sandbags, or, as Riley saw them, moneybags. He had been throwing balls into his collection bags by the handful the entire time he was underwater. When he dragged the heavy bundles up the shore he was pleased to see the

Titleist logo everywhere. There were also plenty of Bridgestone, Taylormade, and Nike balls that had solid demand.

He loaded the first haul onto a flatbed cart that Carlos had provided and moved on to his next dive. The second and third lakes he dove were more of the same: perfect conditions and countless balls. Normally, he picked up everything and then sorted them out later. At Pine Hollow there were so many balls that he focused on spots where they looked whiter underwater with the expectation that those were newer arrivals and better balls.

Riley was working hard and enjoying himself thoroughly. He always appreciated the fact that his profession involved doing something he loved. At one o'clock he knew he needed to take a break and grabbed lunch on the edge of the eighth hole.

He parked his cart in the shade of a large oak tree and pulled out his cooler. There were numerous workers swarming around the course handling the maintenance projects. They exchanged waves and went about their respective business.

A short time later a familiar face drove up.

"Good afternoon, Aquaman," Gryphen said, tipping his hat.

"Hello again, Gryphen," Riley replied cordially.

"It looks like you are making quite a score out here," Gryphen added, motioning to the cart that was already overflowing with balls.

"These lakes are loaded with golf balls. Getting all of these was pretty easy and I've only hit a few spots so far."

"Be careful when you head out near the turn. There is a creek that connects a few of those lakes and it seems to be the most popular spot for the alligators to hang out."

"I saw that, but thanks."

"Have you ever had any run-ins with them?" Gryphen asked

"A couple of times I've gotten close, however, they don't seem to be as interested in things underwater. When they see me they just move along. Nonetheless, I'm always very careful. I'm not a gator fan and you certainly can't trust them. I'm glad they spend most of their time just being lazy."

"Yeah, they sit around a lot, but they're not as lazy as koala bears. Now that's a lazy animal."

Koala bears? Riley thought to himself.

"Are there any koalas here in Florida?"

"Not anymore," Gryphen said with disdain.

"In this area I worry more about the snakes. I've come face-to-face with water moccasins on a few occasions."

"I've killed my share of those and plenty of rattlesnakes, too," Gryphen commented.

"I do my best not to disturb the wildlife, but safety is still a higher priority."

"Well, good luck out there. Be careful and let us know if you need anything."

"Thanks, I appreciate the offer."

He seems like a nice guy, Riley thought, watching as the greens keeper drove away.

***

The summer days were still long and when Riley arrived at the fourteenth hole late in the afternoon he saw the sun's rays hitting the lake at a perfect angle. On this part of the course there was no one around and it felt very peaceful. There were times when Riley would not dive alone, but here he felt secure. He had plenty of remaining daylight and a number of course employees knew he was on the property. For added protection he had also given Carlos a list of the holes he intended to dive each day.

Once his gear was ready, Riley went to the near side of the green and carefully eased himself down the grassy slope. He pulled down his mask, wrapped his lips around his mouthpiece, and plunged into the water.

Below the surface, Riley was immersed in silence. The first and only noise he heard was the hissing of his breath followed by the gurgle of exhaled bubbles. Directly below him were a few random balls that had snagged on uneven spots along the slope. He grabbed those and then slid deeper. Several feet further down, the dark bottom was interrupted by a band of white that flowed out of his field of vision. It was the first shelf and it was overflowing with balls. In less than five minutes he filled three large bags and had to rise to the surface to deposit them. On the edge of the shore he tied them off on an anchor bolt he'd driven into the ground.

He made several more runs and filled the bags with ease. He was already reaching the bolt's capacity and hadn't even arrived at the front of the green yet. On the next descent Riley went deeper and found another shelf covered with balls. This continued for another hour until Riley decided that he'd far exceeded his quota for today.

There was still plenty of daylight so Riley made one more dive for fun. He wanted to see a little more of the lake and determine just how deep it went. He had two powerful lights, one on his wrist and one on his chest, which penetrated the darkness as he reached new depths. The bottom gradually tapered off, but only a short distance from shore Riley was already in over thirty feet of water. He glided toward the front of the green and a strange shape caught his eye. As he approached the item, the details started to emerge. *Ah, the missing lawnmower!* he realized.

It was sitting upright and Riley gave the handle a tug. It appeared to be in decent condition and Riley was confident that he could attach a rope and fish it out the next day. The lake had a very firm bottom so there was not a lot of sediment for the items to sink into. Nearby he found a few bottles and a rusty length of chain. The next find was a stick that was too straight to be natural – it was a putter with a tarnished shaft. Based on his position in the lake he knew that the club had not fallen into the watery grave, rather it had been thrown. He picked up the orphaned club and headed back to shore.

The first day at Pine Hollow had been long, but very successful. Riley had to make three trips from the course to the cart barn to unload all of the harvested balls.

He was weighing the balls near his truck when Carlos pulled up to check on the totals.

"I guess I don't have to ask how it went out there today," Carlos said, smiling at the multitude of balls in the area.

"We're off to an excellent start and I should be able to repeat this each day."

"It certainly looks promising. We'll see you in the morning."

"Have a good night."

Riley finished his work and drove off with his flat bed trailer riding low on the ground.

***

On the afternoon of the second day, Riley was once again probing the depths of number fourteen. After an hour of pulling balls he headed away from shore to explore. He quickly found two more clubs and an assortment of trash. He was cruising along the bottom when something odd caught his attention. His light reflected off a metallic object and made a flash in the darkness. He moved closer and shone his beam on the item. It was a silver revolver. Riley picked it up carefully and shook off the dusting of silt. The chambers were all empty and he rolled it over in his hand. The gun looked old, but was still in very good condition. He clipped it to a carabiner on his belt and continued his search, wondering what else he might find.

On the way in he tied a rope to the handle of the lawn mower. It was no longer the most interesting thing he was going to bring up from the lake today.

Back in the parking lot Riley had one of the attendants call up to the clubhouse for Carlos. He arrived a few minutes later and saw the prize Riley had brought him sitting on the ground.

"Don't tell me you pulled that out of the lake on number fourteen," Carlos said in disbelief.

"Sure did," Riley said proudly, enjoying the look of amazement on Carlos's face.

"It's in surprisingly good shape, but I don't think we'll be putting it back into use on the course."

"That's what I figured. I just wanted to show it to you. I'll drop it by the scrap yard on my way home today if you want."

"That sounds like a good new home for it."

"And I found something else down there, too."

"What's that?"

"This," Riley said, producing the gun from his duffel bag.

"Oh my gosh. You really found that in the lake?"

"Yeah, it was just sitting there on the bottom."

Carlos took the weapon and studied it. The screws were rusted and there was some tarnish in areas, but most of the gun still had a shiny chrome finish. Carlos hefted it and noted its weight. He pulled the pin, released the cylinder, and spun the empty chambers like a gunslinger.

"How do you suppose it got there?"

"No idea," Riley said. "I didn't want to leave it in the lake so I thought the best thing was to turn it over to you. Maybe you can hang it up in the clubhouse as a decoration."

"Thank you, Riley. The county sheriff is a member here and I'll give him call in the morning to see what he says. Is there anything else?"

"A whole bunch more golf balls."

"I like the sound of that. I can't wait to see what you bring me tomorrow."

***

Several police vehicles converged on Pine Hollow the next day. Sheriff Jeb Myers was here on official business, not to squeeze in a quick nine holes of golf. When Carlos called him in the morning and told him what had been found he decided to take appropriate action. Guns did not typically end up in the bottom of lakes by accident. He didn't have a theory as to why the gun would be on the course, but he didn't want to take any chances, particularly due to the fact that he was a member of the club.

"Good morning, Carlos," Sheriff Myers said with his strong southern drawl.

"Hello, Jeb. Thanks for coming out," Carlos replied, shaking hands with the hulking officer who was hiding behind a thick mustache and Ray-Ban aviator glasses.

"What have you got for me?"

"Here's the gun," Carlos said, holding up a large plastic bag.

"Thanks," Myers said, taking it carefully and examining the weapon. "That's an older model so I'm guessing it's been down there a while. We'll run some checks and see if we can get a history on it."

"If it has been in the lake for a long time does it still matter? Isn't there some sort of statute of limitations or something?"

"Not for murder, Carlos," Myers said, as though it had been a silly question.

"Murder?"

"You never know. There have been a lot of unsolved ones over the years. With modern technology and new evidence," the sheriff said, holding up the bag, "a cold case can suddenly become hot again."

"I guess I hadn't really been considering foul play."

"Anyway, you made sure the golf ball diver didn't go back out there, right?"

"Yes. I told him just to stay away from that end of the course today. He's got plenty of other lakes to dive. The guy has a lot of experience and he offered to help if you needed it."

"Thanks, but we better keep him out of there just in case it does become a crime scene. Now, if he happens to find any Titleists with two, black slashes through the logo those need to be returned directly to me as evidence," Myers joked, lightening the mood of the conversation.

"Oh, he's pulled up a few buckets of those already. You've left a whole string of victims out here at Pine Hollow, Jeb."

The sheriff gathered his men and led the divers out to number fourteen. The caravan of divers and officers commandeered several golf carts and wound out along the path. On the way they passed the greens keeper and one of his men.

Gryphen looked up from his work and nodded at the law enforcement officers.

"What do you think they're doing out here?" Gryphen asked his associate.

"I heard one of the guys at lunch say something about the Sheriff coming out to look into some unsolved murder."

"Really?"

"Yeah, all those cops are probably out here to look for evidence."

"Hmm. That's interesting," Gryphen said before returning to his task.

***

The sun was getting low when Sheriff Myers returned with his posse.

"We didn't find anything else out there, Carlos."

"I'm honestly glad to hear that," Carlos said with relief.

"I saw that Riley fella' out there and had a chat with him. He's obviously not involved and I thanked him for bringing in the gun. I asked him to contact me if he came across anything else that seemed suspicious."

"He did pull up some golf clubs and a lawnmower, too. You don't suppose those were used as a murder weapons."

"The lawnmower, no. The golf clubs, maybe."

"Out here perhaps they were used in a mercy killing."

"I hear ya', Carlos. It might take us a while to find information on the gun. I may need to send it off to the FBI lab. Hopefully we can find out something and then we'll see where it leads. I'll keep you posted if there is anything we can share with you. By the way, when will Tobias be back?"

"He is scheduled to return next Friday."

"That's good. I may need to talk to him. He is probably the only person around here with a history going back to when this place was built."

***

68

"Welcome back," Carlos said, greeting Tobias as he entered the executive office area.

"Good to be back, Carlos," Tobias replied, shaking hands with the man he trusted Pine Hollow to during the summer. He hadn't spoken to Carlos in over a month, which was exactly how Tobias wanted it. In the past, even short vacations were invariably interrupted by molehills turning into mountains while he was away from Pine Hollow.

"How were things north of the border?"

"We had a great summer this year. It was very relaxing and I played some solid golf. Last week we finished up by taking a side trip out to the coast to play some new links courses that opened recently."

"I'm glad it went well."

"I take it things have been pretty quiet around here."

"It was a relatively slow summer until the last week or so."

"Oh? What did I miss?"

"Unfortunately we suffered a big loss last week. Gryphen resigned," Carlos said, gauging Tobias's reaction to the news.

"He's leaving?" asked a surprised Tobias.

"He already left."

"Why?"

"Honestly, I don't know. He came in the other day and let me know he was leaving immediately. He said he had been very happy here and appreciated us giving him the opportunity to work at Pine Hollow. He told me it was time to move on to new challenges and said goodbye. He wanted me to pass along his thanks to you and wished you the best of luck with the club going forward."

"Well that was nice. He was an odd fellow, but we're going to have a tough time replacing him."

"This happened the other day and since I knew you'd be back this week I didn't want to spoil the end of your vacation."

"That's alright, Carlos. It is a loss, but something we can deal with."

"I've already quietly put out the word to some of our contacts that we will be looking for a replacement."

"Good. With season approaching we need to be proactive and make sure the members don't get antsy. Anything else?"

"I also hired a diver to pull balls from the lakes."

"You did what?"

"You know, one of those guys who goes down and brings up all the lost balls."

"Why did you do that?"

"It looked like a great way to generate some extra revenue. And don't worry, I had him out here during the maintenance week so he didn't disturb any of the golfers."

"Well, that was good thinking."

"He did a great job retrieving balls, but he also pulled up some other interesting things. Look at this," Carlos said, holding up his phone to show Tobias a picture.

"What's that?" Tobias said, squinting at the grainy picture.

"It's the lawnmower that fell into the lake on number fourteen a while back."

"Oh, I'd forgotten all about that."

"But this was even more surprising," Carlos said, swiping to the next picture.

The photo of a gun was much clearer and Tobias stared at it silently.

"It was also in the lake on fourteen," Carlos said with excitement.

"What did you do with?" Tobias asked.

"I gave it to Jeb."

"Oh..."

"How do you think it ended up out there?"

"I don't know."

"Well, I'm sure you have a lot of things to do so I'll let you get to them. All of your mail is stacked on your desk and there are reports from each of the membership committees. Overall, I think everything looks great."

"Glad to hear it. I'll let you know if I have any questions."

Tobias closed the door to his office and sat down behind his desk. He spun his large, black leather chair around and looked out his broad panoramic window. The clubhouse was situated on a hill affording an expansive view. He gazed out across the course and the property surrounding Pine Hollow at everything he'd spent the last several decades developing.

He turned back around and stared blankly at the meaningless stacks of paper on his desk. Although his office was silent, something seemed to be calling to him. He eventually gave into the urge and opened the bottom drawer on his desk, pulling out a large black and white photo. The picture had his father, Marvin, standing in the middle with his sons on either side of him. He had his arms around the boys who had their hands perched on the ends of golf clubs. Everyone in the picture was smiling.

***

"Hello, this is Sheriff Myers."

"Good morning, Sheriff. This is Pete Kernan calling from the FBI weapons division."

"Agent Kernan, good to hear from you. What have you got for me?"

"We were able to identify an owner, but not much else. We had to go through the old fiche records and finally determined that the last registration was to a gentleman named, Curt Kennedy. Does that ring any bells?"

"It does. I know his brother who is a resident here in Grove County."

"Perhaps he can help you more than we can. It looks like Curt Kennedy disappeared in the 1970s and there is no trace of him since then."

"I never knew Curt, but my understanding is he parted ways with his family around that time and never came back," Sheriff Myers explained.

"We also ran a check on the gun's ballistics and it didn't match up to anything in our database. However, the data starts to get thin as you go further back in time."

"I understand. Anything else I should know?"

"That's about it. I would suggest talking to the brother and see if he can shed any light on it."

"Yeah, I plan to do that," Sheriff Myers said hesitantly.

"We'll have the gun shipped back to you this week. Let us know if there is anything else you need."

"Thanks, Agent Kernan."

The sheriff hung up the phone and debated his next move. It could just be a coincidence; perhaps there was a perfectly valid reason why Curt would have disposed of his gun in the lake. Maybe when he left town he didn't want to take it with him. He was also concerned that his relationship with Tobias and affiliation with the club might cloud his judgment. He knew that he needed to look at the situation as an objective professional. When the gun of a man who disappeared without any further trace suddenly shows up there was no other choice than to open an investigation.

After a quick search on his computer yielded nothing, Sheriff Myers headed down to the library to search older information. He scanned through old news articles and records and found plenty of references to the Kennedy family. There were a number of pictures of Marvin and his sons, but after a certain point there were only mentions of Tobias. Marvin had died and Curt had simply vanished. He also found nothing that pointed to any serious conflict among the family.

***

Sheriff Myers was sitting in Tobias's office waiting for him to arrive. He looked out the window and watched as golf carts zigzagged down several of the visible fairways. Myers was daydreaming about being out among the golfers when he heard the door close behind him.

"Tobias."

"Jeb," Tobias said, sitting down at his desk and facing the sheriff.

"It's a nice day out there today," Myers said, motioning toward the course.

"Sure is. What can I do for you today, Jeb?"

Sheriff Myers lifted his hat from his lap and then tossed the revolver, wrapped in a plastic evidence bag, onto Tobias's desk.

"We've got a problem here, Tobias."

Tobias stared at the gun and said nothing.

The sheriff continued, "I wish I could tell you to take the gun and toss it back into the lake on number fourteen and that would be the end of it. Unfortunately, the diver dredged it up, Carlos gave it to me, and the FBI examined it. Therefore, I now need to deal with it. I decided the easiest thing to do would be to ask you what you may know about it and whether or not it has anything to do with your brother's *departure* from Pine Hollow."

Tobias sat back in his chair and continued to think about what he wanted to say to Sheriff Myers.

"Look, Tobias, we've been friends for a long time. I'm not here to pressure you or make you do something you don't want to do. I simply want to give you the first move and let you know what I will have to do. Given the circumstances, I can't sweep this under the rug. I have to do my job."

"I understand," Tobias finally said in a quiet voice.

"If you want me to leave I will. However, I will have to come back and will bring a lot of men and a lot of shovels. I really don't want to do that to you or Pine Hollow."

"That won't be necessary, Jeb."

Sheriff Myers felt a quick wave of relief followed by the sinking anticipation of what he was about to hear.

"So where is Curt?"

"He's here. He never left Pine Hollow."

"What happened to him?"

"We were here working late one night. Curt had spent the afternoon golfing and drinking. Things were very marginal here as Pine Hollow was just getting started. I confronted him about his commitment to our father's club and we got in a yelling match. I told him to sober up and went back to my office. A few minutes later he came in and started arguing again. This time he had his gun with him," Tobias said, motioning to the weapon on his desk.

"After his wife left him and dad died he had increased his drinking considerably and he seemed to be spinning downward. I tried to calm him down, but he was out of control. He kept coming toward me and waving the gun. When he was right in my face I grabbed the gun, backed off, and held it at him. He charged me and the gun went off and hit him in the chest."

"If it was self defense why didn't you just report it?" Sheriff Myers asked.

"I thought about it, but I was worried about the club. How would it look to prospective members if one of the owners had just shot his brother in the clubhouse? We never would have made it."

"I understand, Tobias, but it still would have been the right choice."

"There was another problem, too."

"And that was?"

"When my father died he had a life insurance trust. It was a half million dollars and he set it up to serve as an emergency reserve for Pine Hollow. One of the clauses was that if either brother left the club, or died, the other one could draw on the principal. I had to have an agreement signed by Curt so I told the trustee that I had sent it to him and then forged his signature. Initially I didn't touch the trust, but eventually when we took a downturn I had to access it. I know someone might look at that and see it as a motive. It had nothing to do with what happened that night, Jeb. You have to believe me."

"I do, Tobias, but I'm the sheriff, not the judge and jury. Where's the body?"

"Under the cart barn. I was able to take it out that night and bury it right before a concrete pour."

"And why didn't you just bury the gun?" the sheriff asked, thinking that they would never be having this conversation if he had.

"I forgot about it and after I'd buried Curt I came back in to clean up and realized it was still in the office. I just panicked and tried to figure out the best place to get rid of it. Number fourteen jumped into my mind so I drove out there and chucked it."

Sheriff Myers nodded. "Well, I think you made the right choice *today*, Tobias. Come on. Let's go and we'll figure this out."

The two men walked out of the offices together without a word as other staff members looked on.

***

Riley picked up the local newspaper in his driveway and unfolded it. On the front page he saw a picture of Tobias Kennedy being led up the courthouse steps by his attorney. The story below indicated that he was arriving for a hearing on the death of his brother, Curt. It stated that Tobias intended to plead not guilty and that he had killed his sibling in self defense.

The dives at Pine Hollow had been a tremendous success and Carlos had contacted Riley about future opportunities to return. Still, after what had happened, Riley's enthusiasm had diminished and he hoped this saga wouldn't doom the club. Riley promised himself that if he did ever dive there again he would stick to retrieving golf balls and leave everything else at the bottom of the lakes.

4. Trespass at Twilight

"Are you ready, Kwin? Let's go see who's playing," Zak yelled.

"Hang on! I have to finish cleaning my room first," Kwin replied.

"Do it later. I don't want to miss anything."

"Alright, I'm coming. Mom's going to be mad."

"Don't worry. We'll be back before she gets home and you can finish then."

"I better not get in trouble," Kwin warned. He received no response as Zak was already out the door.

The two boys walked quietly across the barren field near their house. Zak walked efficiently leaving clean foot prints with each step, while Kwin shuffled his feet lazily kicking up the dusty, gray soil as he went. They made their way up the modest hill that separated them from their destination. Stopping at the crest, they took up a position behind several large rock formations. The perch gave them an excellent vantage point, while still shielding them from the view of the players below.

"Excellent, we're just in time. Here they come now," Zak noted with giddy excitement.

Kwin fiddled with a crag in a boulder displaying far more indifference to the visitors' arrival.

"How can you not be interested in watching this?" Zak asked.

"I am. Just not as much as you are. We get lots of people coming through here; I don't know what's so special about these guys."

"Are you kidding? Do you realize how far they probably traveled just to play here? And look at them. They are all dressed up in their fancy clothes and sporting cutting edge technology in their equipment. I'm impressed," Zak said, justifying his view. "At least they're walking today and not leaving tracks all over the place."

"The cart looks like far more fun. I hope I get to drive one like that some day."

"You? Drive? You'd just wreck the thing," Zak chided.

"I would not!" Kwin shot back, giving his brother a small shove.

"Okay. We'll see. I just want them to finish up and leave so we can sneak out there and play before dark. Now be quiet and watch."

***

Down below the golfers were far too focused on their game to notice the boys watching from above. Their visit was primarily a business trip, but they couldn't skip the chance to work in some golf. None of the men had played here before and likely wouldn't get another chance any time soon.

"I shouldn't complain, but I sure wish I had my own clubs to play with. These are a bit short for me."

"I knew you'd say something like that, Jay. Don't even think about using the equipment as an excuse. These are perfectly good clubs they gave us. Any difference in yardage will be more than compensated for by our elevation."

"And you can't gripe about the conditions either," added Carl, the third player in the group. "The sky is perfectly clear and there's not a puff of wind."

"Okay, okay. It wasn't really a complaint anyway. More of just a way to enhance the experience even further."

"This is about as good as it gets. The only course I've played like this was out in Nebraska. It had rolling hills interspersed with rugged terrain. It appeared flat from a distance, but still felt like a roller coaster ride. Some holes looked basic until they disappeared down into a box canyon," Bud observed.

"I'd compare it to a course I played in the Caribbean. It was woven into a forest of jagged rock spires jutting up from the sea. Obviously no water hazards here and certainly a lot more carry than at sea level, though," Jay added.

"When we get back to Florida next week let's try to get a round in. After that I'm sure we'll all be busy and back on the road for a while. Who knows when we'll get to play again."

"Sounds like a good plan, Carl. Let's play nearest to the flag on this hole. Hit away," Bud said.

The three friends would normally do some minor betting on their rounds. However, since none of them knew this layout they were focusing on specific bets such as longest drive and closest to the pin.

No one played particularly well and no one seemed to care. This was about being away from it all and enjoying hitting the ball.

Although they were together, there was an undeniable sense of loneliness here. There were no houses on the fairways and the lack of trees gave the course an infinite feel of barrenness. Each of the men could feel it and would periodically glance back toward the small clubhouse just to reassure themselves of where they were.

When they made the turn and started the inward holes, however, there was no sense of relief. Rather, each shot took them closer to the end of an unforgettable round.

On their final hole the group stopped on the tee and absorbed the stunning panorama.

"This has been one heck of a round, gentlemen," Carl said. "With all of this land just think of the potential. Endless opportunities for additional holes and they could build an incredible clubhouse up there on that ridge," he added.

"Sure, but there's a lot to be said for playing it in the natural state as well. Pure golf, no gimmicks," commented Bud.

"Alright fellas, we better finish up and hit the road. How about longest drive gets to have the first sleep shift on the way home?" Jay suggested. It had been a long and hectic trip so all of the men were exhausted and sleep would be a valuable prize.

"I'm game," Bud replied, knowing that they were equally matched golfers and it would be a fair contest.

"You've got the honor, Bud. Show us the way home," Carl said, gesturing toward the tee box.

It had been one of those great and memorable rounds for all of the men. As they marched down the fairway to determine the winner, they were infused with a renewed sense of vigor. The trip home would be an arduous one, however, the thought of seeing their families and sleeping in their own beds was a powerful motivator.

When they finished the men shook hands and patted shoulders before walking off to the clubhouse. The round had just finished, but they were already beginning to recount the highlights and lowlights of the afternoon's adventure. Bud's drive had edged out the others and he made notable stretches and yawns to taunt his companions.

The group dropped off the golf clubs and loaded into their vehicle. Bud happily climbed into the back to sleep while Jay and Carl took seats up front. They were also burdened with making the call to check in with the home office before leaving. In a connected world there was truly no escape.

As they departed, the men gazed out the windows and absorbed the dazzling views of the course. They continued to glance back as it faded into the distance before turning their weary eyes toward home.

***

Unbeknownst to the golfers, they were also being watched as they left. Zak and Kwin were eager for the round to conclude so they could finally have their chance. They looked carefully to see when the clubhouse door was closed and locked and made sure the golfers' vehicle was out of view. The boys knew that getting caught would land both of them in serious trouble.

Cautiously they crept out onto the course and made their way to the spot where the others had just departed. The sun was getting very low, but they still had enough time to get in a few holes. Sunset came slowly here, but once the sun went down they would be out of luck.

"Awesome! Some clubs are still out here," Zak said, examining the metallic sticks.

"I've got a couple of balls, too," Kwin added, holding out a handful of white spheres he'd scrounged from the practice area.

The boys looked at each other and then simultaneously turned toward the golf cart parked a short distance away. They dropped their items and broke into a sprint in that direction.

Kwin yelled, "I call first!"

But it didn't matter as his older brother easily won the footrace and flung himself into the driver's seat.

"I called first," Kwin whined as he arrived at the cart.

"Yes, but you were second," Zak replied, shoving his sibling away. "Be happy with shotgun. Get in."

Zak could hardly contain his excitement as he gently slid his fingertips over the hard, black steering wheel and wiggled his butt in the cushy seat. His brother was even more enthusiastic, bouncing up and down on the passenger side.

"Sit still a minute," Zak directed, trying to prepare for his maiden voyage. He pushed a green button on the console and it began flashing, but nothing else happened. Having watched the golfers previously he knew that the foot pedals were somehow involved. He pushed the first one and again there was no response. He looked over to his brother who just shrugged. Zak stepped on the second pedal and the machine sprung to life, snapping the unprepared boys' heads back as the vehicle lunged forward. Zak yanked his foot off the pedal and they flew forward as it rapidly decelerated.

"Don't push so hard," Kwin advised, glaring at his older, and supposedly wiser, brother.

"Okay, okay. I'm sorry," Zak replied, scared, but excited by the power under his foot.

He set his foot back on the pedal and gently eased it down, resulting in an equally smooth forward movement. He eased up and they slowed more gracefully.

"I wonder what the other one does?" Zak asked.

"Beats me," Kwin responded.

Zak began driving forward in a straight line and then hit the second pedal with his left foot. The boys were once again jarred as the brake fought against their acceleration.

"Of course. That one slows you down," Zak observed.

He progressed slowly and started to get the feel of the steering in a nearby open area. His confidence built quickly and he drove faster and more wildly at the constant urging of his brother. They shot up and down the modest hills and Zak slung them hard into ever tighter turns. Zak marveled at how simple it was to drive and couldn't believe just how much fun it was as well.

Finally, Zak slowed down and took a break. Both boys were tired from yelling and laughing so hard.

"Alright, my turn," Kwin proclaimed.

Zak was having a blast and did not want to yield his seat, but thought it was only fair to allow his sibling a go on the driver's side.

"Okay, let me show you what to do," Zak said in his judicious, big brother voice as he climbed out.

Kwin glared at him. "I know what to do! Get in," Kwin said, motioning to the passenger side.

"I'm not so sure about riding with you," Zak said hesitantly.

"Fine," Kwin replied as he tore off, almost running over his brother's foot.

Kwin was a reckless driver indeed. He wanted to show up his brother and performed even more aggressive moves than Zak had made during his turn. At one point he hit an angled rock and had two wheels on one side get slightly airborne. He immediately doubled back and did it again. With his confidence growing he looked around for bigger targets.

Zak watched as Kwin lined up for a run over the edge of a large pot bunker. "Don't do it!" he yelled, watching the stunt unfold. It was too late and Kwin would not be deterred at this point.

The cart picked up as much speed as it could attain and kicked up a modest trail of dust. Right before takeoff Kwin shot a sideways glanced at Zak that clearly said: *watch what I can do big brother*. Kwin held the wheel tight and leaned forward as though it would somehow make him more aerodynamic.

The cart hit the earthen ramp and just when it seemed that Kwin would take off into space the opposite happened; a complete anticlimax. Clearly Kwin had not yet taken a basic physics class. Despite its abilities on flat ground, the vehicle was still far too heavy and could not reach a high enough speed to do what Kwin had hoped. It immediately flopped down over the back edge and came to an angled halt, ejecting Kwin in the process. As he took flight, he looked like a bull rider being tossed by an unwilling animal.

Zak stood still for a moment processing what he'd just witnessed. Then his feet instinctively began running toward the crash. To his relief he found his brother rolling on the ground laughing.

"Did you see that?" Kwin exclaimed with pride, despite the epic failure of his jump.

"Yeah, I saw you crash. Are you okay"

"I think so," Kwin said, sitting up and brushing the gray dirt off his arms and legs. "I bounced off the steering wheel," he added, rubbing his chest to see if anything seemed out of place. "That's really going to hurt tomorrow."

Zak helped Kwin get up and they surveyed the scene. The cart's back wheels were still on the lip and the front bumper was wedged into the sand. They gave it a push and it didn't even budge.

"What do you think we should do?" Kwin asked soberly.

"We?" Zak said with exasperation. "You are the one who wrecked it. What were you thinking? Even if you had made the jump how would you have gotten back out the other side?"

Kwin looked at the bunker and pondered the topography, shifting his head back and forth. "I hadn't really considered the landing part."

"Clearly."

They walked around the trapped machine to see if any other ideas would present themselves. None did.

"I guess just leave it there. There's nothing we can do. They'll find a way to get it out. I just hope they don't figure out who did it,"

Zak said. He looked at the sun in the distance and decided not to let Kwin ruin what remained of the fading afternoon. "Come on, let's go hit some balls while we still have time."

The boys plodded back and gathered up the golf clubs and balls. As was usually the case, Zak quickly forgave Kwin for his youthful indiscretion. There was no one he'd rather play golf with than his brother. They both started making big, easy practice swings, emulating what they'd seen the golfers do earlier. Zak watched with a bit of unease and kept an adequate distance from his brother. Luckily this time Kwin was more careful. He'd at least learned a short-term lesson from his crash.

The boys were both good athletes with excellent hand-eye coordination; however, they quickly discovered that the game of golf was tougher than it looked. They hit some easy chip shots before deciding that they were ready to begin play.

They were each well aware that their sibling rivalry could be an impediment to having an enjoyable time so they agreed to just play for fun, though neither boy really knew what to expect.

Zak was polite and graciously allowed his younger brother to hit first. Kwin lined up toward the small flag in the distance and took a mighty swing. There was a gritty explosion and Kwin looked up optimistically to determine his result. Unable to locate his ball against the dark sky he asked, "Where'd it go?"

Zak couldn't contain himself and laughed loudly while pointing to the ground next to the newly sliced gash in the dirt. "It's right where you left it."

"Quit laughing!" Kwin demanded as he shook the soil from his ball and tried again. This time he swung even harder and made a bigger splash. Once again he couldn't locate this ball and turned to his brother after checking the ground at his feet.

"Well, you at least hit that one, Kwin," Zak replied, pointing far off to the right where the ball was just coming down and skittering to a stop.

"That's your fault!" Kwin accused. "You were laughing during my swing."

"Sorry, but my laughter didn't make the ball go way over there. My turn."

Zak was excited to hit a full length shot, but tried to show some restraint. He made contact on his first attempt; however, it was far from a good shot – low and left. He shrugged and looked at his brother.

"I think we should each get another try for our first full shots. Call it a 'try-again'," Kwin said diplomatically.

"That's an excellent idea, Kwin," Zak agreed.

Their second efforts were both better, though still not stellar. They divided up the clubs and headed off to hit their next shots.

As they followed in the footsteps of the golfers who had played earlier, the brothers slowly made their way up the learning curve. The first few holes featured plenty of hacks, however, by the turn they were showing solid improvement.

In terms of gamesmanship it was just as one would expect with siblings. Despite their pre-round agreement, there was a constantly fluctuating mix of taunts and compliments.

After watching his best tee shot of the round sail down the middle of the fairway, Kwin turned proudly to his brother and asked, "Did you see that one?"

Without skipping a beat, Zak replied, "No. I was looking over that way towards our house. Was it a good shot?" He then waited for his brother to take the bait.

"Are you kidding? That was the best one by far. Can't you show a little respect and watch my shots? I'm watching all of yours."

"Alright, I'll try to watch the next one."

"Great. I probably won't hit another one like that the rest of the day. Unbelievable."

"If it will make you feel better you don't have to watch this one," Zak said nonchalantly as he teed up his ball. "Will that make us even?"

"No it won't. But I'll be the bigger man and watch yours anyway."

Zak enjoyed his brother's stewing and then proceeded to hit a decent shot down the fairway. "That was a good one. Is that what yours looked like?"

"Not even close. Mine was way better than that lousy attempt."

"Lousy? I thought you were being the bigger man?"

"Let's go. It's a long walk past your ball to get to mine."

As they strode off the tee, Zak grabbed Kwin by the neck and shook him playfully. "Lighten up, bro'. I'm just messing with you. I saw your ball and it was an awesome shot. That was the best one either of us has hit."

"Why couldn't you just say so?" Kwin asked, shaking loose from his brother's grip. "Instead you have to play your little game."

"Because it's *fun*! And you make it so easy. If you stop overreacting to everything I won't have a game to play anymore. But until then..."

"Let's go wise guy," Kwin said, glaring back over his shoulder. "We're running out of time."

To get back into good graces with Kwin, Zak was extra complimentary of his brother's game down the home stretch. Of course Kwin was now skeptical as to whether any of the comments were meaningful.

On the final tee the two boys were again emulating the golfers who had played before them. Zak looked happily into the distance and observed, "It's a pretty cool spot up here. You can see so far in every direction."

"Yeah, it's neat. But the terrain is still like everything else around here. I wonder what it's like where those guys are from?"

"Probably a lot different. Can you imagine playing this game with lakes and trees? It's tough enough just to hit the darn ball. We're certainly not ready to play with any obstacles in the way."

"Speak for yourself," Kwin replied boldly, stepping in front of Zak and teeing up his ball.

"Alright, big man. Let's see what you've got besides cockiness."

Kwin backed up his bravado and hit another surprisingly good shot toward the final flag. He picked up the tee and just stared at his brother with a pleased grin.

"Was that another good one?" Zak asked. "I was distracted by something over there."

"Don't even try," Kwin responded. "Hit your ball."

Their final shots had less dispersion than their initial ones and this time they walked together down the fairway. They were joking around and focusing only on the positive aspects of their round. It was one of those moments when brothers who could fight like dogs realized they were truly best friends.

When they reached the putting surface, Zak tapped in his short putt and then held the flag for his brother.

"Come on, Kwin. Knock this one in," Zak said, honestly rooting for him to make it.

It was only about ten feet away, but Kwin studied it carefully using all of the knowledge he'd gained. He took his stroke and immediately knew that he'd hit it too hard. The ball skidded across the ground directly toward the hole.

Zak also sensed the velocity and instinctively backed away as though the ball might hurt if it hit him.

The tension was short lived as the racing ball smacked the hole squarely, popped straight up in the air, and then disappeared into the cup.

"Whoo-hoo!" Kwin bellowed, raising his hands and the club toward the sky above.

"Great shot, Kwin," Zak complimented, waving the flag back and forth in celebration.

Kwin retrieved his ball and held it up like a trophy. "I'm keeping this one."

"That's fine, but we better leave the clubs. Otherwise they might come looking for us."

"Let me see that flag," Kwin said, noting that it was different than the others on the course. This one was larger and had red and white stripes with a small, blue rectangle covered in white stars. "I like the design. Maybe I'll keep this too."

"No. That's a bad idea. This one is different for a reason and we definitely shouldn't mess with it. Put it back and let's head home."

"Yeah, you're right. Let's not ruin a good thing here."

The boys put the equipment back where they'd found it and walked off across the property. As they left, Zak put his arm around Kwin's shoulder and said, "Great playing with you, little brother."

"Thanks, you too, Zak. I'm glad you made me come out here today. Maybe we can do it again tomorrow?" he inquired eagerly.

"We'll see."

"Do you think those guys will be back?" Kwin asked, motioning in the direction where the golfers had exited.

"Perhaps some day. I'm sure they'll tell others about it and more people will come out here."

"That sounds good."

"Maybe. You have to be careful what you wish for, Kwin."

***

Jay sat with his seatbelt on running through checklists in a three-ring binder. He routinely flipped the laminated pages while confirming information with Carl, who was floating above and reading gauges on the ceiling.

"It looks like our oxygen stir was successful so we should be all set until we begin re-entry," Carl reported.

"Is Bud still sleeping back there?" Jay asked, unable to turn around in the large chair to which he was secured.

"Like a baby. Nothing seems to interfere with his nap time."

"Hmm. We should probably do one more test, just for safety sake," Jay mused, with a fiendish smile.

"What's that?"

"The audible alarm circuits. We wouldn't want something to go wrong and not know about it."

"Excellent idea, Jay," Carl agreed, knowing there was no legitimate reason to run the test at this moment.

"Ready?"

"Beginning sequence."

Carl flicked a row of steel toggle switches and the tiny cabin was quickly filled with a cacophony of sirens and whistles.

"What the hell?" Bud immediately shouted from the back. "What's going on?"

Carl reset the controls and quiet was restored. "Oh, sorry, Bud. No problem, just running some final tests."

"On what?" Bud asked, still trying to get his bearings.

"I wanted to make sure you were still alive back there, Bud."

"Thanks alot, jackass," Bud grumbled, realizing the nature of the prank.

"I was just following orders," Carl replied.

"Okay, *jackasses*," Bud said with added emphasis for his commander's benefit.

Their conversation was interrupted by a deep voice from above, "Everything alright up there, boys?"

"Yes, sir," Jay responded. "Just testing some systems. Needed to make sure that Bud wasn't malfunctioning."

"Okay, Jay. We heard the noise, but it didn't look like any actual alarms. I just came on shift and didn't want to start with an emergency."

"Only smooth sailing to report, Houston."

"So how was your afternoon up there?"

"Like the rest of the trip: spectacular. I'm glad we were able to get in a little recreation before we left," Jay answered.

"Good for you. How was the course?"

"Challenging, but worthwhile. It was strange playing on a gray surface rather than a green one. I don't think my son, Gryphen, would care for it. He loves to mow the lawn and make it look perfect. I've never seen a kid so engrossed in grass."

"As long as he's not smoking it then I'm sure he'll turn out just fine, Jay."

"One similarity with courses down on Earth: no sign of intelligent life."

"Isn't that the truth," the voice from Houston affirmed, lamenting his own golfing woes. "As serious as you are, Jay, I figured you'd find some little green men to caddie for you."

"Maybe next time. I sure hope we get to go back."

"We'll have people living up there before you know it."

"There's plenty of real estate," Carl added. "I'm looking at it right now through the top hatch. From here all of the craters look like dimples on a golf ball. I still can't believe we were just there."

"We already have the pictures you took to prove it. Now all we need is the three of you back here soon. Everyone is looking forward to seeing you splash down safely. God speed, gentlemen."

5. The Devil Down in Atlanta

"Ethan, is your foot alright?"

"Yes, sir. Why?"

"I was just wondering if there was a reason why you couldn't push the gas pedal further toward the floor," Paul Bailey said sarcastically.

"Sorry, I'm doing the speed limit already."

"It's really more of a guideline than a limit. Pick up the pace, Ethan. I want to get there and get this done fast. Some of us have tee times this afternoon."

Ethan Collins checked the road ahead for any signs of law enforcement before suddenly pushing the pedal. He made sure the burst of acceleration was noticeable enough for his boss and then settled in at five miles per hour over the limit. A minute later Paul groaned and threw his head back when Ethan braked and stopped on a yellow light at a major intersection.

They were on their way to visit Bramco, which had been a client of Infinity Bank for nearly twenty years. Paul Bailey had only been with Infinity for eighteen months. His resume showed how he'd hop-scotched between different institutions for years. The purpose of this stop at Infinity was to help shore up the commercial lending portfolio. He took his job very seriously and had no problem putting Infinity's interests before those of the clients.

Pulling into the company's parking lot Ethan was relieved that his ride with Paul was over. However, he was now bracing himself for what he knew was going to be an unpleasant meeting. Ethan had seen Paul in action a few times with borrowers who were delinquent and it wasn't pretty. Bramco had been Ethan's client for seven years and he enjoyed working with their management team. Unfortunately, their industry was in transition and Bramco was struggling to change how it did business in order to keep pace.

"The building at least looks pretty good," Paul grumbled as he got out of the car. Clearly he was sizing up his collateral. He noticed his own reflection in the mirrored glass by the entrance. Paul was nearing fifty and thought he still looked pretty good, too. He was an even six feet in height and spent a couple of days each week in the gym. His light brown hair was thinning gradually and retreating, but he still had more than a lot of men his age. The light tone camouflaged the gray hairs that were steadily appearing.

"You've re-checked all of our collateral and mortgage agreements, right, Bruce? Water-tight, no loop holes?" Paul asked.

"The documents are very clean, Paul. We're good," responded Bruce Daugherty, the third member of the team. He was the bank's attorney. He did his job by the book. He didn't have much in the way of customer service skills, but at least he didn't take enjoyment from putting the screws to borrowers.

The three men marched into the waiting area of the corporate offices. Paul and Daugherty took seats while Ethan went and said hello to Iliana, the receptionist. Another reason that Ethan liked handling this account was being able to flirt with her. She had caramel skin and long, black hair. She always wore loose blouses that were buttoned only half way up, putting her ample cleavage on display. Ethan had asked once and determined that she had a mix of Latin American heritage. She possessed an exotic beauty that was rare in this part of Georgia.

"Hola, Iliana," Ethan said, expending most of his Spanish skills in one shot.

"Buenos dias, Ethan," Iliana said, raising her eyebrows seductively.

"We're here for our meeting with Mr. Kronos."

"I'll let him know you're here," she said cheerfully. Clearly she had no idea what the meeting was about.

Ethan wanted to stay and ogle Iliana, but felt obliged to wait with the others. He sat down next to Bruce and then Paul revisited the game plan for the meeting for the third time today.

"Listen, Ethan. I know you like these guys, but we have reached the end of our rope. If you want to be the *good cop*, that's fine. You know I have no problem being the bad cop. We've given them all of the breathing room that we can. Unless there are some strong signs of improvement we are pulling the plug. I'm guessing that he's still going to want more time and money. I hope I'm wrong."

Ethan nodded in required agreement. He looked over to Iliana and wondered what would happen to her. Maybe a spot would open up at Infinity Bank and he could get her a job there.

At one point several years ago, Mr. Kronos had made overtures toward Ethan to leave Infinity and join his company as the head of finance. The company was still profitable at that point and Ethan had given it real consideration. There were some cracks starting to show in the business so in the end Ethan stayed put. Despite his dislike of Paul, today he was glad to still be on this side of the bargaining table.

Iliana approached and told them she would walk them back to Mr. Kronos's office. The three men followed obediently, all of them thoroughly enjoying the view from behind Iliana who was wearing high heels and a tight skirt.

Mario Kronos greeted Ethan warmly and gave a courteous hello to Paul, who he'd met previously. Ethan introduced Bruce, who was here for the first time. Mario looked Bruce up and down, sensing that this new team member's presence was not a positive development in the relationship.

They sat down at a glass topped conference table with four seats. Mario was now surrounded. Paul allowed for about two minutes of pleasantries and then cut right to the chase.

"Alright, Mario. You know why we are here today. Show us the numbers – and I hope they are good."

Mario had a blue folder sitting on the table next to him with their accountant's logo embossed on the cover. He clearly wasn't in a hurry to open it up and spread good cheer.

"Before we get to those, let me first tell you about some exciting developments," Mario said, waiting to see the reaction he received.

"The only way I'm going to give a damn about any new developments is if they are reflected in your current numbers," Paul barked, leaning over and smashing his index finger into the folder.

"This is a deal we've been working on for a long time and it is now coming to fruition."

"Is...it...in...your...numbers?" Paul said as if he was speaking to a young child.

Mario paused and looked to Ethan for help.

"No."

"Then it means nothing. Let's see the numbers."

Mario began opening the folder and made one last try. "The contract is ready and we'll be signing it tomorrow..."

Paul shook his head and motioned with his fingers for Mario to hand over the financial statements.

Mario slid a copy of the report to each of the three men at the table. He sat back in his chair to let them read and prepared himself for the inevitable response.

Ethan thumbed through the major line items and could see it was bad. He was desperately looking for any kind of positive data point that he could put a good spin on to help his friend. It was a tall order. He kept glancing up at Paul, waiting for an eruption.

"Do I look like I have a sense of humor?" Paul finally asked.

There was no reply.

"Because these numbers are a joke. Were you so busy working on your magical new contract this quarter that you forgot to sell anything to your other customers? What a disaster!"

"I know the numbers appear weak," Mario began in a pleading voice.

"*Weak?* I think you're giving yourself a compliment there, Mario."

"That's because we have been working so hard to push into new markets."

"Just stop, Mario. You're wasting everyone's time," Paul said, waving toward the others at the table. "I guess I should actually thank you. You've made this decision a lot easier and hence, this meeting is going to be much shorter," Paul continued, checking his watch for effect. "I can probably get some extra time on the range now."

Ethan cringed. It was painful to hear Paul brag about golfing when he was preparing to crush the company a man had spent his life building.

"You have been in violation of your loan covenants for over a year and these numbers only put you further out of compliance. We are at the end of the line. From here on out your contact at the bank will be Mr. Daugherty here. Ethan will no longer be handling your relationship. Bruce will be taking care of the details, but in a nutshell we're calling your term loan and foreclosing on this property. Your secured line of credit has been frozen and we will be paying off the entire balance with the funds in your collateral account. Oh, and don't forget, you and your wife are personal guarantors. If you are able to find alternative financing please feel free to contact Bruce."

Ethan watched Mario closely and could see the papers he was holding in his hands trembling.

"How will I make payroll?"

Paul shrugged. "I don't know and I don't care. My only concern right now is *making* my tee time. Bruce, give him the docs."

Daugherty took a large manila folder from his portfolio and set it in front of Mario.

"These are for you. You'll probably want to contact your attorney," Daugherty said, indifferent to the drama encircling the table.

Paul stood up to leave and motioned for the others to join him.

Ethan placed his hand on Mario's shoulder and simply said, "Sorry."

Although it was clearly over, Mario was compelled to make one last effort.

"Why can't you just give me one more day, Mr. Bailey? Please. That's all I'm asking for...one...single...day." Tears were now streaming down his face.

Paul turned.

"Oh, jeez. Now you're crying. One day, one week, one month – it wouldn't matter. This place has been crumbling under your feet for years. The bank kept telling you that, but you were too blind to see it. At least try to go out with dignity."

"Don't lecture me on dignity. You have no idea what you're talking about. You've never built anything. All you do is parade around wielding someone else's power. You are an evil person and you're going to hell!"

Paul almost seemed worried for a second, and then it passed.

"Maybe someday that's where I'll be going. But not today! I'm going golfing."

He walked out, proud of his wordplay, leaving Mario reeling in his sorrow.

Ethan followed, knowing there was nothing else he could do and not wanting to witness any more anguish.

Outside they loaded back into the car and Paul was immediately on his phone checking with the office. A few minutes into the drive Paul held the phone to the side and again badgered Ethan. "Come on. Come on," he said, circling his hand forward.

Ethan slammed on the brakes and stopped dead in the middle of the road. The car behind them skidded to a halt just short of a collision. Ethan turned and gave Paul one of his own evil glares.

Paul, who actually liked Ethan relative to most of his other reports, could sense the seething anger.

"Okay, okay. You drive; I'll talk on the phone."

Ethan resumed his course and followed the posted speed limit all the way back to their building.

On the way back to their offices Paul pulled Ethan aside.

"Listen, Ethan, I know Mario was a good client and friend of yours. But things have headed south and we have to protect the bank

91

and our shareholders. You can't let personal feelings get in the way of business decisions. Allow Bruce to handle it now. Let it go."

"I fully understand and support the business decision. I have no problem with that. The problem is how you handled it. There was no need to crush the man."

"Maybe not. You've got your style, I've got mine. I focus on the business side, which is why I'm the right man for this job. We'll leave it at that."

Ethan turned, went back to his office, and closed the door. He spent the next hour staring at a blank page on his computer screen where he considered writing his resignation letter. Ethan thought to himself, *if Paul is the right person for this job, then I must be the wrong one.*

***

Paul arrived at his club right at one o'clock. He was in a good mood having cut the cord on Bramco this morning and then getting all of his other loose ends tied up before leaving the office. He grabbed a sandwich at the bar and then headed out to the range where he found his partners.

This group normally played together a couple of times per month. Cam was still working part time as a consultant, while Frank and Gary were both recently retired. They weren't close friends yet, but had enough in common to form a bond. Like so many of Paul's acquaintances, the other players were forced to take the good with the bad.

For Paul, the *good* was his game. He was an excellent all around player, which was the primary draw for his companions. The *bad* was his behavior. He did a decent job observing proper golf etiquette, though his manners – particularly toward club employees – left a lot to be desired.

Today's round had been going smoothly until the sixth hole when they saw the beverage girl approaching. Paul was sharing a cart with Cam, who always tried to limit Paul's interactions with the staff.

The girl working on the drink cart today was a young blond named Cali. She knew that the best way to score bigger tips was to flirt with the male golfers. For Paul, however, she made an exception. She parked next to the other two golfers and called out to Paul and Cam to see if they wanted anything.

Paul, not to be deterred, fished his wallet out of his bag and walked over.

"Hey, Cali," he said, eyeing her up and down. "How about a couple of cold beers?"

"Sure, let me just finish with these gentlemen first."

Paul waited by leaning against the cart and watching Cali's every move. When she finished with the others she slid open the beer cooler for Paul.

He peered inside and said, "Give me two of the Yuenglings. Open one and I'll put the other one in our cooler on the cart."

She did as she was told and then asked, "Anything else, Mr. Bailey?" She called many members by their first name, but always stayed formal and called Paul by his last name.

"Nope, that's it for now."

"It's twelve dollars. I can just put that on your member account," she said, moving around him to get back in her cart.

"No, I'll pay cash. Here's twenty, you keep the rest," he said, forcing the bill toward her chest.

She grabbed the bill delicately as though he'd just wiped himself with it.

"Thank you, Mr. Bailey."

"Oh, my pleasure," he replied, giving her a look like she now owed him something.

Cali thanked the others with actual sincerity and drove off rapidly.

Returning to the cart to join Cam, Paul couldn't help himself.

"Damn, that girl has a tight little body, doesn't she?"

"I would hope so, Paul. She just finished high school."

"Hey, Cam, high school is a lot different now than when we were in it. I'm sure she's already screwed a bunch of guys. I'd just like to add myself to the list," Paul said, as though it might somehow be even a remote possibility.

"Really, Paul?" Cam groaned. "I've got daughters almost that age. Cali is someone's daughter, too, so I can't think that way."

"Yeah, that's one of the reasons why I never had kids."

"We can all be thankful for that!" Cam said, only half joking. "Come on. Close your filthy mouth and stick to playing golf."

The next infraction took place after the turn. Paul had stumbled for a few holes and flared his approach wide and into a greenside bunker. A maintenance employee had been working near the green when they drove up to it, but he stopped and moved off to the side politely. Paul immediately blamed his poor shot on the inconsiderate worker who had somehow forced him to hurry.

When they got to the green Paul grabbed his wedges and headed off to the bunker still grumbling in a number of four-letter words. The maintenance worker was standing well back from the green and waved at the players tentatively.

As Paul arrived at the edge of the bunker, he lost it.

"Son of a bitch! Look at this lie!"

The other players ignored him and focused on lining up their putts.

Getting no response, Paul refocused his anger.

"I don't know what you were doing up here before we arrived, but it clearly wasn't tending to the bunkers," Paul yelled at the timid worker. "Is this one of your footprints my ball is sitting in? Didn't they have rakes in the country you came from?"

"Enough, Paul," said a deep voice behind him. "It's not his fault that you suck. Hit your damn shot and join the rest of us on the green," Frank instructed. Frank also put up with Paul, but the line had just been crossed. Frank had been in banking and had retired from a much more senior position than Paul currently held. In the "man hierarchy" Frank maintained a higher rank.

Paul stopped his attack and hacked his shot out. It stayed on the green; however, Paul proceeded to three-putt from there.

Departing the green, Frank turned to the employee, who hadn't moved a muscle for the last ten minutes.

"Sorry about that. You're doing a great job. Thanks."

Paul, whose tail was already between his legs, felt as if it had crawled even higher.

On the following tee Paul tried unsuccessfully to regain a little bit of face.

"You know those guys work for *us*, right? We pay their salaries. You don't have to defend them."

"Shut up, Paul. What we pay them barely qualifies as a *salary*. So you can afford to pay them a little respect. You're a good golfer and I keep telling myself that you're a decent guy. But when you pull crap like that it becomes tough to stomach. Hit your drive."

Paul meekly teed up and hit a high fade of into the trees on the right.

"Who are you going to blame for that beauty?" Frank chided as he walked back to his cart.

Paul was about to start swearing, but couldn't find his voice. He bent over to pick up his tee and fell to his knees. A vice-like pain gripped the left side of his torso.

Frank saw this out of the corner of his eye and snapped out of his scolding mode. He knew something was seriously wrong.

"Help me get him in your cart, Cam. We're going straight in. I'll call 911."

***

Lying in a hospital bed, Paul glanced from the wall to the ceiling and back. It was like playing visual ping pong. He was alone and had nothing to do but wait.

The other three golfers had accompanied him to the hospital and made sure he was stabilized. After several hours they all had to leave to get back to their families. The doctors in the emergency room ran numerous tests and then placed him in a room to get some rest. He had only drifted in and out of sleep all night, constantly waking and having to re-determine where he was.

The monotony was interrupted briefly by the arrival of the breakfast cart. Paul picked through the bland breakfast that had been delivered on a covered, tan tray. He tried not to look at the clock too often, but it proved difficult.

Earlier a nurse had told him that a doctor would be in to see him at nine thirty to review his test results. Paul grew increasingly impatient as the hands slid past nine thirty-five and nine forty. At nine forty-five he began tapping the "call" button next to his bed.

"Yes?" said a raspy, female voice through the speaker.

"This is Paul Bailey. I was told the doctor would be here at nine thirty. It's nine forty-five. Can you tell me when he'll be here?"

"Let me check," she said, which was followed by the sound of computer keys typing. "She's running behind schedule. It's probably going to be closer to ten thirty."

"Are you kidding? Isn't there anyone else who can be here sooner?"

"No, sir."

"Alright," Paul said, knowing he really had no choice.

He had already called into his office and told them he would not be in today. He decided not to tell them he was in the hospital until he had some idea of what was wrong with him and how long he might be here. With no other option, Paul paged through a magazine and looked at the pictures, unable to concentrate long enough to read any of the articles.

After two more unproductive calls, Paul was relieved to finally see the large, wooden door swing open just after eleven o'clock. His normal urge would be to complain about the late arrival, but he did his best to bite his tongue.

"Good morning, Mr. Bailey. I'm Dr. Radeem," the woman said as she approached the bed. She was very tall and thin with dark skin. She had straight, black hair that was pulled back tight.

"Hello," Paul replied. He was anxious to get his diagnosis, but fear had been building for hours. "So what can you tell me about what happened?"

"I've looked over the scans and consulted with several different physicians and radiologists already. I apologize for being late, but I was waiting to hear back from another doctor who is very familiar with cases such as yours. I think we have a pretty clear picture of what is wrong with you," she said before stopping and making direct eye contact with him.

"And?"

"It says you're not married," she said, flipping through his data sheet.

"No."

"Any other close loved ones that are local?"

"Not really," he admitted. He didn't like the direction her questions were leading.

"I wanted to ask because what I have to tell you is not good news."

"I understand. Go ahead."

She pulled out a chest x-ray and showed him a set of cancerous masses growing near his left lung.

"Because of the way these are developing you probably haven't experienced many of the normal symptoms of lung cancer. Have you had any issues with a cough or blood coming up?"

"No blood. Some coughing, but nothing that I would call significant. Can they be removed?"

"Yes, but at this point it won't matter."

"Why?"

"It has metastasized to your brain," she said frankly, holding up another scan that showed what resided betweens Paul's ears. She pointed to several spots that appeared out of place. "Similar to those on the lung, the way these tumors have grown would allow them to go unnoticed. Have you had any head pain or headaches?"

"Some. I'd say I've seen an increase more recently. I kind of attributed it to work."

"Unfortunately they've grown to the point where full removal is now impossible. What you experienced yesterday was actually more of a seizure. That was probably the first sign of more and worse things to come."

"So we're talking about terminal cancer?"

"Without question."

"No radiation or chemotherapy options?"

"They might forestall it slightly, but at this point it would be like trying to stop a freight train. The tumors are going after the brain from several different directions. We've seen a few cases like this before and nothing worked. I can give you some references if you want a second opinion."

"How long do you think I have left?"

"Only a few months at most. As yesterday showed, it could even be an acute incident on any given day."

Paul leaned back against the pillow and gazed ahead at the wall. He looked at the clock and couldn't decide if minutes even mattered. The hours he'd spent waiting to see the doctor this morning suddenly represented a large portion of his remaining life.

"So what do you suggest I do?"

"We can discharge you today and allow you to begin dealing with your affairs. Here is an information package that the hospital prepares. It has a number of recommended service providers for issues you may face, including hospice. My personal advice is to do what you want within reason. Try to have someone else drive you when possible, in case you have another episode."

"Thank you, doctor," Paul said earnestly. "I'm ready to get out of here."

"I certainly understand. I wish there was more we could do. I'll let the nurse know you're ready for release. We have a shuttle bus service that can take you home. Good luck," she said before leaving.

Twenty minutes later Paul stood alone at the front entrance of the hospital waiting for his ride. He was oblivious to the other people coming and going. Paul had always rationalized being alone as "independence." Suddenly the idea of dying alone was terrifying.

***

Paul had plenty of vacation time accrued so he informed the office that he would be out for the coming week. The job that he'd taken so seriously now seemed unimportant.

The first few days were a blur for Paul. A mix of pain killers left over from a recent dental treatment and alcohol kept him in a comfortable state of numbness. This, and the fact that he'd hidden all of the clocks in his house, made the passage of time more bearable.

On Wednesday Paul slept until late in the morning. After watching game shows and eating leftovers for lunch, Paul decided to go golfing. He checked the tee sheet online and saw that the course was wide open. He had no idea what to expect so he didn't try to get a group together. He'd simply told his friends that his "episode" was stress related and that he needed to take it easy at work.

The round was rather mediocre. He hit some decent shots mixed in with some forgettable ones. He was nice and relaxed because nothing was riding on his play. Unfortunately, his concentration was limited and he sprayed a few shots to whereabouts unknown. Getting out lifted his spirits and on the back nine he started to formulate a plan. Over the years he'd played a lot of top venues so his bucket list was short. Searching through his memory bank, he made a list of several favorite courses that he wanted to play one last time. He had plenty of money that he couldn't take with him and no heirs to leave it to. By the time he walked off number eighteen he'd resolved to start laying out an itinerary on his computer when he got home.

He wasn't in such a hurry, however, that he couldn't stop at the bar for a drink, or two, or three. He took a seat where he could watch TV and still see the sunset down the tenth fairway. Paul caught a glimpse of himself in a mirror behind the bar. His hair was matted down and his face looked dark from the thick carpet of stubble.

There were a few people in the bar area, but Paul wasn't feeling chatty. He was starting a fresh drink when his eyes took another look at the mirror. He did a double-take when he noticed someone sitting right next to him. *What the hell?*

"How'd you hit them today?" asked the stranger, now that eye contact had been made.

"Okay," Paul said hesitantly, turning to see the man face-to-face. "You startled me. I didn't realize anyone had sat down there."

"Sorry about that. You've got a good view from here," the man said, motioning toward the horizon, which was turning to a flaming

98

orange color at the moment. "And it looked like you could use some company."

Paul found a smile, "I look like I could use a shower."

"It was pretty hot out there today."

"Did you play?"

"Absolutely. I just finished."

"Really? You look pretty clean," Paul said, looking at the stranger's clothes that were freshly pressed and dry.

"The heat doesn't bother me much."

"Are you a new member? I don't think I've seen you before."

"No, only visiting for the day. I have some good connections who can get me in just about anywhere."

"Sounds like people I'd like to meet. What's your name?"

"Desi. Desi Valant," the man said, extending his hand out.

"Desi? Like the actor, Desi Arnaz?"

"Yes. Although fewer people make that comparison anymore."

"Nice to meet you, Desi. I'm Paul Bailey," he said, shaking hands.

"Do you play here often, Paul?"

"I've been a member for a few years now. I try to get out at least twice a week."

"Good for you. I thought it was a very nice course. The bunkers on the back side were very well maintained."

Paul paused. *That's a strange observation to make*, he thought. Then he remembered how he'd reamed the employee about that during his last round, right before he'd gone down. *Coincidence?*

"I'm getting ready to take a golf road trip," Paul declared.

"Ooo, that sounds like fun," Desi said with interest.

"Hopefully it will be enjoyable. It's really more of something that I *need* to do."

"Is it important?"

"For me it is. I think it's going to be the last one I ever take."

"Tired of traveling?"

"No, I'm dying," Paul said plainly. He was surprised that he said it to a guy he'd just met, but it actually made him feel better to say it aloud to someone.

"I'm sorry to hear that, Paul. Maybe I can help you with your trip."

Paul thought Desi was just being nice, but then recalled what he had said about having "connections."

"I wouldn't want to impose."

"No imposition at all. I help people all of the time, it's part of my job. Where were you thinking about playing?"

"I figure I've got a couple of good weeks so I was going to focus on the East Coast. Start up in Maine at Ancient Links, I've always wanted to play there. Work my way through New York. Maybe hit Bethpage, see if I can get into The Peninsula Club out on Long Island. Then head back through the Carolinas. I've a got a buddy with a place out at Kiawah. Depending on how things are going I'll probably finish up with some of my favorites here in Georgia."

"That sounds like a fabulous adventure. I know I can get you into all of those and some other great tracks. Peninsula will comp me all the rounds you can play, I've got a close friend there," Desi said enthusiastically. "And when you get back here to Georgia I can get you into the best of the best, including Augusta."

Paul's ears perked up when he heard the final name. He had tried for years, but had never been able to finagle a round at Augusta National. He wondered if this was his chance or if Desi was just a braggart blowing smoke.

"Augusta? Really? You're not messing with a dying man, are you? I'm not sure God can even get a tee time there."

"Sure he can. He plays there all the time," Desi said with a straight face. "I'm not just blowing smoke. But I can..." he added before exhaling a few faint smoke circles from his mouth. He then waited for Paul's reaction.

Paul was perplexed. *How did this guy know I was thinking about blowing smoke? And where'd that smoke come from?* Paul thought while checking Desi's hands for a cigarette.

"This is a rather strange conversation. I'm starting to wonder if I overdid it on the pain killers."

"Don't worry, Paul, you're not imagining this. I'm just not the normal kind of guy you meet at a bar. Meeting you tonight was not accidental. I've been watching you for a while."

Paul felt a wave of discomfort crawl across his skin. *This guy must be some kind of con man or an insurance salesman with a scam for people who are dying.*

"No, I'm not selling insurance. But I do have a deal to offer you. While I've been keeping tabs on you I've seen you belittle people, crush dreams, and be downright mean. Every time I think: 'Hey, Paul is my kind of guy.' So, would you like to hear more?"

Paul stared speechlessly at him.

"I'll take that as a yes. You see I go by Desi, but some people also call me Lucy. As in Lucifer."

Desi's black eyes glowed with red flames as he said this. Paul again questioned whether or not he'd just seen that or if it was a freak reflection from the sunset.

"My deal is simple. I can't save you or extend your life. That's out of my hands, the die has been cast. However, I can make your remaining days on Earth the best of your life. You'll play scratch golf on some of the finest venues in the world with perfect weather every day. Everything will be set up for you, think of me as your personal golf concierge. You'll also get some 'perks.' I can't tell you about those other than they'll be the fondest golf memories you'll ever have.

Physically you'll feel great and have stamina that the cancer wouldn't allow. Play dawn to dusk every day if you please. Hell, play at night if you want! But when your time is up – that's it. I can give you a lot, but not everything. It's kind of like three wishes from a genie. You can't use one of them to ask for more wishes. How does that sound?"

"Insane."

"Yeah, I get that a lot. It comes with the territory," Desi shrugged.

"Let me ask you this: should I expect a similar offer from God?"

"You?" Desi chuckled. "Don't hold your breath. We play a lot of golf together – usually just a five dollar Nassau – although sometimes the wagers can get real interesting. Anyway, when God heard I was trying to recruit you he pretty much called it a 'gimme'."

Paul considered it and honestly wasn't that offended or surprised. He'd had a lot of chances to live a better life.

"So what's hell like?" Paul said, as if he were asking a waiter to describe the specials at a restaurant.

"It's what you make it. It's one place, but it is different and unique for everyone who goes there."

Paul raised his eyebrows questioningly.

"For instance, Saddam Hussein. He spent his life in the dry heat of the desert. He thought he'd be perfect for fire and brimstone. But his hell is Seattle. It's cold and rainy every day. Instead of a Starbucks on every corner there's a synagogue. Oh, and the rain is even bespoke, we mix in a little napalm. So each day his skin blisters and peels off. He wakes up the next day and does it again."

"I don't suppose God fought you too hard for him."

"Heck, he conceded that hole before it was even played," Desi said, continuing his golf analogy.

"Can you tell me what my hell will be?"

"I can't describe it for you, but deep inside you already know what it will be."

"What if I don't go with you and God doesn't put me in his foursome?"

"Then you go to the middle ground: purgatory. It's kind of like muni golf. But eventually you end up going one way or another. Any more questions?"

"Well this has been a very interesting chat, but I'm going to have to think about it."

"I understand, Paul. Pretty heavy stuff for bar chat. Here's my card. You can call or text me. Sorry I'm not on Twitter or Facebook, but who needs that nonsense when you're already in hell! Just remember the clock is ticking and I can't stop it."

"Thanks, I'll give it some thought," Paul said. He turned briefly to look at the end of the sunset. When he turned back Desi was gone. *Did I image that?* Then he saw the red business card sitting on the bar. He picked it up and it felt warm in his fingers, almost alive. He tucked it safely in his pocket and returned his attention to his drink.

***

Paul woke up at seven o'clock the next morning and felt great. He bounced out of bed and went into his bathroom. He didn't like what he saw in the mirror so he took a shower and shaved. His appetite had also returned so he went to the kitchen for breakfast.

He stopped when he saw the red rectangle sitting on the counter. It was one of those things that instantly triggered a memory. Like seeing something that made you remember a dream from the night before. The card was real, however, and Paul knew it hadn't been a dream. It was very quiet in the room, but one noise stood out. One of the wall clocks he'd taken down was in a drawer and he could hear the steady ticking getting louder and louder. He didn't need a more obvious metaphor.

The card drew him closer. Paul leaned on the counter and stared down at it. He knew that if he was going to make a decision it had to be now.

There was no reason he couldn't organize the road trip on his own. He had plenty of money and his club pro could set up rounds at a lot of top clubs. But that would be the extent of it. At different points during his golfing career he had gotten to low single digits. He had never been able to get all the way down to scratch. Playing the best courses with that caliber of game would be a whole different experience. The idea of having Desi as his concierge was also quite appealing. Paul had scheduled numerous trips over the years and there were always problems and headaches. It was particularly frustrating when buddies decided to throw a wrench in his well laid plans and he had to pick up the pieces. He hoped there was a special place in hell for those guys.

And the weather – always an unknown – would be a non-issue. As all of these factors bounced around in his head, Paul found himself seriously considering the offer.

The deal obviously sold itself. It all boiled down to the trade off. What would be awaiting him on the other side? And what if he didn't take Desi's offer and went to purgatory? Who was to say he might not end up in hell anyway? That would be the worst case scenario. He might as well get what he could out of it now.

With everything that had happened in the last few days it was very difficult to come up with a logical decision. Flipping a coin almost seemed like a viable option. Most people would seek out others to weigh the choice. Again, Paul's independence meant that the decision was his own. His parents were both deceased and he was an only child.

He decided to give it one day and then make a final call.

After breakfast he headed over to the club to hit some balls and practice putting. It was a hot, hazy day and Paul was sweating as soon as he got out of his car. As he approached the range, he saw several small signs dotting the green ridge. *Oh come on!* he thought, as soon as he read them. Sure enough the grass portion for hitting was closed off. That meant he had to hit off of the synthetic turf mats along the edge, which he hated. The ball did funny things and the material left green streaks across the bottom of his clubs. He went ahead and hit through his practice routine, complaining after every shot. He spent a short time chipping and did okay.

Finally, he walked to the putting green and began rolling balls. Everything seemed off. He was pulling *and* pushing short ones and his speed control was abysmal. He changed his grip a bit and still struggled. He took a break and got a drink of water to try and cool down. Feeling somewhat refreshed he returned to the green and set up a few practice drills. Eventually more balls started to click around in the bottom of the cup.

"There you go, Paul," he said out loud.

Right then he felt a slight tap on his shoulder; then another one and another one. He looked up and the hazy cloud above had morphed into a dark, gray monster. The sound of drops pattering on a nearby roof picked up speed.

Frustrated by the timing, Paul gathered his clubs and trotted toward his car in the growing downpour. By the time he was in the driver's seat he was soaked in a combination of perspiration and precipitation. He checked the rearview mirror, half expecting to see Desi sitting in the back seat and gloating about how his offer stacked up against this misery. He also wondered if Desi could stack the odds by impacting what happened today, or if it was only a coincidence. At this point it didn't matter. Paul had no intention of spending his remaining days like this. He wanted to go out with a bang.

***

Back at home, Paul was eating lunch in the kitchen. The small piece of red cardstock commanded his full attention. He wanted to jump up from the table and call right now, but he used what little will power he had to hold off. Some part of his conscience was searching for a reason not to contact Desi.

By the time he cleaned his plate he'd come up empty. He'd wiped down his clubs and already had a suitcase packed with golf clothes waiting by the door. He set his phone on the counter and dialed Desi's number.

"Good morning, Paul."

"Were you expecting my call?"

"Sooner or later I was hoping to hear from you. How are you doing today?"

"Doing great, Desi. Thanks for asking."

"What can I do for you, Paul?"

"I'm in."

"That's great to hear. We're glad to have you on the team," Desi said as though his top draft pick had agreed to sign.

"Obviously this is the first time selling my soul. What do I have to do next? Is there an online form I need to fill out? Some office where I need to stand in line waiting to speak with an overweight bureaucrat?"

Desi laughed. "We used to process through the DMV, but there were simply too many errors."

Paul's doorbell rang.

"Hang on a second, Desi, someone's here," Paul said, going to the front door. He pulled back the drape over one of the glass panes and saw his visitor. Desi put his face close to the window and waved cheerily.

Paul opened the door and invited Desi inside. He was still having trouble grasping the idea that he was willingly allowing the Devil inside his home.

"Come on back and we'll sit in the kitchen."

"Nice place you've got here, Paul," Desi said, taking note of the decor.

"Thanks. They'll be having an estate sale soon so you'll be able to pick up some bargains."

"I certainly can't use any of these wood pieces. Do you know if that couch is flame-resistant, though?" Desi asked, enjoying his satanic humor as always.

They sat down at the table and Paul waited for Desi to begin.

"I know this is a big decision to make in a short period of time so I'll make this as simple as possible. First, I do need to be one hundred percent sure you're ready to commit. I can entice you, but our etiquette dictates that I don't coerce you."

"Yeah, that could be a fine line when dealing with the dying. This is my call and I'm making it."

"Good. I do have some paperwork to complete," Desi said, pulling a single page of paper from the inside pocket of the black suit vest he was wearing. He laid it out in front of Paul to review. "This is just like one of your loan closings, Paul. No need to read any of the fine print. Just sign at the bottom."

"You're really a smart ass aren't you?" Paul said with a cynical expression as he snatched up the paper to examine it.

"They don't call it a *devilish* sense of humor for nothing."

Paul looked at the sheet and, after years of working with tedious loan documentation, was shocked by its brevity.

I, Paul Bailey, do hereby relinquish and transfer my soul for all eternity to Desi Lavant, aka Lucifer, aka Satan, aka Prince of Darkness, his successors and/or assignors. In consideration for this pledge, Paul Bailey shall receive all of the promises included on Schedule A (attached) and any other perquisites provided.

Paul immediately turned the page over looking for the attachment.

"Here you go," Desi said, sliding another sheet across the table.

Paul perused the listing and saw an itinerary of dream tee times spanning the Eastern Seaboard of the United States.

"I hope you like it. I added a few extra special ones in there just for you."

"Amazing."

"If you are ready to go all you need to do is sign."

Paul went back to the contract. There was only one thing printed in a small font at the bottom: NOT FDIC INSURED. He laughed modestly.

"Come on, Paul. I put that in there just for you."

"Yeah, that's funny. So can I use a pen?"

"For tradition we still go with blood. Although ink, pencil, and even coal are all perfectly legal and binding."

Desi pointed at Paul's index finger and a small droplet of deep red blood appeared at the tip. Paul stared at it for a moment and then swirled it around on the line on the contract. The fluid seeped into the paper's fiber and dried instantly. Paul flipped the paper back to Desi. He felt a sudden surge of adrenaline as though his body had strengthened.

"Here you go, Paul," Desi said, passing across a folio of plane tickets and a red credit card that matched Desi's business card.

Paul opened the ticket folder.

"Two first-class tickets?" he asked.

"You don't want to get stuck with some chatterbox sitting next to you on a long flight do you?"

"Good point."

Then Paul fondled the credit card.

"Whatever you want related to your journey," Desi explained. "Clothes, clubs, balls, booze. Indulge!"

"Here I thought you were going to make me regret this as soon as I signed."

"Hey, I'm the Prince of Darkness – not a banker! This game is like golf – it's one of honor."

"I don't consider myself a banker any longer. From here on out I'm a golfer."

"I agree. Now why don't you stop wasting your very limited time and get on your way. Remember, I can't control when you go. When it happens it happens. Have fun," Desi said, shooing Paul away.

Paul got up and started to leave before turning back to Desi. Desi answered before Paul could say anything.

"Don't worry, I'll let myself out and lock up. Go! Go!"

***

The first leg of Paul's farewell tour had been smooth as silk. His direct flight to Maine had left on time and arrived early. He was greeted at the terminal by a driver holding a small "Bailey" sign. The gentleman showed him to the car and handled his clubs and luggage.

It was a perfect ride out to the coast along winding, scenic roads. Paul had rolled down the window to breathe in the air that smelled fresh and new compared to what he was used to inhaling down in Georgia. Watching the trees flicker by had relaxed Paul and put him into a trance-like state. All of the tension and angst he'd accumulated during his career had drifted away. He had stopped caring where he'd been and was now focused on where he was going.

Paul had never been to Ancient Links before and was enchanted as soon as the lodge came into view. He felt like a kid approaching an amusement park while catching glimpses of seaside holes on the drive in. Check in took less than a minute and he was shown to a sprawling room with an ocean view. After a light snack in the quaint restaurant, Paul emerged onto the back lawn to find a caddie standing ready with his clubs. The young man assured Paul that he had two good hours of playing time left. Paul didn't care how many holes they got in, he just wanted to play.

The first few holes were phenomenal. The caddie told Paul where to hit it and that's where it went. Paul didn't feel like Desi was doing anything magical to his shots. Rather, he had unlocked all of the best shots that Paul was capable of hitting and removed any mental baggage that had prevented him from consistently executing those shots.

The outward holes provided only teasing glimpses of the water. A full view was obstructed by rolling dunes and a medley of small trees. Finally, after departing the fourth green, Paul snaked up a steep rise and the full expanse of the black Atlantic swallowed everything past the coastline. Paul took a seat on the planked bench near the tee box and waited for his caddie to join him. The caddie stopped nearby and popped out the legs on the carry bag. He remained standing, stoically awaiting direction from Paul.

"Sit down," Paul said, patting the empty space next to him on the bench.

"Okay," the caddie replied, surprised by the invitation.

"Do you go back and forth for the seasons?" Paul asked. He knew that many full-time caddies traveled north for their summers and south for their winters, following migrating golfers. Numerous caddies bounced between the same two courses for years.

"I did for a few years. I started school again last fall so now I'm only here for the summers."

"Good for you," Paul said. He was listening while his eyes were absorbing the view.

"What's your story?" the caddie asked.

"Me? I'm dying."

"Whoa, really?"

"Yes."

"Sorry to hear that. Are you okay to be out here?"

"I feel fine. I feel great in fact. Don't worry I'm not going to drop dead on you out here," Paul said, realizing it wasn't necessarily assured. He didn't tell the caddie about his situation to get a reaction. He did it simply because it was true. He didn't have anything to hide in that aspect. Paul did, however, hold back on any details about his satanic travel agent.

They sat there silently for several minutes. Paul wasn't feeling sentimental, but he did want to soak up all the moments he had left. This was one of the most breathtaking views he'd ever seen on a golf course. As the sun was setting over the hills in the west, broad bands of pale blue light extended all the way to the horizon in the east. It was a mild evening with cool breezes blowing up from the rocky beach below.

When Paul felt that his thirst had been quenched he stood up and tapped his caddie.

"Alright. Let's play some more golf."

The round continued like a twilight dream for Paul. He watched as towering drives and approaches flew forever against an impressionist's painting of a sky. He was putting on grass that was a deeper and more beautiful shade of green that he'd previously thought possible. Although the day was ending, the sky seemed to be getting lighter. Paul could see everything in perfect detail.

On the elevated eighth tee Paul stood and marveled. *Amazing! Perhaps God is indeed making a play for my soul*, Paul thought. Although he had his caddie in tow, it felt like there wasn't another soul on the course.

The solitary golfer was able to complete fifteen holes before darkness finally claimed the round. Paul was in awe of how much faster a round could move when every shot went where it was supposed to go.

Paul thanked his caddie, gave him a generous tip, and wished him well. Paul then wandered the grounds near the clubhouse. He relaxed in an Adirondack chair next to a fire pit that contained a calming blaze. Paul stared into the glowing, red heart of the pile of small timbers. As the cool night air took over, the warmth of the fire was inviting. He moved closer. Each crackle and pop spoke to him. *Is that my hell?* he wondered. *It wouldn't be so bad.*

With heavy eyes Paul retreated to his suite. He opened the doors facing the ocean and listened to the rolling surf in the distance. A large moon was whitewashing a wide stripe on the black water. Paul stretched out on the vast bed and drifted quickly off to sleep with the sounds of nature's white noise.

***

The next few days provided more of the same: perfect weather, perfect golf. Desi clearly knew the game of golf and had lived up to his promise of a first-rate experience.

It was a Tuesday morning and Paul was riding in the back of a limousine as they entered today's venue: Devil's Valley Country Club. The club had an imposing entrance with a massive stone wall and a black, iron gate that looked to be at least thirty feet tall. The guard at the check-in office spoke to the driver and then waved them in.

Driving past, Paul glanced at the guard. The man looked familiar, but Paul had never been here before. In fact he'd never even heard of the course before. The man peered into the car's passenger compartment and seemed to look right at Paul, despite the heavily tinted windows. Paul did a double-take as the man appeared to mouth the words: *Have fun.*

The car dropped him off and Paul climbed the black, slate steps to the front doors. The edifice was constructed of black stone and timbers. The facade was lined with dark, narrow windows that rose to pinched arches near the roof.

The inside was even more bizarre. The black wood carried over from the exterior. Long beams crossed the ceiling and matched the ornate trim and moldings. Everything else was red.

Paul proceeded down the main hallway running his fingers along the rough, ruby colored wall paper. He was debating whether he was entering a golf clubhouse or a whore house. *What the hell?* Paul thought. It took him a moment to answer his own question. Toward the back he finally located the pro shop. The racks of golf equipment, combined with the outlandish decor, made it look like a dungeon.

"Interesting place you have here," Paul said to the pro.

"Yeah, they got a little carried away with the whole devil theme. But it's definitely memorable and one of a kind. Have you visited us before?"

"Nope, first time."

"I think you'll find the course to be very unique as well. It's a special track."

"I can't wait."

"You're all set. If you need any balls, help yourself. We'll have your clubs ready out back with your caddie. She'll help you get around out there today."

"She?"

"Yes. Would you prefer a male caddie?"

"Umm...is she good?"

"Excellent."

"Well, I've never had a female caddie before. What the hell, you only live once. I'll give her a shot."

"Enjoy."

Out back Paul was immediately greeted by his caddie. She wasn't so much tending his clubs as she was guarding them. The tall, athletic woman was standing next to his bag with her arms folded behind her. The caddie attire consisted of a tight red golf shirt and black skirt and hat, all embroidered with the club's pitchfork logo. She was about five foot ten with broad shoulders and large breasts. Her face was almost masculine in its features, but still attractive, and there was a long mane of black hair running down her back. She looked like a libidinous Amazon warrior.

"Good morning, Mr. Bailey. I'm Sephanie, I will be your caddie for the round today," she said with an accent that sounded Eastern European.

"Nice to meet you Stephanie," Paul said, trying not to stare at her chest, but failing badly.

110

"It's Sephanie, sir," she said politely. "Like Stephanie, but without the 't' in it."

"Sorry," he said, worried that she might crush his skull for making such an error.

"No problem, it happens all the time. Would you like to warm up on the range, Mr. Bailey?"

"No, I'm ready to play. Lead the way," Paul said, happy to enjoy the view from behind Sephanie. Paul had stopped spending any time practicing before his rounds. At this point it was a waste of precious time. He was also amazed that he could walk courses all day long and not get tired.

Paul was now curious about the course itself. From the clubhouse most of the view was obscured. The grounds were impeccably maintained, but he didn't see anything that would separate it from other top tier facilities.

Arriving at the first hole, Paul teed up behind the obligatory wrought iron, pitchfork tee markers. The hole was a gorgeous rolling par four, but again, it didn't seem overly unique.

"So what's so special about this place?" Paul asked.

"You'll see," Sephanie said with a wicked grin.

On the second hole Paul got his first taste of the true course. It was a short par three with a tiny green across the water – except that it wasn't water. There was a strong chemical smell in the air and the dark liquid appeared to be bubbling.

"What the?..." Paul said as he evaluated the surreal hazard.

"That's an example of our signature tar pits, Mr. Bailey. It's one of a number of unique geothermal features that make up Devil's Valley. It's not just a catchy name chosen by the developer, we back it up with some real fire and brimstone," Sephanie said proudly.

"I guess so. You don't want to stick a ball retriever in that mess."

"Definitely not. There are spots in this one hot enough to melt it. Watch," she directed, producing a ball from under the edge of her skirt and throwing it toward a particularly active spot.

The ball stuck to the surface like Velcro. It sat stationary for a moment before its white skin began to slough off. Quickly the fuchsia colored core of the ball emerged and it now looked like a psychedelic fried egg. The core then began to pop and split. Within a minute all that remained was a technicolor swirl on the dark surface.

"So I better take enough club to reach is what you're saying."

"There's a reason we offer extra golf balls to all of our guests," she said.

Paul hit his nine-iron to the center of the green and walked away happy with a two-putt par.

Over the next few holes Paul encountered more of the same with holes carved out of strange, rocky formations. He noticed that the air temperature had increased only slightly, but the ground temperature seemed to be increasing even faster. Sephanie confirmed his observation and warned him that it was only going to get hotter.

By the ninth hole there was no sign that they were going to be making a turn back to the clubhouse. Instead, they seemed to be going deeper into the strange wilderness.

Paul was dripping with sweat and becoming savagely thirsty. There had been some water coolers along the way, but the heat was now getting critical.

"Are we going to see any drink girls out here today?" Paul asked.

"Getting thirsty, Mr. Bailey?" Sephanie observed.

"Very."

"No problem. This is right about the time they usually show up."

Again she finished with her wicked grin, which Paul now took as a warning.

They were walking down the next fairway when Paul heard a gas powered motor behind them. He turned to see a drink cart with a black and red striped roof approaching. Even at a distance he could hear the driver calling out their names in a loud, sensuous voice.

"Sephanie...Mr. Bailey...Sephanie...Mr. Bailey..."

"Are you ready to have your thirst quenched, Mr. Bailey?" Sephanie asked.

Paul didn't even bother to look in her direction because he knew what the expression on her face would be. He also couldn't shift his attention away from the approaching cart. He was captivated. What finally distracted him was the sound of another cart coming from the other direction. Paul turned and saw an identical cart hurtling toward them. Once again a sexy voice called out their names.

"Oh, there are two of them today," Sephanie noted. "This should be fun!"

The carts pulled up and skidded to a stereophonic halt. The girls dismounted at the same time and Paul's eyes couldn't move fast enough to take in the sights. They were both wearing outfits similar to Sephanie's, but smaller and even tighter.

The first girl, a stunning redhead, rushed over to Paul and said, "I'm Serena. What would *you* like, Mr.Bailey?" She was holding his hand with one of hers and stroking his right arm up and down with the other hand.

His other arm was then taken and he turned to see a ravishing young, blond girl on his left side.

"I'm Siri. Please let me serve you, Mr. Bailey."

"No me!" pleaded Serena.

"Go back under your rock, Serena. I'll service him," Siri snapped.

"Ladies, ladies," Paul said with joy. "There's no need to argue. I'm so thirsty I can have something from both of you. Right now I could really use an icy, cold beer."

"Well, to drink here at Devil's Valley you have to be a 'member' of the club. That means you need to fill out one of these forms," Serena said, producing a small, white card.

This seemed rather bizarre so he looked to Sephanie for advice.

"Yes, Mr. Bailey, you need to fill out the card to 'join'. I know it's a crazy vestige of days long past, but we do have to comply with all local government rules. It's only good for the day, so go ahead and fill out the card."

"Thanks," Paul said, quickly scribbling down the few pieces of information required on the card.

"Here's your beer, Mr. Bailey," Serena and Siri said in unison, each handing him a chilled bottle of beer.

Paul took a deep belt from each bottle. It was the best tasting beer he'd ever had.

"So what else do you have in those carts?" Paul asked.

"Anything you want," Serena said suggestively.

"Anything," echoed Siri, running her finger along his neck behind his ear.

"Now to me that means things beyond food items."

"You can have whatever you're hungry for. We will sate your appetite," Serena added as she rubbed her breasts against his arm.

Paul was now concerned that he'd already died and had mistakenly been sent to heaven. He looked to his caddie again for advice.

Sephanie had clearly been in this position before. "Why don't you take a little break from golf, Mr. Bailey. I'll wait here until you return."

"I guess my caddie is telling me to go for it."

"Come with us, Mr. Bailey," Siri said, pushing him forcefully toward her cart. Serena joined them and they all sat in the front seat with Paul sandwiched between the two gorgeous vixens.

Siri drove through a narrow opening in the trees and then emerged near a strange looking creek. She flew across a rickety wooden bridge.

"What the hell is that?" Paul asked, looking down at the colorful water swirling below.

"The River Styx of course," laughed Serena.

When they reached the other side it felt as though they were no longer on the golf course property and the temperature had risen significantly.

"It's getting pretty hot," Paul noted.

"Hold on tight, Mr. Bailey, it's about to get hotter!" Serena said as her eyes lit up and she shoved her hand down his shorts.

The two women took Paul to a stone grotto and threw him down. There they performed every sexual act he could imagine and some he'd never even considered possible. At some point during the proceedings Paul passed out from exhaustion.

When he awoke Siri was driving back out from the woods. Sephanie was standing right where they'd left her with her hands clasped behind her.

"It looks like you enjoyed your 'perks'. Desi thought that would be an appropriate diversion for you," Sephanie said.

Paul was still speechless.

"Enjoy the next few holes," Serena said as she drove away.

"We'll see you in a little while, Mr. Bailey," chimed Siri.

The thought of seeing them again was both very arousing and very scary to Paul.

"Shall we play on?" Sephanie asked.

"Honestly, I'm a little worn out," Paul admitted.

"Ha! From those two? You're a light weight, Mr. Bailey. I could take you places they don't even know about," Sephanie bragged.

Paul didn't doubt her at all.

"Here, drink this," she said, handing him a narrow can.

He chugged the liquid and quickly felt alert and refreshed.

"Is that some kind of magic elixir?"

"Uhh, no, Mr. Bailey. It's a Red Bull. Read the can!"

"Oh."

They resumed their round and Sephanie abused him the rest of the way. He loved it. The golf was good, but it couldn't top another visit from Serena and Siri on the sixteenth hole.

After only playing eighteen holes, Paul decided he couldn't go on. Sephanie helped him to the limousine and threw him into the back seat.

"Take care, Mr. Bailey. Hope to see you again sometime soon," Sephanie said before slamming the door.

***

The door opened and Paul stepped out once again to the fresh smell of ocean air. After several days of inland play, Paul had returned to the coast. Today's line item on the bucket list was The Peninsula Club on Long Island. It was an older club, but was now said to have the best greens in the northeastern U.S. Rumor had it that golfers were challenged to find even the tiniest of weeds or to locate a single differentiated circle from a prior pin location on any of the greens.

Paul was already draining everything so he could not wait to see what his putter could do here.

When he checked in he was told that he would be paired up with another single for his round. The gentleman was a member of the club so Paul thought it would be helpful having someone with course knowledge along.

On the first hole the starter introduced the two men.

"Mr. Bailey, this is Mr. Wilcuff. Mr. Wilcuff, this is Mr. Bailey. He's a guest at the club today."

"Nice to meet you, call me Chuck," Wilcuff said extending his hand.

"Chuck, I'm Paul."

Wilcuff gave Paul's hand a heavy squeeze and Paul reciprocated. He'd met plenty of people over the years in banking who tried to somehow intimidate him with overly aggressive handshakes. It didn't phase him normally and certainly not today.

"First time out here at Peninsula?" Wilcuff asked.

"Yes, it is. I've heard wonderful things about it, but I'll need you to show me around a bit."

"Will do. Let's get going."

The first holes were non-eventful as Paul took in the sights and the course while Wilcuff sized up his playing companion. They were riding in separate carts, but both were playing well and finding the fairways and greens.

By the fourth tee Wilcuff was ready to start betting.

"Are you up for a little wagering the rest of the way, Paul?"

Paul had been expecting the question at some point.

"Sure. What were you thinking?"

"Straight up, no strokes. Maybe a thousand bucks a hole?" Wilcuff suggested. He was used to playing for higher stakes, but didn't want to scare Paul away.

"I figured you guys up here played for more than that," Paul replied, goading Wilcuff a bit.

"Okay, how about five thousand?"

"Now that's more sporting!" Paul exclaimed. He hadn't done any betting so far on the trip and he knew that he was going to run out of life before he did money.

The fourth was a par three that was playing about one hundred and seventy-five yards with a slight cross breeze. Wilcuff teed up and promptly put his shot to about ten feet. He strutted off the tee box proudly. The wealthy investment banker wanted Paul to know that such trivial wagers didn't impact his confidence at all.

"Nice shot," Paul complimented. He casually tossed his ball down on the turf behind the tee markers and addressed it. He seemed to suddenly have this energy flowing through him that made him feel like he was going to hit a good shot no matter what. It wasn't confidence, though, it was something else.

He made his swing with a completely clear mind and flushed the ball. It arced up nicely and then began riding the breeze back toward the pin. The ball hit, hopped, rolled, and went in. Paul celebrated. Wilcuff swore profusely.

"What the hell?" Wilcuff finally said to Paul in total disbelief.

"Just a nice little ace. And at the perfect time, too."

"I've seen dumb luck before, but nothing like that," Wilcuff grumbled. He didn't even bother to compliment Paul on his rare feat.

"I am feeling lucky. How about you, Wilcuff? What if I give you another shot to win *this* hole?"

"What do you mean?"

"Double or nothing on another set of tee shots from here. One shot only. If you hit it closest we're back to even. But if I hit it inside of you I'm up ten grand."

Wilcuff didn't know what to make of the offer. It seemed like a test of manliness, though, so he had no intention of backing down.

"Let's do it."

"You can even have the honors," Paul said, holding his arm out to the tee.

Wilcuff was mad, but he had no intention of letting that impact his next shot. He took a deep breath and went through his routine. He hit another great shot. This time to about five feet.

"Ooo, nice one," Paul said. "Really putting the pressure on me."

Again, Paul simply dropped a ball and then swung. His ball flight was a carbon copy of the first one, as was the result: it went in.

"You've got to be kidding me," Wilcuff said, staring hard at the hole as though it might somehow cause the ball to pop back out.

"How about that," Paul mocked.

"Let me see your balls!" Wilcuff demanded.

Paul couldn't prevent a giggle.

"Well, Chuck, I usually don't go that far on a first date."

Wilcuff snarled at the flippant comment.

"Here you go," Paul said, tossing him one from his bag.

Wilcuff squeezed it, tapped it, and shook it. It looked and felt like a normal ball. He simply couldn't believe that Paul had made back-to-back aces without somehow cheating.

"One more time, double or nothing," Wilcuff finally declared, not even waiting for a response from Paul before bending over to tee up his next attempt.

Paul nodded his affirmation and smiled.

Wilcuff tried to focus and follow his routine. He was clearly now getting rattled. He hit the shot and then watched as it faded lazily away from the pin. It landed on the green, but it was the worst of his three shots. He muttered a few obscenities under his breath before stepping away.

"I saw you were testing my ball. What are you playing?"

"Titleist, of course."

"Alright, give me one of yours. I don't want any questions about fairness."

Wilcuff grabbed another ball from his bag and tossed it to Paul.

Paul dropped it and hit it. The ball landed and started rolling out toward the hole. It looked like it was going to go in again, but this time it lipped the cup and then stopped a few inches away.

"Yeah, definitely the ball makes a difference. I didn't hit that one the way I wanted."

The taunting and the quick loss of twenty thousand dollars before they'd even left the tee were too much for Wilcuff to swallow.

"You cheating son of a bitch! The best golfers in the world couldn't do that. There's no way you did it."

"What do you mean? You were standing right here. I even used your ball. Do I have to hit your *club* too in order to make it fair?" Paul continued. He was enjoying the game he was playing with Wilcuff.

"Screw you, Paul."

"Hey, you're the one who wanted to start betting, not me."

"You tricked me into that."

"I tricked you? How old are you? Five? With that kind of attitude I think our game is over. Let's settle up on the twenty thousand and you can go on ahead."

"I'm not about to pay you."

Wilcuff had plenty of money so twenty grand wasn't something he would worry about. This was about principles, or perhaps a lack thereof.

"That's pathetic. We have a lot more integrity when we make a wager down in Atlanta."

"Screw Atlanta and screw you," Wilcuff said. His anger continued to grow and he continued to move closer to Paul.

Paul almost found it funny when he suddenly wondered if this was where he was actually going to die. Going out on twin aces wouldn't be bad.

Fate and the course's greens keeper intervened, however.

"Everything going alright over here, gentlemen?" Gryphen Reed said, seemingly appearing from out of nowhere.

"Sorry if we're moving too slowly," Paul said. "I was just waiting to settle my bet with Mr. Wilcuff here."

"That's fine. Mr. Wilcuff is well aware of our policy here: if you bet, you pay – no matter what."

Wilcuff was ready to explode, but didn't want to screw up his membership at Peninsula because of some crazy visitor. He grudgingly went to his bag and pulled out a checkbook.

"Please make it out to Paul Bailey. Thanks."

Wilcuff scribbled out the check and tossed it on the ground before driving away without another word.

"Thanks for helping to facilitate payment," Paul said.

"No problem, sir," Gryphen said. "Enjoy the rest of your round."

Paul did just that. He was glad to be rid of Wilcuff and played great golf, but did not make any more holes-in-one.

***

The next two weeks of Paul's quickly fading life were spent rolling down the East Coast. He logged a few days around the Washington, D.C. area before the journey moved into the Carolinas. With each stop the clock ticking in Paul's head seemed to grow louder and louder.

His anxiety level also started to grow as he approached his home state. It felt like he was moving closer to the inevitable death that he was trying not to face. Each day, each round, each shot grew more precious.

Paul was staying in an ocean-side villa in Kiawah when the phone rang.

"Hello?"

"Paul, my friend. How is the trip going?" Desi asked.

"Playing the best golf of my life. And the variety of courses is wonderful. Playing all of these different venues really keeps it interesting."

"That's great to hear. Speaking of variety, it looks like I've been able to get one more course added to your upcoming calendar."

"Seriously?"

"Yep. I should have everything firmed up today to have a tee time for you at Augusta late next week."

"That's awesome. I really appreciate it. I know how hard that tee time is to get, even for you."

"My pleasure. I just wanted to call and tell you the news. I'll let you get back to enjoying yourself. Take care, Paul. I'll be seeing you *very* soon."

Paul hung up the phone and walked out on his balcony to watch the waves roll in. He was astounded at just how well his deal with Desi was working out right now.

***

Today was the day. It was the day that Paul had been waiting for his entire golfing life.

He woke up early and had a full breakfast at his hotel. His car picked him up and drove him down Washington Road. The route was non-descript and Paul hadn't noticed anything during the drive until the car turned onto Magnolia Lane. Instantly it was as though his vision had gone from black and white to vibrant color.

Paul sat upright and looked at the driveway lined by lush, mature Magnolia trees. It felt like they were in a tunnel and Paul stared ahead toward the white light at the end of it. The driver took him directly to the clubhouse, dropped him off, and handed his clubs to a waiting attendant.

Under the large oak tree nearby Paul saw a familiar face. Dressed impeccably in black pants and a red shirt was Desi Valant.

"Good morning, Paul. Welcome to Augusta National," Desi said, shaking hands with the man whose eternity would soon be in his hands.

"Hello, Desi," Paul replied graciously. "I can't believe you pulled this off. And what an incredible day; more of that superb weather you promised. I've been here as a spectator for the tournament, but it seems even more beautiful than I remember. I've never seen so many flowers on a golf course before."

"It is nice. A little too showy for my tastes, but the golf course is exquisite."

"So are we playing together today?"

"Unfortunately no. I've got a later tee time with some billionaire, I forget his name. You're actually going to be paired with the CEO of one of the banks you used to work for. Good guy, solid golfer. He's a regular so between him and your caddie you should have a decent amount of help on the course."

Desi took Paul on a brief tour around the clubhouse and then escorted him to the practice range.

"I'll let you warm up and see you later. Enjoy your day."

"Thanks, Desi. This is amazing," Paul said. He was still surprised at how likeable he found Satan to be.

Paul didn't need much practice, but he savored the chance to even use the driving range at this legendary venue. The weather was perfect, the course conditions were perfect, and every shot he hit was perfect.

A short time later a starter stopped by and let Paul know it was time to proceed to the course. His caddie loaded up the clubs and Paul followed him across the manicured, deep green grass.

As the tee box came into sight, Paul felt an incredible wave of nervous energy come over his body. His heart began to race and his legs felt wobbly. Then his vision began to shake. He fell hard and was now looking at the course from ground level. He watched as the caddie dropped his clubs and raced over to check on him. He saw others in the area coming toward him as well. Someone was on his cell phone calling for an ambulance. Paul could see that they were all yelling, but he didn't hear a sound.

Paul no longer had any sense of time either. The commotion surrounding his body went on for a while and then Paul finally heard a voice.

"That's a shame, Paul. You were so close," Desi said.

Paul could see the black pant legs approaching behind the other golfers.

"This can't be it," Paul moaned.

"I'm sorry, but it is. This is the end. And the beginning..."

"Please, Desi, please. Just one more day!" Paul begged.

"Did you ever give anyone *just one more day*?" Desi asked, already knowing the answer.

"No," Paul admitted.

"That's right. Time to go, Paul. Let's roll."

Desi lifted Paul from the ground and led him toward the black car that was waiting in the driveway. Paul looked back over his shoulder and could see his body still lying prone on the ground surrounded by others who knew that he was dead.

The car squealed its tires and tore down Magnolia lane at breakneck speed. An ambulance raced past in the opposite direction and Paul turned one last time to look out the back window at his carcass spread across the grass. He was now just a soul in the hands of the Prince of Darkness.

As the car drove faster and the sights outside became a blur, the driver turned and addressed Paul.

"Am I driving fast enough for you, Paul?" the man asked.

Paul saw that it was Ethan Collins.

Desi and Ethan shared a hearty laugh.

"Are you going to miss your round now, Desi?" Paul asked.

"No, I'll be back in plenty of time. But when work calls I have to be ready to respond."

"Am I going straight to hell?"

"Non-stop! Do not pass GO and do not collect $200," Desi said. He was clearly enjoying himself.

121

***

Seconds later the car came to a screeching halt. Paul could see that they had without a doubt arrived in hell. When the door of the car opened there was an awful chorus of screaming and yelling. He exited the vehicle with Desi and saw a landscape that surpassed any Biblical artwork by a wide margin. There were demons torturing souls in every imaginable way as far as the eye could see. The structure felt like a massive room within a cave with passages heading off in countless directions. Fire was everywhere and molten rock seeped from cracks and bubbled from the floor. It was worse than Paul had ever expected.

"Ahh, nothing like being home!" Desi declared.

A number of hideous creatures approached Desi and discussed operational concerns with him. He signed some paperwork and issued orders quickly.

"So much work to keep this place running smoothly. You have to be efficient, though, if you want to have time to get your rounds in, right?"

"Certainly," Paul agreed.

"Follow me," Desi said, starting out across a narrow rock bridge crossing orange pools of lava. "This isn't your hell."

Desi continued on and it looked like he was going to walk directly into a wall of solid rock. At the last second an opening appeared and he passed through. It quickly disappeared so Paul stopped as he approached the stone wall. He stood there for a moment before Desi's hand materialized from the rock and dragged him through to the other side.

He emerged on the first tee of a beautiful golf course. It was bright and the sky was a dazzling shade of blue. The grass looked perfect and the first hole was wide open.

Paul's first thought was that somehow he'd made it to heaven and Desi was just dropping him off.

Desi snuffed that thought out immediately.

"No, you're not playing here. You're playing over there on the back nine," Desi said, pointing across to what looked like an entirely different course.

On the tenth tee the skies were gray, the grass was dead, and there was a large number of horrible golfers standing in line to tee off. The waiting players were a motley crew of sloppy middle-aged men who were overweight and dressed in untucked T-shirts and cutoff shorts. The outlook was changing fast.

"Let's head over there and meet your foursome, Paul."

They walked toward the chaos and Paul's stomach sank as soon as he recognized one of the faces in the crowd. *Oh no*, he thought.

"Paul, I'm sure you remember your ex-wife, Cheryl," Desi said.

"Good to see you finally made it, loser," Cheryl said, scowling at Paul.

"She doesn't even play golf," Paul noted.

"Oh, I know. You're not playing with Cheryl. You're playing with her mom, Ethel."

"Ma! Get over here," Cheryl yelled.

A wrinkled and wizened old woman emerged from the group and made her way over to where Paul was standing. She had lit cigarettes in both hands.

"Hey, Pauly. How about giving me a big kiss," Ethel said sarcastically, blowing smoke in Paul's face. Her voice was like nails running down a chalkboard. "We'll get to see you perform on the course today. Hopefully it's better than your work between the sheets. Cheryl always told everyone how lousy you were in bed."

The crowd standing nearby laughed at her comments.

"And next up we have Mrs. Stubben, your second grade teacher," Desi said.

Yet another prehistoric looking woman approached.

"You sure didn't turn out to be much," Mrs. Stubben said, looking Paul up and down. "Just like I expected. Put your hands out, boy."

He hesitantly held his hands out in front of him and out of nowhere Mrs. Stubben swung a metal ruler and lashed it across his knuckles, slicing the skin wide open.

"Jesus!" Paul screamed in surprise and pain.

"No, I don't think you'll find him here, Paul," Desi deadpanned. "Ethel and Mrs. Stubben will be riding together and playing the tips today. And here comes your fourth now."

A short, chubby man who Paul did not recognize approached. The man had his arm out as though he wanted to shake hands. When Paul reciprocated the man reared back and sucker punched Paul in the face. He fell to the ground and quickly took a hard kick to the rib cage.

"Come on!" Paul complained.

"Don't you recognize Johnny Byrum?" Desi asked. "The boy who used to live down the street from you as a kid. The boy you spent years tormenting and bullying. I'd keep your eye on him out on the course. As you can see, he is still quite pissed off at you."

"What have I done?" Paul moaned as he tried to get back on his feet.

"Well, it looks like you've got a good wait before you tee off so we're going to go grab a bite to eat," Desi said, walking off with Cheryl on his arm. "We'll be back to watch you later."

***

An hour of the worst golf Paul had ever seen passed on the tee before their group was called. Ethel and Mrs. Stubben each topped several shots before they even made it to where Paul and Johnny were teeing up.

Paul finally teed up his ball and tried to think about playing golf to take his mind off the misery. His fingers were still bleeding and he winced in pain when he tried to turn with his now injured ribs. He noticed that many of the waiting golfers had encircled the tee and were watching him intently. Desi and Cheryl had also returned.

"We get a gallery?" Paul asked.

"Not really. They're your hecklers. They are going to scream all kinds of stupid random things when you hit. We've got the moron who yells 'mashed potato' at PGA events. You also have one that will say, 'You da' man!' after every shot and, 'In the hole!' after every putt."

Paul focused on the ball and swung. As soon as the club went back, the hecklers went wild. Paul still made good contact, but hooked it toward some trees.

When he found his ball is was sitting down in a vine-like weed. He stepped in to take his stance and quickly realized the vine was covered in thorns. They dug into his ankles and broke off when he lifted his feet. He stopped and picked the brown spurs from his skin. Small droplets appeared at each spot. Paul was now getting angry and wanted to show Desi that he could still play even in these conditions. He hacked the ball out into the fairway and marched after it.

From his next location Paul only had about one hundred and fifty yards to the hole. He looked at the green and saw that a worker was crossing it on some kind of equipment.

"What are they doing up there? Rolling the greens to make them faster?" Paul complained.

"No, they're not rolling them. They're aerating them. We do it every day!" Desi informed him from nearby.

Once the equipment cleared, he lined up and took a practice swing and some deep breaths. When he addressed the ball pain returned suddenly to his lower legs. He jumped back and saw that he was covered in red ants. He swatted them off and danced around in the fairway while swearing continuously.

"Come on, you baby! Hit the ball!" the hecklers yelled.

Once his now swollen ankles were insect free Paul took a drop from the ant piles and hit his approach. It was well struck and landed about two feet from the pin.

"Ha! That's for par," Paul announced, pointing at Desi.

"Nice shot, Paul," Desi said while giving a polite golf clap. "Two footers aren't guaranteed here, though."

On the way to the green Paul saw a drink cart coming toward him. He immediately recognized the driver. It was Cali from his club back home.

"What can I get for you Mr. Bailey?" she asked politely.

"Should I even ask if you have beer?" he said. He was already dripping with sweat and was incredibly thirsty.

"Sure," she replied, retrieving a bottle for him.

The bottle was ice cold and Paul rolled it across his forehead. He then held it up against his inflamed ankles.

"Oh, that's perfect. Thanks, Cali."

"We only take cash here, Mr. Bailey," Cali said, holding out her hand.

"Umm," Paul said, not sure if he even had money with him. He fished in his pocket and found that there was a twenty dollar bill. "Here you go, keep the change," he said, grinning and enjoying the chance to look over her firm, young body.

"No, I can't accept tips. Here's your change," she said, coming closer to him. She stepped in and kicked him viciously in the groin.

Once again he fell to the ground and writhed in pain.

"I'll see you later," Cali said before driving away.

Paul eventually sat up and reached for his beer that was sitting on the ground. Half of it had spilled out. He put it to his lips and let the liquid flow into his mouth. He then spit it out violently. The bottle was still ice cold, but the beer was warm and flat.

"Damn you!" he yelled at Desi.

"No, damn *you*," Desi replied.

After a half hour of pure insanity Paul finally arrived at the first green. Ethel five putted, while Mrs. Stubben took six to find the bottom of the cup. Paul looked over his two-footer across freshly punched aeration holes. It was dead straight, slightly uphill. All he had to do was hit it firm and it would go in. He took a practice swing and then addressed the ball. As the putter went back, a bolt of lightning dropped from the sky and struck Paul violently. He pulled the putt to the left and missed it.

"Noooo!!!" he yelled while shaking his fists at the sky.

Desi laughed heinously.

"Good luck, Paul. This is only your first hole!"

6. Out of the Fog

"You need to go."

"I know. In just a minute. I'm enjoying this. It will be a nice memory to reflect on when I need to zone out during the round."

"Okay. As long as it's positive. I don't want you worrying about them, or me. Today I want you to focus on yourself and playing your best," Tracy West said. She wrapped her arm tighter around her husband's midsection and leaned up to put her chin on his shoulder, peering out from behind him at the scene he was watching through the wide, bay window.

They stood there silently for a moment before Cody West spoke. "I will. I promise."

She squeezed a little tighter as a reminder that he needed to live up to that commitment. She wanted for him to leave without saying another word, but he didn't.

"I want this one so bad. I want it for you and them. You deserve it," he said, intertwining his rough fingers into hers, which were cool and soft.

"We're going to be just fine. Now go play some golf, Cody."

Cody reached forward and touched the glass in front of him, waving a silent goodbye to his daughters who were playing below. Their joyous screams indicated how oblivious they were to the pressure that was mounting on their father.

Cody turned and kissed Tracy on the forehead. "I love you."

She smiled warmly. "I love you too. You can do it."

***

As he pulled out of the driveway, Cody glanced back up at his house. It had become their home and he didn't want to uproot his family. They had steadily been falling behind on the mortgage over the past year and he didn't know how much longer they could hold on to it. Cody had lived in tiny apartments and shared rooms in homes with buddies before; he knew he could live anywhere. However, his life had changed and he no longer considered those places to be viable options. He was also acutely aware that how he tried to support his family was going to have to change soon. The reality of raising a family was clashing with his dream of being a professional golfer.

Today's event was likely his last good chance to get to the next level – from subsistence to sustainability. He had been grinding away for nearly a decade now. Several times he thought he had made it only to slide back to the same spot. Cody had just turned twenty-nine and every day that went by meant one less opportunity. Every season brought a new crop of younger players shooting for the same goal that he was.

Tracy had maintained an unwavering level of support throughout their time together. She always knew the right thing to say and had been his rock during some painful failures. But despite the strong facade, he knew that even her conviction was being tested.

The girls were different. As toddlers they would be ecstatic when he arrived home with an occasional, shiny trophy. To Cody that was the only thing trophies had become good for. Now his daughters were starting to understand winning and losing. They were beginning to grasp the connection between how well he golfed and what the family could afford to buy. They would still greet him at the door with excitement and ask how he'd done. A part of him would want to lie in order to extend their joy, but he couldn't. He'd tell them the truth and, per their mother's coaching, they'd reassure him that they knew he'd still done his best. It always felt like a punch to the gut. The scene was repeating far too often and, despite every effort to block it out, it was constantly gnawing at his mind. He was even starting to wonder if some hidden region of his brain was trying to sabotage his golf game in order to end his career sooner and stop the pain that awaited him.

Cody quickly slammed on the brakes, realizing at the last second that he was about to sail through a red light. "Damn, get a hold of yourself, Cody," he said quietly to himself. His heart was now racing and he knew that he'd worked himself into a mental frenzy already.

"You've got to focus on golf now, Cody. If you are going to show up on the first tee like this you might as well turn around and drive home now. Alright, time to get your head in the game," he said assertively.

The light changed and Cody checked for traffic in both directions before proceeding cautiously. Once he cleared the intersection he reached down and selected one of the CDs he had in the car's player. He skipped forward through several tracks using the tactile buttons on his steering wheel.

A few seconds later the calm voice of a middle-aged man began to fill the car's cabin with positive messages and mantras. Cody took deep breaths, leaned back in his seat, and relaxed his grip on the wheel.

The motivational speaker wasn't terrible, but after several minutes Cody knew that it wasn't what he needed today. He clicked the controls again and switched to another disc in the player. The first few notes of AWOLNATION's song, *Sail*, danced around the car's interior before a heavy storm of bass rained down upon him.

"Ahh, that's better," Cody exhaled with a grin.

The music quickly soothed him and shook the other thoughts from his head. The rhythmic beats accentuated the steady thumping in his chest and pumped a feeling of strength through his body. His focus finally shifted from the concerns behind him to the challenges at the course ahead. He started the process of walking through each hole on the course and what his gameplan was for every shot.

The Cypress Grove Club was located near the Pacific coast and as Cody made the drive down the last few miles the fog grew progressively thicker. This was very normal for the area and Cody expected that by the time play got under way the thickest portion of the moist haze would be burned away.

Cody knew the route to the golf course well; however, he was starting to have difficulty even seeing the street signs. He had plenty of time, but didn't want to take any wrong turns nonetheless. Just to be safe he tapped on his phone and opened up the GPS application.

With the music blaring and his full focus now on navigation any golf anxiety that Cody had been feeling was pushed aside.

Up ahead he saw the stoplight for one of the main crossroads. He slowed down and craned his neck up toward the windshield to see the street name as he passed through the intersection, confirming he only had one more stoplight before the course entrance. As he returned to a normal position in his seat, he felt a sharp pinch in his neck.

"What the hell?" Cody said, wincing from the acute pain. He immediately began rubbing the sore spot and rolling his head in circles. He was also instantly immersed in fear. Cody had experienced several neck injuries over the course of his career and each time the problem had been worse and longer lasting than the prior occurrence.

"I don't need this now," he barked, banging his fist on the steering wheel. "Why does this have to happen to me?"

He threaded his way the remaining mile to the club and was glad when he finally pulled into a parking spot. He flipped down the visor and looked into his own eyes in the small mirror. "Get it together, Cody. It's game time."

After popping the trunk, he unloaded his equipment and made one final check to be sure he had everything in his bag. He changed shoes and headed toward the check in area. There were a number of other golfers arriving and they exchanged lukewarm nods of acknowledgement when they passed one another. Cody knew most of them by sight, but today was not the day for friendly chit-chat.

Scanning the rows of cars, he finally located his brother's red Honda. Knowing that his caddie was already here at least eased one of his worries.

Cody deliberately avoided the bag drop. He had no intention of letting anyone touch his clubs until he handed them off directly to his trusted sibling. He proceeded to the check-in area behind the clubhouse and went through the motions. Situated behind the table was the large leader board where scores had been carefully tallied in colorful calligraphy. He tried his best to keep his eyes down; however, the call was too strong. Medusa herself could have been standing there and Cody would have been powerless not to steal a glance.

He already knew exactly where he stood so seeing his name written in the second place spot was in no way a surprise. Entering the final round he was right where he needed to be.

The first sheet of poster board had ten players listed. As he scanned up and down the names, calculations and computations of different scenarios filled his head. However, for Cody the math was really quite simple. At the end of the day he *had* to be in first place. A win would catapult him to a number of additional opportunities; anything else would leave him right where he was – treading water.

His train of thought was derailed by the force of someone clamping their hand on his shoulder.

"Hey, bro'. How are you feeling?"

Cody turned and faced his older brother, Shane. "I'm ready."

Standing next to Shane was their father, Rudy West. Cody instantly sensed that something was wrong and then, for whatever reason, glanced down at his brother's foot. There he saw a thick, black walking brace secured with wide Velcro straps.

"Had a little stumble last night on the basketball court, Cody. I didn't want to call you and have you worrying about it."

"Are you still going to be able to carry my bag?" Cody asked nervously.

"That's one of those good news/bad news things. Unfortunately I don't get to be on the winner's bag today. However, I was able to locate an excellent replacement on short notice," Shane said, pointing at their dad.

"I'd love to loop for you today, if you'll have me."

"Of course, Dad. It will be just like old times when I played junior golf. Are you sure you're up for it?" Cody asked, considering the litany of health problems his father was dealing with. The flip side was that his dad had played the course many times and knew the greens even better than Shane.

"I've lost a step or two, but I'll be able to keep up with you for eighteen holes," Rudy said boldly.

"Alright, let's get going," Cody said, starting toward the range with his bag.

"Gim'me the clubs, Cody," his dad instructed.

"Okay, okay. I was just going to let you conserve some energy."

"You've got a different family member on your bag, but it's going to be business as usual out there. I'm not here for a nostalgia trip. I'm here to help you win."

"Thanks, Dad," Cody replied, appreciating his father's confident words.

Cody and Rudy walked side by side to the practice range while Shane hobbled along after them.

Rudy instinctively knew Cody's warm-up routine and handed his son clubs and casually tossed him balls. Rudy was not going to do any coaching, rather he would take up a position behind his son to check alignment and nod when Cody hit particularly solid shots.

All three of the West men were just under six feet tall and had similar appearances, with collar-length brown hair and well tanned skin from years spent on the course. Cody was dressed for play in a royal blue shirt and light pewter pants that matched his Titleist hat. Cody was looking forward to a day in the not too distant future when he might be able to wear the same hat and get paid for it.

Shane and Rudy were both nicely clad, although one notch down in dress code, with khaki shorts, fresh polo shirts, and comfortable athletic shoes.

The fog seemed to be thinning slightly and most of the shots were visible with the exception of the longest drives that would disappear at the far end of the range. After about twenty minutes the group made their way to the putting green to sharpen up the short game. Cody was stroking the ball smoothly and felt very comfortable having his family there for support.

Cody and Shane were two years apart in age. Growing up they had gotten along more than they had fought and had remained close through the college years and thereafter. Their other brother, Dylan, was three years older than Shane and had always been more distant. He had gone to school in the northeast and remained there after graduation, returning home only for periodic holidays. Dylan had also never been interested in golf so he did not join the rest of the family when they got together on the course.

Cody's mother was a decent golfer, but would not normally come out to watch her son play. It was too nerve-racking and she did not want to be a distraction.

Rudy watched the large post clock near the putting green and let Cody know when they should start heading toward the first tee. Most of the other players were already out and the modest gallery of friends, family, and club members was spreading out across the course.

They would be playing in threesomes today and on the tee box Cody greeted Mason Silva, who was one shot ahead of him, and Neil Oliver, who was two shots behind. Both players were solid competitors and Cody wasn't worried about gamesmanship or getting along with them.

Based on the grouping Cody would obviously be able to keep tabs on the two nearest players. He always tried to focus only on his game, but in this situation it was important to know where you stood in order to make certain decisions on course management.

He was acutely aware of the fact that two of the golfers in the group ahead of them were streaky and could go very low at times. Beyond that there were only a few other players who could realistically make a run at the title. With the fog still blanketing the course it would be hard to see the group ahead, however, Cody hoped to be able to pick up some information from the gallery and possibly send his gimpy brother on occasional scouting missions.

By this point Cody had expected the fog to be lifting. The course was playable, but the moisture was still hanging tough.

Nearby, the tournament director was discussing the course conditions with Cypress Grove's head greens keeper, Gryphen Reed.

"Everything is in great shape out there, but this fog is going to make it play slow. To be safe, make sure your staff is keeping adequate space between the groups on the course," Gryphen reported.

"How about the holes along the ocean?" the director asked.

"We placed additional ropes along the edges, but the golfers still need to be careful on the cliff side holes. That's where the fog is the thickest. I would hate to have a player disappear out there. I'll be out on the course monitoring conditions until all of the rounds are complete."

"Thanks, Gryphen. Your staff has done an excellent job this week. These are the best greens in California."

The caller announced each of the players in Cody's group and all three hit excellent tee shots in the first fairway. The final group was away and they marched off down the damp path mown in the grass.

Cody's gameplan for today had broken the round into three pieces. For the first five holes he wanted to play solid, steady golf and simply avoid mistakes. Perception was huge among the players and he did not want to be seen as a front runner who was going to crumble early and never be heard from again. It was a regular occurrence even on the PGA Tour where you knew a player was in the final group, but the networks mercifully didn't show a single shot as the player had imploded and was no longer in contention. Additionally, the course began with a difficult opening stretch and there were limited scoring opportunities until later in the outward nine.

The middle section of the course is where Cody would try to make his move and play more aggressively. That section contained three scorable par five holes and there were fewer chances to put up a really big number.

The strategy for the final four holes would depend on where he stood in the tournament. If he was behind he would have no choice other than to go for broke and try to make up ground. However, if he had a lead he would simply try to hold it – but not "defend" it. There was a big difference in that "defensive" golf was scared golf – not a good way to play. Fear made the club do funny things. Holding the lead meant that he knew he was on top and was going to continue playing like it. It meant carefully picking where you want your shots to go – not where you *don't* want them to go. He knew most of the other players probably had similar plans; however, Cody's only focus was successfully implementing his plan.

The first several holes unfolded without incident for the members of the group. On the fourth tee the course claimed its first victim. Neil, who was still trailing Cody by two strokes, began leaning to the left and groaning as soon as his tee shot was away. He had blocked his drive well right and was headed for trouble. He waited for Mason to hit and then announced a provisional ball. It went safely down the middle and Neil hustled off the tee muttering under his breath.

Cody walked to his ball in the fairway and had his father set down the bag before heading to the right to help Neil search for his first shot. Neil's caddie had located the ball in a clump of bushes and they were discussing their options.

"All set?" Cody inquired politely.

"We found it. Just trying to figure out what's next," Neil replied.

Cody held up his hand in acknowledgement and turned to walk away.

Neil called after him quickly, "Cody, I'm going to go ahead and take an unplayable and drop it here, okay?"

Looking back over his shoulder with disinterest Cody answered, "No problem. You make the call." He noticed the concern in Neil's voice and sensed that the next shot would be crucial. Neil knew that his choice was acceptable, but by asking Cody he was subliminally looking for reassurance about the decision he was making.

Back in the fairway, Cody watched as Neil lined up. The drop had still left him blocked from a direct line to the green. Cody could tell that Neil was going to try to shape a shot around the trees from a sketchy lie. The ball came out clean and hot. Unfortunately it did not bend enough and crossed the fairway before ending up in some deep rough short and left of the green. Even worse, there was a large bunker between the ball and a short side pin. It was going to be difficult to get up and down from there. Cody looked forward and saw Neil's provisional ball further up the right side of the fairway in perfect position. It would have been a far better location to play the fourth shot from. Cody realized that it would have been advantageous if Neil had not found the first ball at all. Neil was going to come to the same realization when he arrived back in the fairway.

Cody and Mason both hit the green and waited for Neil to get there. Neil's flop shot from the rough sailed over the flag and bounced off the back edge of the green. He and his caddie walked all the way around and prepared once again. Cody had been in that situation before and knew how agonizing it could be. Neil's chip finally found the putting surface, but settled about ten feet short of the hole, leaving more work for a double bogey. Cody and Mason hit their birdie putts close and tapped in for pars, clearing the stage for their competitor. Neil spent a lot of time over the putt before making a tentative stroke. The ball just barely crawled to the edge of the cup before tumbling in. He raced over to the hole with a sigh of relief and retrieved his ball.

"Nice recovery," Cody said half-heartedly. He didn't want to root against anyone, but he knew he'd just doubled his lead over Neil and was very content with the additional breathing room.

The fifth hole was a long par three with a large cypress tree guarding the left side of the green and a vast bunker protecting the right. With the pin tucked tight left, almost behind the tree, a high draw to the middle was all the players wanted here. Cody achieved that and Mason came up just short, but safely on the fringe. Neil teed his ball and took a few extra breaths while trying to visualize the shot. He made a good swing, but the draw was too low. As the ball descended near the green, everyone who was watching braced for impact. It was like watching a plane prepare to crash. The ball slammed into the vertical face of the bunker with a white, granular explosion. Everyone waited breathlessly for the ball to roll out. It didn't. Neil was plugged.

"Whoa. Tough break, Neil," Mason offered.

"Sorry, man," Cody added before walking on.

Neil didn't respond. He stood motionless on the tee staring at the bunker as though the ball might still decide to appear.

On the green Cody marked his ball and then waited for the next act of the Neil drama to unfold. The lie was horrific. Only a small portion of the ball's surface could be seen and Neil could barely even find a stance because of the steep slope. The sand on the embankment kept collapsing as he tried to dig in while not influencing the ball in any way.

Once he was set Neil took several hard check swings. With that lie and that swing Cody knew the ball could go anywhere. Neil heaved at the ball and buried the club with a muffled thud. A fan of sand sprayed up and the ball briefly appeared to hover in the air just above the edge of the bunker. It did not clear it, however, and it started falling right back toward the fresh divot. Neil had lost his footing and was falling back and to the right. He was still holding onto his wedge with one hand as it had stopped dead in the sand.

Almost simultaneously the ball tapped the head of Neil's club and Neil fell uncontrollably into the sand below. Cody was entranced as he watched the ball's next move. It seemed to pause for a second before rolling down the slope and finally coming to rest against Neil's prone body. Neil appeared to be dead in many ways.

He gradually rose up to silence. No one knew what to say. Cody had seen double hits before and had seen shots hit players, but had never seen them both happen with one swing of the club

Neil shook his head and hit the ball casually to within three feet of the flag. He would have an easy putt for triple bogey. Cody continued to keep his mouth shut as Neil emerged from the pit, caked with white sand. It was one of those moments when nothing you could say would do any good. Cody's dad nudged him and they refocused on their putt. There was nothing left to see regarding Neil. Cody thought: *Neil was no longer in the telecast for today.*

Cody made a routine par and headed to the next hole still one shot down to Mason. "Time to start making a move," he said quietly to his father.

"That's my boy," Rudy said, putting his hand confidently on Cody's shoulder as they walked.

Thus far in the round there had been a minimal level of conversation between Cody and Rudy. So far things were going as planned and there was no need for pep talks – just a father trying to keep his son on target.

Number six was a modest par five while number seven was a short par four. Cody and Mason each birdied both holes to get into the red for their rounds, but stayed in the same relative position.

They once again matched each other by hitting close approaches onto the eighth green. Cody putted first and just missed a fifteen-footer for birdie. He tapped in the short remainder and watched as Mason lined up his effort from about ten feet out. Cody could sense Mason's eagerness. Mason knew this was a chance to gain some ground and made an aggressive stroke. The ball rolled true and vectored off the edge of the cup. The speed, however, had flung it nearly four feet past. He marked and waited for Neil to finish up his short putt. Mason scrutinized the line from both sides and took his stance. Again he gave it a solid run and again it just caught the lip and spun out. He finished his bogey and walked off with his head down.

Cody and his dad exchanged glances. Rudy gave a smile and a nod recognizing what a pivotal sequence that had been. Mason turning a good birdie opportunity into a bogey was huge and the leaders were now tied.

On the ninth tee, Cody had the honor and he stood looking down the length of the hole for a moment before teeing his ball. This was the first time he was going to be hitting a shot as a co-leader of the tournament. Instead of feeling tense or stressed he was becoming more relaxed with every second that passed. A sense of peace was spreading like a wave of warmth across his body. Occasionally, Cody had experienced this sensation on the golf course during casual and practice rounds. Never before had it appeared during a competitive event.

He looked down the fairway again and saw his drive arching slowly from the right edge to the center. It hit silently and rolled out to a perfect position. He knew he'd just hit a stellar tee shot, but felt as though it had happened without any conscious thought on his behalf.

In the fairway Cody waited for his playing companions to hit, having easily out driven both of them. He listened to their shots, but didn't watch either one. He then turned to his father who had already pulled a club. His dad held the sole out for Cody's approval. Cody accepted the selection without discussion and took his stance. He looked up and closely scrutinized the flag position and again time seemed to shift as he watched the ball plummet from the sky and nestle within a few feet of the pin. He handed the club back to his father and they just smiled at each other.

Cody knocked in his short putt for birdie and took a one shot lead over Mason who only managed a par.

There was a modest walk to the next hole and Cody covered the distance looking up at the trees and the sky. The high fog combined with the midday sun to give the sky a pure, bright white appearance. It created a strong contrast to the dark, jagged treetops. Although Cody didn't notice, both Mason and Neil walked the same stretch with their eyes following the worn path on the ground.

Along the way Rudy stopped and had a brief conversation with Shane, who had been getting updates from ahead. Two other challengers had made a move and were now also just one stroke behind Cody. However, they were running out of holes and entering the final stretch that members called *The Gauntlet*. Rudy had no intention of sharing the information with Cody. They still had a few holes before they would need to consider any strategy changes.

Cody seemed to be on auto pilot as he rolled through the next several holes. He added two more strokes to his lead when Mason made another careless bogey on number eleven and then could not match Cody's birdie on thirteen.

When they arrived at number fifteen Neil said what everyone was thinking, "This is it guys – the toughest closing stretch around. Good luck."

"Let's do it," Mason added.

Cody was silent. He teed up his ball, went through his routine, and found the narrow, sloping fairway. He wasn't being rude, just playing his own game. Cody was the leader and he intended to act like it. He knew that he only needed four pars; however, he refused to go on the defensive.

Rudy on the other hand was being a keen observer of the competitors. He watched their body language and eavesdropped on the detailed conversations they were having with their caddies. He knew that Neil was just trying to hold steady and manage a reasonable finish while Mason was going to try and make a closing push to win.

There were no changes on the fifteenth hole. On number sixteen Cody confidently hit the middle of the green on the long par three. Mason debated between two different irons before finally making a selection. He was attempting to hit a draw to the pin that was tucked on the front, left side and protected by a step-faced bunker.

He went through his whole routine and then, when he finally appeared ready, stepped away. He stared at the pin and then restarted his entire preparation dance. Rudy looked on and tried not to smile, confident that he knew something bad was about to happen.

Mason swung and hit a low ball that started right at the flag. However, the shot quickly showed its true intentions and hooked left.

"Get in the sand!" Mason pleaded in agony.

The shot hit right on the front edge of the trap and then bounced up and away from the green. It completely cleared the bunker and came to rest in some heavy grass. The real problem was that it was now under low tree branches that would make the required high flop shot nearly impossible. All of the players knew that the best choice from over there might be to intentionally hit the second shot into the sand.

Mason pounded his club on the tee and stood there while Neil waited to hit his ball. Neil was patient knowing that it was another one of those shots where there was nothing beneficial that could be said.

Near the green, Mason walked around his ball looking for any possible solution for reaching the green. The only option was trying to thread it somehow through the thick branches. He took a vicious swing with his sixty-degree sand wedge and the ball sprung straight up. It instantly interacted with the tree and, after a few quick ricochets, plummeted into the sand with a muffled thud. From there he only managed to stop it twenty feet past the hole. Two putts later he lost two more shots to Cody's par.

On the seventeenth Rudy received another update from Shane. The players that had been making moves had faded down the stretch. Cody was sitting on a five shot lead with two holes to go.

Cody looked to his father. He didn't want details, but he did want reassurance.

"It's a clear road home, Cody," Rudy said, smiling warmly at his son with pride.

Cody knew that he was safe and hit an excellent drive with a fluid swing. He missed the tiny green on the par four, but made up for it with his chip shot from the thick rough. It was a little too hard, but rolled out on a perfect line. The ball slammed into the flagstick and dropped straight down – a rare birdie on seventeen.

A winding path through a grove of stubby cypress trees led the players to the final tee box. As Cody walked the trail next to his dad, he could feel the air become colder and damper. Emerging from the far end, a swirling mist surrounded the group. Cody felt like a football player jogging out of the tunnel at the start of the game with fog canisters erupting. The similarity ended there. Rather than being greeted by a massive stadium of screaming fans, they were welcomed by a small gallery of family members and other players who'd already finished their rounds.

Cody grinned and touched the brim of his hat as he climbed the rock steps leading to the tee. He was somewhat caught off guard by how much thicker the fog was here on the closing hole along the ocean. The fairway was drifting in and out of sight and he could only hear the obscured waves below.

He was still somewhat lost in thought when his father tapped him with the grip of his driver. "Are you ready, Cody? Everybody is waiting for you, Son."

"Sorry, I'm ready."

He did not seem focused, but it didn't matter. He easily pounded another huge drive that bounced in sight and then disappeared down the fairway.

After the other two players hit his father had to rouse him yet again. "Come on, Cody. You're not quite done. Let's finish this thing up right."

"I know. I'm just really enjoying being here right now. The finish line is right up there, just a couple of hundred yards away and I'm not sure if I'm ready to cross it yet."

"You're more than ready, Son. Take all the time you want to savor it," Rudy said and then let out an inadvertent laugh.

"What?" Cody asked, wondering the cause of the outburst.

"I was just thinking back to one of your first junior tour event wins. You were so proud of yourself and weren't afraid to show it. You were strutting up the last hole pumping your fist and barking, 'yeah! yeah!' It was a little bit over the top and I think it was making the other kids you were playing with very uncomfortable. I wanted to stop you, but it looked like you were having so much fun."

"Oh, I remember that," Cody said, shaking his head with embarrassment. "I'm having even more fun right now, despite the lack of sound effects."

Cody and his father walked right down the middle of the broad fairway together while Mason and Neil and their caddies respectfully remained slightly behind and to the sides until they reached their balls. This was a well deserved victory lap for Cody.

Cody continued, "Thanks again for being out here with me. I really appreciate it, Dad. I couldn't have done this without you. And I don't mean just today. I mean all of these years of positive support and encouragement. You were always able to keep me going without yelling at me or punishing me."

"Well, you did plenty of yelling at yourself. I didn't think you needed any more from me."

"You did a great job, especially compared to a lot of the other parents who were beyond intense. There were plenty of times that I tested your patience and you never failed."

"As long as you're happy then it was all worth it," Rudy said.

"The last few years have been a struggle, but right now I'm very happy."

"Good. Now let me get you a yardage for this shot," Rudy said, getting back to business.

The fog swirled around them in heavy, flowing blankets. Rudy was able to obtain a good yardage from a fairway marker and their pin sheet. He hoped the number was accurate because he kept losing sight of the flag. In terms of aiming, there were two trees in front of the green on either side that normally framed the approach shot. Rudy directed Cody to favor the one on the left side and stepped away.

Cody addressed the shot with a completely clear mind. His body motions were unconscious; his muscles just did what they were supposed to do. His eyes tracked the ball to its apex in the sky before it disappeared. He let his head drop and then listened carefully. A moment later he heard a muffled *thump* right where he thought he should. It was followed by a round of clapping and cheering from the gallery up around the green. He knew he'd hit a great shot.

His father reached for the club and then handed Cody his putter. "This should be all you need now, Son."

Mason hit his shot and then the group began their march toward the green. The players and caddies all walked together with no animosity as the eventual result had been known for some time. Given the scores, Mason and Neil felt that this was the appropriate place to begin offering congratulations.

"Nice work today, Cody," Mason said, patting Cody on the shoulder. "You certainly earned the victory and the spoils that will go with it. This could be a real life-changing win."

"Thanks. It's a big one, but I'm not going to get ahead of myself. I'll still need to play good golf."

"Yeah, but you'll have a spot reserved for you with all of the exemptions. You won't have to go out and fight for it every week. That takes a lot of the pressure off and will free you up to just play," Mason added, knowing how close he'd been to being in the same position.

"And you should pick up some sponsorships," Neil said. "That's the kind of money that can help you make it through the season even if you're not bringing home a lot of consistent checks from events."

"We'll see," Cody replied humbly. He knew they were right and was trying to contain his enthusiasm.

Looking at the others, he evaluated where they stood in their careers. Mason was getting closer to Cody's situation. He had been working the mini tours for a while and had not broken through. He was married, but didn't have children yet. Although he had some time left, the clock was definitely ticking.

Neil was in his early twenties and seemed to come from a family with plenty of money. He was still out here to compete and win; however, he had a safety net if things didn't work out.

Cody only considered the others for a moment and then let the thoughts go. He finally allowed himself a feeling of self-congratulation. He'd done his job today and done it well. He couldn't wait to tell Tracy that he'd won. More than that, he really wanted to see the look on his daughters' faces when he showed them his trophy. For the first time in a while this one would really mean something.

Shortly before reaching the green Cody's dad left him to go set down the golf bag. "You're on your own now, Cody," he said, sauntering away.

Cody normally read all of his own putts so it didn't surprise him that his father would leave him alone at this stage. Mason and Neil also headed off in different directions and Cody was suddenly all by himself. There was polite clapping from the nearby crowd, but he couldn't make out any of the faces through the fog.

There was a murmur among the crowd and he thought he heard his name being called: "Cody...Cody..." He instinctively looked toward the sound, but saw nothing. He heard it again and recognized it as a female voice. This time it was louder. He realized it was Tracy's voice. His heart leaped knowing that she had come out to see him finish. Then he heard the girls calling: "Daddy...daddy..." He wanted to run to them, however, he still needed to putt.

He looked around and blinked his eyes hard several times. His vision started to clear and it looked like the sun was breaking through a gap in the fog. He tried to start walking toward the voices, but found he couldn't move. He blinked again and could finally start to make out the outline of Tracy's face. She was suddenly right in front of him.

He closed his eyes one more time and kept them shut. Something was telling him that he was imagining this. He opened his eyes slowly and there she was. He tried to turn and see his daughters, but couldn't. His head wouldn't move.

He quietly asked, " Wha...wha...what?"

"Sssh," Tracy said reassuringly, sliding her hand down the side of his face. "You don't need to talk. Just blink your eyes if you can hear me."

He did as he was told and she smiled at him with tears streaming down her face. To her side he could see his daughters edging into view. He shifted his eyes as far as he could to see them. The first thing he noticed was that they were dressed differently than when he'd left the house this morning.

He looked back to his wife and asked again, "What?"

"You're in the hospital. You've been in a coma for two weeks. Don't worry, you're going to be okay. I promise."

Cody had nothing but questions whizzing through his mind. He decided to wait to move his mouth again. He jaw was extremely sore. Instead he tried to raise his right hand and was relieved when he felt his arm leave the bed and enter his peripheral view. He did the same thing on the left side. A blanket was covering his legs, but he was able to push both knees up a little and flex his feet back and forth.

His wife watched the display with wide eyes. "It looks like everything is still working. The doctors didn't think that there would be any paralysis. You've got a neck brace on that is immobilizing your head."

He sat still, thinking for a moment. "Did...I...win?" he finally managed.

Tracy choked back an urge to cry. "No, honey, you didn't win."

"You're sure? I was just there. I had a big lead and just needed to finish eighteen."

"That was two weeks ago, Cody. You never made it to the course that day. Right outside of the club another driver went through a stop sign and slammed into the side of your car. You've been in a coma since then. The doctors expected you to come out of it, but had no way of being sure. We've all been so worried, especially your mother. She couldn't bear the thought of losing you so soon after your father died."

He gave her a confused look. "My dad? But he was..." It started to dawn on him that the round he was just finishing was never actually played.

"He was what?" Tracy asked, trying to understand what her husband wanted to know.

"He was caddying for me," Cody said, now knowing it wasn't true.

"But he couldn't have."

"I see..." He looked over to his daughters and held up his hand again. They both took hold of it and put their cheeks up against it. He gave a slow smile that hurt. "You two are awfully quiet."

They looked up to their mother before saying anything. "We missed you so much, Daddy. We've been asking you to wake up every day," said his older daughter.

"Today you did it!" chimed the younger one.

"Thanks for doing that girls. Sorry it took me so long."

"Can you stay awake for a while? I'm afraid if you go back to sleep you won't wake back up," his younger daughter said fearfully.

"Sure, don't worry. I'm tired, but I'm back and don't plan to leave again."

"Do you remember anything else?" Tracy asked curiously.

"Nothing other than playing golf that day. I can't believe it's been two weeks. It feels like I just left you at the house this morning. I remember driving through the fog and listening to music. Then...I looked up and...my neck...my neck hurt. That must have been it. I couldn't figure out why my neck had started to bother me. And then I drove the rest of the way to the course."

"You were unconscious when the paramedics arrived and they assumed that you had been knocked out immediately."

"So where do we go from here?" he asked.

She knew that he was asking the question at several levels. "Waking up was the first big step. They'll be able to do some other tests now and get your responses. Then you'll need to do rehabilitation depending on what they find. It could be weeks or even months. We'll just have to take it day-by-day."

"I don't imagine that golf figures into the equation anymore?" he said, managing a grin of acceptance.

"You know that was one of the first things I asked the doctors," she said proudly. "It will depend on you. Physically, they think you should be able to heal and rehab so you can at least play, even if it's not competitively."

"Well I haven't been that *competitive* recently anyway. I'll have to start pursuing those other career paths."

"Probably so, Cody. But there may have been a silver lining in all of those fog clouds the day of the accident."

"And what's that?"

"The gentleman that hit you is a very wealthy man. He was not severely injured and spoke with the police when they arrived. He admitted that he was taking medication and was not supposed to be driving at all, let alone in thick fog. He's also a golfer and was very upset when he found out where you were going and where you stood in the tournament. His lawyer contacted us and I have put him in touch with our attorney. In all likelihood there will be a sizeable settlement of some sort. I'm not counting on winning the lottery, but we will hopefully have some breathing room to get back on our feet."

"That is good news...I guess..." Cody said thoughtfully

"I'd better go get the doctor and let him know you are awake," she said, kissing Cody on the forehead and then getting up to go. "I'm sorry you didn't get a chance to play that day. I know you would have won."

"Thanks. It felt nice to win even if it was just a dream. But this is still better. I'm glad I came out of the fog."

7. Idyl Hands

"Hit a few more iron shots, Josh."

"We've warmed up enough already, Dad. I'm ready to play. Can't we go out now?"

"Give me ten more and then we'll play. Deal?"

"Okay," Josh Fischer said, giving in to his father's demand. He casually knocked another ball off the pile and slapped it down the range.

"Ten *good* ones, Josh," Darren Fischer clarified.

"Alright."

The boy forced himself to hit decent shots to appease his dad.

"Great work, Josh. The practice will pay off on the course. I promise."

"Can we play now, Dad?"

"Definitely."

The Fischer family had just moved to Idylstream and was beginning to enjoy all of the amenities that the community offered. It was a relatively new master planned community located near the coast in South Carolina. Darren Fischer had recently been offered a promotion and he jumped at the opportunity to leave upstate New York. As an avid golfer, he was looking forward to a greatly extended golf season. He also saw it as a chance for his son and daughter to improve their games and start junior golf careers. Both of the Fischer children liked golf; but as middle school students, their ambitions were far smaller than their father's at this time.

When they arrived at the first tee the starter was busy checking sports scores on his phone.

"Good afternoon, gentlemen."

"Hi, we're the Fischers. The pro shop said that we could go out whenever we were ready."

"The course is pretty open so you should have no problems out there today. Try to stay on the cart paths as much as you can and enjoy your round."

"Thanks."

They had already played the Forest course several times. This would be their first time on the Lakes course. Darren Fischer was a reasonably strong golfer and, after consulting the scorecard, decided to play from the gold tees. His son hit the ball well, but was not big enough to get a lot of distance yet. Darren let him play from the green tees, which made the course a more manageable length.

It was a Saturday in late spring and many of the course's part time residents had already headed north for the summer. The weather was mild and sunny with a steady breeze blowing in off the ocean. So far, Darren thought he had found the perfect place to live and raise his family.

The family was also a perfect fit in the community. Darren and his wife were both in their late forties and were active and in shape. The entire family was attractive and a number of neighbors had already told them that they looked like a stereotypical family in the development's marketing brochure. Darren was tall, with a full head of brown hair that he kept closely trimmed. Josh was a close replica of his father, but had a buzz cut and a mouth recently filled with braces.

Darren got off to a good start and after a few holes was highly focused on his game. Josh was playing mediocre and quickly became bored.

"Dad, can I drive the cart now?"

"No, Josh. You know you aren't old enough yet."

"Why not?"

"I just told you why."

"But grandpa let me drive the cart at his club in New York."

"Well, grandpa's *club* isn't quite the same kind of place as Idylstream. Grandpa and his buddies do a lot of things out there that they probably shouldn't."

Grandpa had also let Josh have sips of beer and take a puff on a cigar, which Josh vowed to never do again. Josh didn't relay that information to his dad.

"But there's no one around, Dad," Josh countered, motioning toward the empty fairway.

"Well, if a ranger decides to drive by I'll be the one that gets in trouble. We just joined here and it's important that we follow the rules and show that we know proper etiquette."

"What's the point of playing if we can't have any fun?"

"We're having lots of fun."

Josh rolled his eyes and decided to table his argument for another day. Perhaps if he played with his mother she would be more flexible.

As they headed up toward the seventh green, Josh saw something across the way that caught his eye. He took his putter and jumped out of the cart before jogging to the edge of the course.

"Look at this, Dad!" Josh said as he jumped on the back of an enormous alligator.

"Get off of there, Josh!" his father yelled.

"How big do you think it is?"

"I don't know. Get away from there, Josh," his agitated father repeated.

Josh ignored his father and walked the beast from head to tail like a tightrope walker, steadying himself with his outstretched putter.

"This thing must be ten feet long."

"Get over here right now before you get hurt."

Josh finally jumped off the animal and then squatted down next to its immense head. He looked into its marble-like, green eyes and could see his reflection. Slowly, he reached forward and touched the smooth, glassy orb.

"It looks so real, Dad."

"Yes, I can see that. Now get over here," Darren said more imperatively as he approached his disobedient son.

"Okay, I'm coming."

Although angry at his son, Darren was also impressed by the imposing concrete creature. He looked across the yard at the owner's house and it didn't appear that anyone was home right now. He hoped that no one had seen his son jumping on the yard decoration and walked with Josh back to the green.

"Josh, you know that you shouldn't be dancing on other people's property. Playing out here is a privilege and if you can't handle it you won't be coming out on the course."

"Okay, let's go home then," Josh said, quickly calling his father's bluff.

"That's not what I said. You need to follow the rules and show proper behavior here on the course and throughout the community."

"I'll try, Dad," Josh relented, not interested in hearing any more lecturing from his father.

***

After dinner that night, Josh headed out on his bike to cruise the neighborhood. It had just gotten dark and he met up with some of his friends near the community pool. The parking lot was well lit and the boys took turns jumping the curbs on their bikes. It only took a short time for boredom to set in.

"This is lame," Josh's new friend, Anthony, declared. He had lived in Idylstream the longest and was the senior member of the local bike gang. He was tall and skinny with pale skin and black hair. Anthony liked to swear a lot and act like he came from a broken home. However, his father was a cardiologist and his mother was an endodontist. They were still happily married, doting parents.

"Yeah, these jumps suck," confirmed another boy named Taylor.

"I wish they'd let us build some bigger ones," Josh added. "Back in New York we had way better jumps than this."

"I'm going home," another younger boy declared.

"Yeah, me too," said the kid on the bike next to him.

Both pretended they were leaving due to the weak biking choices; however, they actually had curfews to meet and were already running late. They knew they'd be in trouble if they didn't get home quickly.

"What else did you do up in New York?" Anthony asked.

"We skated a lot, but you could only do that in the summer. In the winter we had some hills near our house where we snowboarded. They weren't big, but we made some sweet jumps and grinds," Josh said, trying to sound cool.

"That sounds cool," affirmed Taylor, who was chubby and nerdy looking.

"The only people who get to do anything around Idylstream are the old people. I can't believe they won't let us ride skateboards here," Anthony said, pointing to the sign declaring it to be off limits.

"My dad won't even allow me get a basketball hoop for our driveway. He said the deed restrictions require him to roll it into the garage at night and he doesn't want the hassle," Taylor complained.

"Same thing with my hitting net for baseball," Josh added. "Even when I go golfing my dad doesn't let me have any fun."

"Come on, let's go find some fun, guys," Anthony said, heading off with Josh and Taylor in tow.

The boys raced up and down the smoothly paved streets, occasionally veering off to slalom through the manicured parkways. They stopped near a lot where a new home was currently under construction. With only the framing complete and no electricity, the hulking shell looked very foreboding.

"Do you guys want to go in there?" Anthony asked. He wasn't thrilled about the idea himself, but would consider it if the others agreed to go.

Taylor looked at the other two boys and then up at the house. He didn't think a new home would be haunted, but compared to everything else in Idylstream it was the scariest thing around.

"I will if you guys go."

"We better not," Josh said, noting the *Trespassers Will Be Prosecuted* signs. The image of his dad coming to retrieve him from a jail cell was a powerful disincentive.

"Yeah, besides, I've got a better idea," Anthony said, looking across the street. "Leave your bikes here."

The three boys crept across the road and took up a position along a tall hedge.

"Check out those yard decorations," Anthony whispered.

Standing in the home's landscaping were several strange looking statues. They were small figures that looked like characters out of a fairy tale. There were also two odd birds with sharp beaks.

"Alright, I'll keep watch while you go out and grab one, Taylor."

"Why me?" Taylor protested.

"It was my idea," Anthony said. "You need to do some of the work."

"I'll go," Josh volunteered. He wanted to impress his new friends and prove that the kid from New York wasn't a chicken.

"See. He gets it, Taylor," Anthony scolded.

"Alright, I'll grab one and be right back," Josh said. "Keep an eye out and whistle if you see anyone coming."

Josh scampered out into the garden and grabbed the closest statue. He was surprised when he lifted it. He had assumed it was constructed of stone and would be heavy, despite its small size. Instead, it was made of some type of lightweight plaster. Josh tucked it under his arm and ran back to their hiding spot.

"Here, catch," Josh said in a quiet voice, tossing the statue casually to an unsuspecting Taylor.

"Wow, that's light," Taylor said after barely hanging on to the figurine.

"I'll get the next one," Anthony said, now feeling brave after Josh's successful run.

After a few more shuttle runs, the boys had gathered all of the little, plaster men and both of the birds.

151

"What are we going to do with them now?" Taylor asked.

"They looked bored sitting there in the yard. Let's take them on a trip around Idylstream," Anthony suggested.

They gathered the decorations under their arms and slunk away into the darkness. The boys left their bikes in the bushes and headed off on foot. The first yard gnome was placed in the middle of another home's front porch. The next one was shoved sideways into a mailbox with its small, red elf hat poking out the front. Another one was set on the hood of a car, which made it look like a gaudy hood ornament.

When they were down to just the two birds, the three returned to their bikes and pedaled back the recreation center. Anthony placed one on top of the monument sign at the entryway and then asked, "Where should we put the last one?"

"It has to be somewhere good," Taylor said.

"How about out there," Josh said, pointing to the diving board by the pool.

"But the gates are locked," Taylor noted.

"I can climb the fence and then you can throw the bird over to me," Josh replied.

"That would be awesome," Anthony said, wishing he'd come up with the idea.

"Come on, we'll go down there near the end. It will be easier to get over."

The boys followed the fence line and Josh quickly scaled it and dropped down to the other side. Anthony threw the bird over and Josh took it out to the end of the diving board. He placed it at the end, perched precariously over the water, before returning to his friends.

"That is so cool," Anthony said as they admired the prank. "People are going to be totally freaked out tomorrow morning when they find these things."

"Totally," Taylor seconded.

"Alright, I better get going," Josh said.

"Yeah, me too," Anthony agreed. "I'll see you guys later."

Josh hurried home and parked his bike up against the side of their house. Normally, he would take it into the garage, but at this time of night he didn't want to bother. Pranking had made him hungry and he wanted to have a snack before he needed to get ready for bed.

***

The next morning, Darren Fischer left their home at seven o'clock to make an early tee time at the course. While checking in at the pro shop he heard the two men behind the counter discussing some vandalism that had occurred the previous night at Idylstream.

"Was the course damaged at all?" Fisher asked.

"No, it was in one of the residential sections and at the community pool," the pro assured him.

Darren didn't think twice about it since it wasn't going to impact his game this morning and he knew that his son, Josh, would never be involved in something like that.

***

Earlier in the day, Gryphen Reed, Idylstream's head greens keeper, was up at his usual time and had breakfast before heading out to the club's maintenance facility. He locked the door and walked down the front steps to the driveway. It was a brand new home and Gryphen had been able to rent it from the absentee owners who weren't planning to move in until later the following year. The couple had, however, done some interior decorating and had dictated the landscaping plan. They were from England and had a passion for yard gnomes so there was a small colony of the tiny men in front of the house and another group out back along the eighth hole of the Forest Course. The characters were silly, but they always seemed to put Gryphen in a good mood.

"See you guys later. Keep an eye on the house while I'm away," Gryphen said before getting in his car and driving away.

***

Josh Fischer walked into the garage and then remembered he'd left his bike outside the night before. It jogged his memory of the prior evening's exploits and he chuckled, thinking about what they'd done. He exited the side door expecting to see his bike leaning against the wall. To his surprise it wasn't there. *That's weird*, he thought. He went back into the garage and looked around, thinking perhaps his dad had brought it in before heading out to the golf course. It was nowhere to be found. After one more search outside, he went into the house to find his mom.

"Mom, have you seen my bike?" he asked.

"Have you looked in the garage?" she replied with disinterest as she read the newspaper.

"Yeah, it's not there. I parked it outside last night, but it's not where I left it."

"Maybe your father moved it this morning."

"Where?"

"How should I know, sweetie. Why don't you look again. I'm sure it's around somewhere."

Josh marched back out in frustration and did an entire circle around the perimeter of their house. Still nothing.

"Mom, I can't find it anywhere. Can you drive me down to the rec center so I can shoot baskets?"

"It's a nice day outside. You can walk."

"Please!"

"It's not that far, off you go."

Josh really wanted to play basketball and could worry about his bike later when his dad came home. He grabbed his ball and dribbled down the street.

Ten minutes later Josh arrived at the recreation center. He immediately saw that the bird they had left on the entrance way was gone. As he made his way toward the basketball court, he could see the pool area and noted that the diving board was now clear.
He didn't see the bird anywhere around, but over in a corner of the pool deck he did see something that surprised him. There were two bikes lying on their side. One of them looked suspiciously similar to his while the other one appeared to be Taylor's.

Josh made his way around to the pool gate and walked over to the bikes. It was clearly his bike, however, it looked like someone had dragged it behind a car and then thrown it off a cliff. The rims and handlebars were mangled and even the frame was bent. The tires were shredded and had holes punched in them.

What the heck? Josh wondered as he tried to stand the bike upright.

"Is that yours, son?" came a voice from behind.

"Yeah, I guess so," Josh stammered, still not sure what could have happened.

"Do you know how it ended up here this morning?" the man asked pointedly.

"No, I really don't."

"Well, when I showed up to open the center this morning these bikes were at the bottom of the pool. Whoever put them there damaged the pool deck and the pool coating and now someone is going to have to repair that," the man said.

Josh wasn't really worried about the pool. He examined his bike and tried to push it forward. The rims were so badly bent that it wobbled and would only roll a few inches.

"What is your name, son?"

"Josh."

"Josh, what?"

"Josh Fischer."

"I'm going to need to call your parents."

"Okay," Josh said, lamenting his loss.

Josh sat down and waited by the pool while the property manager went to the office and called the Fischer home. He no longer felt like shooting hoops and reclined on a lounge chair trying to figure out what could have possibly happened last night. His first instinct was that the person who lived at the house with the gnomes had seen the boys and somehow followed them home. It seemed unlikely; however, as there were almost no cars out and all of the boys went in different directions.

Twenty minutes passed before his father finally arrived, still dressed in his golf attire.

"What in the world is this?" Josh's dad said as he walked out onto the pool deck and saw the bikes.

Josh just shrugged.

"Josh, did you do this? And if so, why?"

"I swear I didn't, Dad," Josh said, in no way lying about the bikes. He had, however, decided not to mention the traveling birds and yard gnomes unless it became necessary at some point. "I rode home last night and parked my bike on the side of the house. I couldn't find it earlier so I walked down to play basketball and saw it sitting out here."

Judging by the state of the bikes, Darren believed his son. He wasn't sure how they could have ended up looking like that. Or how they could have made it to the bottom of the pool.

"Whose bike is the other one, Josh?"

"It's Taylor's."

"Alright, we'll take it to his house on the way home. I'm going to need to speak with his parents anyway."

Darren had to lift each bike up and carry it as rolling them was no longer an option.

On their way out, his father stopped to talk with the property manager.

"I'm sorry about all this. I'll call the homeowner's association tomorrow and let them know that we will pay for the damage."

"Thank you, Mr. Fischer. I appreciate you taking responsibility," the manager said, giving Josh a suspicious glance.

Darren loaded the bikes in the back of his SUV before driving to Taylor's house and then heading home.

***

"Good morning, this is Darren Fischer calling about the little incident at the community pool yesterday."

"From what I could see, I wouldn't necessarily characterize it as a *little incident*, Mr. Fischer," Roger McAdams, the board president replied.

"Well, okay," Darren said with acceptance, not wanting to get into a semantics discussion. "Since those were our boys' bikes, my wife and I and the other boy's parents will pay the full cost of any repairs that need to be done."

"I hope you also punish him accordingly for the vandalism."

"I am going to have him pay for part of a new bike, but I do believe him when he told me that he didn't destroy the bikes and put them in the pool."

"Yesterday afternoon we were finally able to review the footage from the center's security cameras. Your son, and several other boys, clearly had a hand in what occurred last night."

"You saw them put the bikes in the pool?" Darren asked with surprise.

"Not exactly. I did see the boys loitering on their bikes in the parking lot after dark. Then, a short time later, they returned and one of the boys jumped the fence and placed a stolen bird statue on the diving board. The property manager was able to identify that individual as your son, Mr. Fischer."

"How did they get the bikes in there?" Darren asked with more curiosity than anger.

"Well, that I don't know. For some strange reason the camera system stopped recording a short time after that. When it came back on line early in the morning you could see the bikes were in the pool."

"That is strange," Darren agreed. He didn't think Josh had the technical know-how to override a security system and even if he did there would be no reason to do it *after* he had already been caught on tape. "Would it be possible for me to see the video footage?"

"Certainly. If you want to meet me at the recreation center later I will be glad to show it to you."

"Thanks. I'm hoping it might answer a few questions or at least give me some new ones to ask the boys. I can't believe Josh would be involved in something like this."

"Parents never do. But boys will be boys, Mr. Fischer."

"Thank you, Mr. McAdams, I'll see you this afternoon."

***

"Josh, do you have something you want to tell me?"

"What do you mean, Dad? I already told you that I don't know how the bikes got in the pool."

"Yeah, I don't know that either, Josh. But I now *do* know how a large bird made it onto the diving board down at the pool last night."

Josh's stomach took a dive. He had been busted.

"Do I need to repeat the question, Josh?"

"No," Josh replied, mentally trying to build his defense case as fast as possible.

"They have cameras down there. I saw the clip with the bird a little while ago. You had nice balance on the diving board, Josh, but it was a very dumb idea nonetheless."

"I know. We were just goofing around and trying to have some fun."

"Do you think I had fun today, Josh?"

"No."

"That's right. I had to deal with the aftermath of your *fun*."

"But, Dad, all we did was move the birds and the gnomes. We didn't break anything and we didn't wreck our own bikes. Didn't the video show someone else doing that?"

"Actually, no. For some reason it stopped recording before that happened. I asked Mr. McAdams about the bird and he told me that he knew the home where it came from. He spoke with the gentleman who lives there and he claimed nothing had been taken. The man said the birds and gnomes were exactly where they were supposed to be this morning."

"But how? We *did* take those things."

"I don't know. Maybe he is lying and then took your bikes as revenge?"

"That's what I thought, but I don't know how he could have done it."

"Maybe he had cameras too and knew where to find you."

Darren was still upset, but continued to believe Josh about the bikes and was now interested in solving the mystery.

"Hopefully we can figure out what happened last night. In the meantime, I still need to ground you for what I know you did."

"I understand. I'm sorry, Dad. I won't do it again."

***

Gryphen Reed looked up from the work he was doing near the green on the fifth hole of the Forest Course. He heard a commotion back down the fairway where two sloppy looking golfers were approaching. Gryphen moved toward the nearby trees to allow the golfers to pass without interruption.

He leaned on his rake and watched the two men. Both were overweight and smoking. One of them chunked his shot and yelled an expletive. The golfer pounded the ground with his club next to the giant divot he'd just gouged before going back to the cart and slamming the club into his bag.

The twosome finally made it to the green and didn't seem to notice Gryphen's presence. One of them had sprayed a fat sand shot that barely flopped onto the edge of the putting surface. He then exited the bunker without bothering to rake his mess. After a pair of three-putts the men shuffled off, leaving a track of scuff marks behind them.

I really wish they'd do a better job restricting the people they let play here, Gryphen thought to himself while shaking his head.

***

"Damn it!"

"Oh man, that ball is a mile right."

"No, that should be okay. There's some room over there."

"Not that much room, Andy."

"I think that one is still in play."

"I think you need to reload."

"Come on, let's go find it, Dave."

"You are quite the optimist, aren't you?"

The two men drove up the right side of the eighth hole to the area where Andy claimed the ball had finally fallen from the sky. He got out and started shuffling his feet through the rough.

"Keep going," Dave instructed. "It's got to be further toward that house."

"I think I see it!" Andy exclaimed.

He jogged over to the back yard adjoining the golf course. There among a group of yard gnomes was his ball.

"I got it, Dave," he hollered.

"Okay, pick it up and come on back. I told you it was out of bounds."

"This isn't OB," Andy countered.

"My ass it isn't."

"Come look at the white stakes. This part of the yard is still in play."

"Then a stake must be missing, because your land of little people there is *not* in play."

"It goes by the stakes that are here, Dave. Come see for yourself."

Dave grudgingly climbed out of the cart and went to examine Andy's lie. He went to the nearest out of bounds stake and plumbed it across. Sure enough, Andy was inside the line.

"I think that's total BS, but go ahead," Dave conceded.

Andy had taken his four-iron with him and thought that he could take a line toward the green with it. The better play would have been to switch to a wedge and punch out into the fairway, but he was feeling lucky now.

He hacked at the ball with a mighty chop and it shot out barely above the grass. It only traveled a few feet before smashing into the face of one of the yard gnomes. The gnome went down hard and the ball ricocheted toward the house.

Dave went down laughing.

"That one is definitely OB, Andy. But you get to hit again from the same spot. At least that poor elf won't be in your way this time."

"Screw you, Dave."

Andy dropped another ball from his pocket and took an angry whack at it. This one came out high with a hook.

"That one is all the way across to the other side. It's not out of bounds, but you are probably in that lake," Dave said, trying to manage his laughter.

159

Andy flew into a rage and marched toward the prone gnome. He pounded on it several times like he was swinging a sledgehammer. Chunks of material flew up from the elf's body. Andy then stood the creature back up and took a stance. He smacked the gnome with a full four-iron swing and sent it tumbling head over foot toward a nearby patch of trees.

Dave stood by idly and watched the meltdown with joy. He knew that after this display there would be plenty more to come during the round.

Andy threw his club at the cart and then marched off toward the trees.

"I need to take a leak," he declared.

He found the beaten gnome next to a large oak. Andy unzipped and aimed his stream at the fallen yard soldier.

"Not smiling now are you, buddy?" Andy asked the damaged, plaster character.

He had just finished and turned to pull up his pants and tuck in his shirt when something moved near his feet. A thick, patterned snake had emerged from the leaves and was starting to coil.

"Shit!" Andy yelled has he tried to run. His shorts, however, were too low and his upper legs wouldn't move in conjunction with the lower portion. He fell face down and skidded into the brush and weeds. He scrambled to his feet and pulled up his shorts. He ran back toward the cart with his shorts still undone.

"What in hell are you doing, Andy?" Dave asked as his disheveled friend ran toward him.

"Snake," Andy said, panting.

"I don't know if you can call that little thing a snake," Dave said, gesturing toward Andy's crotch. "Maybe an inch worm."

"Shut the hell up, Dave," Andy said, picking debris and burrs from his underwear. He finally straightened himself up and returned to the cart. "Let's go."

Over the next several holes, Andy's game only got worse. His tee shot on number nine ended up directly behind the trunk of a tree and he had taken an unplayable, dropping two clubs to the left. He was trying to refocus on golf; however, it was difficult as he began to feel an uncontrollable itch around his genitals. He thought he'd cleared everything out of his underwear, but the sensation kept getting worse.

He stood above the ball trying to clear his mind. Unfortunately, more thoughts kept emerging. He became increasingly tense and when he finally swung the club buried into the ground. The ball popped up and then the club came to an immediate halt when it impacted an unseen tree root. Andy bawled in anguish.

"Ouch!" Dave said, seeing the horrific swing.

Andy dropped the club and crumbled to the ground.

"Ahh, my wrist," he said, grasping it in pain. For a moment it was so bad he forgot about the burning itch between his legs.

"Are you okay?" Dave said, racing over.

"No, I'm not okay. I think I broke my wrist. Get me off this damn course, Dave."

Dave had been enjoying Andy's suffering up until that point, but knew this was serious. He drove straight in and then took his friend to the hospital. There, after several hours of waiting in misery, doctors set the compound fracture and told Andy that he wouldn't be playing golf for quite some time. They were also kind enough to treat the severe case of poison ivy that Andy had contracted below the waist.

***

"Hurry along now, Freddy," Jean McAdams said as she tugged on the thin leash tethered to her small, white Bichon Frise. They were walking past a home in Idylstream that was owned by an eccentric English couple. Freddy always became finicky when they approached the house on walks. Today he pulled a little harder to reach one of the yard gnomes standing in a flowerbed near the sidewalk. He growled and made a few, sad yappy barks at the small fellow whose countenance remained unchanged.

Mrs. McAdams allowed a bit of slack on the leash and Freddy got closer. The dog pawed at the mulch and then turned and quickly lifted its leg to spray a yellow stream on the poor elf who was unable to move out of the line of fire.

"Oh, that's a good tinkle, Freddy," Mrs. McAdams said with a chuckle before they moved on.

Later that night, Mrs. McAdams tucked Freddy into his tiny, fleece bed in the kitchen and made sure the nightlight was on. She said good night and headed upstairs to bed.

A short time later Freddy woke up and heard a noise outside. The McAdams home had a doggy door installed in the kitchen so Freddy could let himself out if need be. Freddy's curiosity caused him to leave his warm bed and scurry outside to see what was in his yard.

"Freeddy. Freeddy. Fre-fre-freeddy," Mrs. McAdams called. She was surprised to wake up in the morning and not find her beloved dog snuggled in his cozy bed. She had looked all over the house and was now searching on the porch near the pool. After going back inside to put on a pair of shoes, Mrs. McAdams went out into the back yard, still calling out Freddy's name. Toward the edge of the golf course she could see that the grass was matted down and torn up. She headed to the spot and gasped at what she saw.

"Freddy!" she shrieked, as she looked down at the few wisps of bloodied, white fur. Crying uncontrollably, she ran back inside to inform her husband.

***

The recreation center at Idylstream was abuzz with activity. After the incident two weeks earlier, Darren was hesitant to attend this homeowner's meeting, but he wanted to be part of the community and thought it was important to know what was going on. Darren had learned that Josh's friend Anthony's bike had also been swiped that evening. It was completely destroyed and parts of it were strewn across the neighborhood where the gnomes had been kidnapped. It seemed like retaliation, however, they still had absolutely no idea what had happened that night.

He and Josh had already visited the local bike store to replace the damaged bike. Darren's main caveat was that the new bike was to be stored in the garage at all times.

Everyone seemed to be in a good mood as they munched on cookies and swilled cups of lemonade. The president, Mr. McAdams, called the meeting to order at seven o'clock and went through the typical formalities and administrative matters. It appeared that it was going to be a very boring evening until the new business and homeowner's comment period began.

"Now that we've taken care of our normal business we will discuss the troubling events that have taken place recently at Idylstream. We all moved to this wonderful community to enjoy a tranquil and secure lifestyle. I, for one, feel very uneasy being outside at night right now."

Darren slid down in his chair and quickly looked for the closest exit.

McAdams continued, "I'm going to open the session with a letter from my wife, Jean. She was not comfortable attending tonight's

162

meeting in person after the terrible tragedy she suffered last week. Her precious Bichon Frise, Freddy, was assaulted in our yard and is feared dead. It is pertinent that we immediately find the person or animal that did this and ensure that it doesn't happen again."

He then read the long, sappy letter aloud. Some homeowners were clearly upset and sympathized with Mrs. McAdams; others picked at their nails and checked their watches.

"She wouldn't be nearly as upset if *he* had died," the homeowner sitting next to Darren snickered under his breath as he motioned toward Mr. McAdams.

After he finished with the letter Mr. McAdams laid out his proposed course of action.

"I have put together a list of proposals that I am recommending we implement to improve safety here at Idylstream. We have a token number of security cameras now. I have prepared a map indicating key locations where additional cameras should be installed," he said, producing a large poster board from below the table. It was a map of Idylstream with small camera icons pasted on it. There were cameras everywhere; it looked like Idylstream had a contracted a severe case of camera-pox.

"The cameras will be a good start, but we also need feet on the street. For that I am suggesting a two-prong approach of volunteer neighborhood watches and private security officers. I will also be gathering bids from animal control companies to install traps around the community.

To greater control illicit activity I have drawn up some amendments to the deed restrictions that will institute tighter limits on our curfew rules and restrict the movement of unattended minors in the community," he added, holding up a legal-sized sheet of paper.

"There will of course be costs, a burden that will have to be shared by all homeowners, however, I feel they are necessary and will be offset by the preservation of value in our property."

During his rant Mr. McAdams had ignored a number of homeowners who were clearly looking to voice their opinions. Between breaths, a woman near the front stood up and interrupted him.

"Excuse me, Mr. McAdams. Two months ago, when our dog disappeared, I brought it the board's attention and you did absolutely nothing. Now precious Fluffy dies and we're supposed to instantly institute your Gestapo regime?"

"It's Freddy, not Fluffy!" Mr. McAdams corrected haughtily.

The woman waved her hands at him dismissively and sat down in disgust.

Before Mr. McAdams could start again another homeowner stood up.

"I just want to say that I think you've really put together a great program, Mr. McAdams. I can see that a lot of time and effort went into it," the man said.

"Thank you," Mr. McAdams said with a pleased smile.

"However, it is really just a good start. We should really consider taking away inmates – I mean homeowner's – belts and restrict the possession of sharp objects. The cameras are great, but we should really look into a system of monitoring devices installed in residents' necks. Finally, our landscaping would really be spruced up with the addition of lots of shiny, silver razor wire."

His comments drew a good laugh from the audience and even a few of the board members who were obviously not on board with the president's plan.

Mr. McAdams' smile quickly disappeared.

"I think it would serve us all to keep our comments constructive in this forum," he directed.

Across the room another homeowner popped up.

"We also had our family dog disappear and your *proposal* at that time was that we should simply adopt a new one and move on!"

"Well, at least when your mutt vanished our barking complaints dropped off a cliff," another board member griped.

"What?" the man retorted. "Maybe you're the one snatching all of these animals!"

An older woman sitting in Darren's row was next up. She was one of the people moved by Mrs. McAdams' letter and still seemed emotional.

"I have to agree with these residents, Mr. McAdams," she said as loud as her meek voice would allow. "When my kitty, Trixy, went missing you wouldn't even allow me to put up fliers in the community. You were heartless and should be ashamed."

Her protest garnered a loud round of applause.

Mr. McAdams tried to regain control, but the meeting was deteriorating quickly. There was clearly a lot of dirty laundry to be aired and the complaints soon moved away from animals to an assortment of other grievances.

Darren walked over to get more cookies and lemonade and watched the proceedings from the sidelines. It reminded him of an

Asian parliament meeting gone wrong like he'd seen on TV. He wondered if fists would soon be flying.

His wife and kids had been lobbying for a dog recently and Darren had been considering it seriously until now. The scene was comical, but he was worried about what was going on at Idylstream. It seemed like a great community so he hoped these issues could be rectified.

***

Several weeks had passed and Darren had not heard of any further issues at Idylstream. He was glad things were quiet as the meeting had caused him to start worrying about their property value. It was a Saturday afternoon and he was golfing again with Josh. The humidity was on the rise and the days were getting hot.

Darren had forgotten about the massive alligator along the seventh hole until Josh pushed his approach shot in that direction. As he drove up, he could see Josh's ball sitting in the rough near the beast. He dropped his son off and headed back to the cart path.

Josh took his wedge and putter and walked over to play his shot. When he took his stance he could see the gator in his peripheral vision. For some reason it was bothering him. He stepped back and went through his routine again. He addressed the ball and skulled the shot into a greenside bunker.

"Darn it!" he whined.

He walked over and tapped his club on the gator's snout.

"Stupid gator. That was your fault."

He looked down at the statue's huge, shiny eye and then ran toward the green in terror.

"Dad! Dad!"

"What's wrong Josh?"

"The gator's eye...it moved!"

8. The Recklessly Curious Golfer

"Head over that way, Doc. I pushed that drive a touch. It should be just into the trees," Grant LoPario said. "There it is."

"That's not too bad. I'm not sure you're going to have a shot at the pin though," Dr. Jonas Anelo replied as LoPario surveyed his situation.

"Too early in the round to be cavalier. This one has punch-out written all over it."

"I thought a guy like you always goes for it," Dr. Anelo taunted.

"With the ladies – yes. On the golf course – no."

Dr. Anelo rolled his eyes, despite knowing LoPario's reputation.

"Alright, that was cheesy," LoPario admitted. "It would be more appropriate to say that I need to try harder to make fewer bad choices on and off the golf course."

He eyed his escape path one last time, dug his feet into the long, patchy grass, and then hit down with a check swing that popped the ball safely back into the fairway.

"Nicely executed," Dr. Anelo said. He swung the cart around to pick up LoPario and then headed off to play their next shots.

Dr. Anelo hit the green safely in regulation and LoPario knocked his third shot close to the pin. Once on the green, Dr. Anelo made an easy two-putt for par. He stepped back and watched as LoPario drained his short putt for a four.

"Nice par, Grant," said Clark, another of their playing companions.

"Yeah, great recovery," added Trent, who was the fourth member of the group.

Dr. Anelo walked off feeling a bit disappointed. Although he and LoPario had carded the same score, it somehow felt like LoPario's was better. He had played the hole the way he was supposed to while LoPario's poor tee shot brought added risk and excitement. Today the golfers were playing a team game against other foursomes so theoretically no one should have been rooting against anyone else in the group. Still, some resentful part of Dr. Anelo was unhappy when LoPario's ball hit the bottom of the cup.

As they put their clubs back in their bags, Dr. Anelo gave an obligatory compliment, "Good job saving one for us there."

"Oh, thanks. You did it the right way though, Doc."

"Thanks," Dr. Anelo replied half-heartedly. He drove off to the next hole determined to outplay his companion.

The two golfers stood side-by-side leaning on their drivers on the tee box while Clark and Trent hit their shots. Dr. Anelo glanced sideways at LoPario. The two men had similar appearances; however, LoPario was just a little bit more of everything good and a bit less of everything bad relative to Dr. Anelo. Dr. Anelo was just under six feet tall, LoPario was just over. Dr. Anelo was in excellent shape for his late fifties. LoPario was a few years younger with a chest and arms that were slightly bigger and a belly that was a bit smaller. Dr. Anelo had a nice looking face, but LoPario was a man that most women would describe as "attractive". LoPario had dark hair with some gray creeping in. Dr. Anelo had gray hair with some black strands hanging on. Dr. Anelo didn't think he had self confidence issues, but from a masculine standpoint he did feel somewhat envious of LoPario.

That feeling also carried over to their golf games. Both players were above average with Dr. Anelo playing to a six handicap, slightly behind LoPario who maintained a solid three. The two were usually quite close in score, but more often than not LoPario ended up edging out Dr. Anelo. Dr. Anelo probably had a better short game; however, LoPario consistently outdrove Dr. Anelo by ten to twenty yards. As is common in golf, other players tended to note the latter rather than the former.

The two had known each other for several years through playing together at the club. They were good friends, but not close friends. Their social interaction was limited by the differences in their personal lives. Dr. Anelo was married and participated primarily in couple's activities. LoPario was a confirmed bachelor who had cultivated a reputation as a local playboy.

On the course LoPario wasn't at all conceited, played by the rules, and had impeccable etiquette. Most of the men that played with LoPario liked him as a person. They viewed LoPario like the "cool kid" back in school. They had long-term, monogamous marriages while he had a steady stream of girlfriends. They assumed the grass was greener on the other side and he was living life to the fullest while their fires slowly dwindled away.

The women at the club also enjoyed being around LoPario. Many of the more conservative, married ladies would scoff at his philandering in private, but at dinner parties they would happily play along with his flirtatious overtures. If nothing else, they loved him for providing them with a steady stream of gossip fodder.

Over the next few holes, as the normal topics of conversation ran out, Dr. Anelo eventually led the discussion toward LoPario's personal life. Sitting in the cart waiting for the green to clear Dr. Anelo asked, "So who was that gal I saw you with last week?"

"Just a friend," LoPario replied casually. He was used to personal questions on the golf course, but tried not to elaborate too much. He knew that other men at the club were attuned to his activities; however, he was typically quite modest around them. He lived his life the way he wanted to. It wasn't some kind of show he put on to prove he was more of a man than everyone else.

"Nice looking young lady," Dr. Anelo said, prodding further.

"Indeed. And you should know, Doc. You've got yourself a beautiful young girl yourself," LoPario replied, quickly turning the tables.

"Uhh...thanks," Dr. Anelo said, somewhat taken off guard by LoPario's reference to his wife as a "girl". Lauren was Dr. Anelo's second wife and she was twelve years younger. At this stage in life it wasn't a drastic difference, but it was enough for most people to still note. Dr. Anelo had been married and raised two children with his first wife. As often happens, they divorced after the kids finished college. The current Mrs. Anelo had worked in the medical field previously and had always been focused on her career over a family. This was her first marriage, and with no desire for having kids, she was comfortable marrying someone older who also no longer had such inclinations. "So nothing serious?" Dr. Anelo added, not knowing what else to say.

"Well, not for her anyway. She's just using me as a rebound guy," LoPario joked. "Paula is coming off a recent divorce – her third. She wants to get out a little and seems to think that I won't be proposing to her any time soon, which is a pretty safe bet. So far we're having a good time and enjoying each other's company."

"Married three times already. Really? How old is she?"

"Just turned forty. The first time she was young. Had a kid and then it only lasted two years. The second time was a good one; unfortunately she lost him in a car accident. The third one was simply a mistake. That's how I actually met her – the guy was a buddy of mine. They were both in bad places emotionally and just latched onto each other. It didn't take long to realize they weren't compatible in many ways, physically in particular."

"Interesting." Dr. Anelo said, raising his eyebrows. The hint of sexual discussion immediately snapped his attention completely away from golf.

"Yeah, she still has a pretty strong drive. My buddy has already run into some serious prostate problems so he had a tough time keeping up. Right away he started to get a complex about it and things went south from there."

Dr. Anelo had heard rumors about LoPario's involvement with several married women over the years. He didn't want to cross the line, but couldn't help himself so he jumped in with both feet, "So...did you have to help him meet the demand?" He laughed after he said it to imply it was light-hearted, however, he was dying to know the answer.

LoPario hesitated for a moment, clearly gauging his answer. "No, I couldn't do that to a buddy. I even asked his permission after they divorced if he was okay with me dating her. He had no problem with it because he knew he could trust me. They had an amicable spilt and they both only wanted to see the other one find some happiness."

"Well that's good."

"How long have you been married now, Doc?" LoPario asked.

"It was five years in April."

"Congratulations. Are you still in the honeymoon phase?"

"Oh, it never lasts," Dr. Anelo said, feeling as though he'd answered too quickly.

"I know, Doc. One of the many reasons I'm not married. The initial excitement always fades, but is everything alright?"

"Oh sure, sure," Dr. Anelo said dismissively. "We're still having plenty of fun. Things settle down and you kind of fall into a routine."

"Routines are okay, just be sure it doesn't turn into a rut. That's where you have to be careful with the younger ladies."

It seemed like more of an observation than an insinuation by LoPario. Nonetheless, Dr. Anelo suddenly felt unnerved about his marital situation.

After a moment of uncomfortable silence LoPario continued, "Well, the last time I saw her, Lauren looked extremely happy. I'm sure you've got nothing to worry about, Doc."

"I only need to worry about sticking this one close," Dr. Anelo said, getting out of the cart and starting toward the tee. He was glad to have an excuse to end the conversation.

Dr. Anelo plugged his shot into a bunker and ended up taking a double bogey. Walking off the green they ran into the head greens keeper, Gryphen Reed.

"Hello, Gryphen. The greens are rolling pure," LoPario complimented.

"Yes, they look awesome. I would enjoy them even more if I could reach them in fewer shots," Dr. Anelo added.

"Thank you, gentlemen. I have been refining the fertilizer mix and the last batch was absolutely killer," Gryphen said with a wry smile.

Riding to the next hole, LoPario said, "Now that guy is someone to keep your wife away from, Doc. His greens are amazing, but something about him has always bothered me."

"You're right. I've never trusted him. He seems like one of those guys that's hiding something."

Dr. Anelo tried unsuccessfully to forget about the discussion regarding his wife for the rest of the round. He played mediocre golf and finished eight shots behind LoPario, which certainly didn't help their team. After the round he found himself rushing home to an empty house.

***

Dr. Anelo spent the afternoon tidying up the house and trying to find projects to distract his mind. Almost uncontrollably he kept stealing glances at clocks throughout the house, wondering what time his wife, Lauren, would return. Dr. Anelo had occasionally worried about the age difference with his wife. This, however, was different. For some reason LoPario's comment had triggered a powerful response. Dr. Anelo felt like he was having a steadily increasing anxiety attack.

He sat down in a deep leather chair in the living room, closed his eyes, and took some deep breaths. He checked his pulse – slightly elevated, but not racing. After just a few quiet moments he couldn't seem to sit still. He reached for the remote and turned on the TV. It was on the Golf Channel of course and they were airing a Champions Tour event. *Old guys golfing – great! The last thing I need to see right now*, he thought, immediately turning it back off.

"This is nuts," he said to the dark screen in front of him. "What is wrong with you?"

He looked over at a small clock on the mantle. Five o'clock. She should be here any minute. After spending the afternoon desperate for her to arrive, he was now suddenly petrified about her return. Dr. Anelo popped up and walked quickly to the master bathroom. He opened the medicine cabinet and sorted through a number of small prescription bottles. Finding the ones he wanted, he shook a few tablets onto the counter. He grabbed a Xanax and a Viagra and threw them down his throat with a swig of water.

Exhaling, he looked in the mirror. "Ah, what the hell," he said, picking up another Xanax and sending it chasing after the other pills.

The faint, mechanical rumbling of the garage door caught his attention and he ran back to the kitchen. He tried to look natural waiting for her to come through the door.

"Hi, sweetie," he said as soon as her face appeared.

"Oh, hey, Jonas," she said with surprise. "I didn't see you standing there."

"Sorry, I was just coming in for a drink."

"Perfect, I need one too. It was hot out there today," she said, gliding toward the fridge. She grabbed a Gatorade. "What do you want?"

"A water would be fine."

She slid the plastic bottle down the granite island counter toward him and then unscrewed her drink and chugged the red liquid greedily.

"I was thinking of going out to dinner tonight. What do you think?"

"I had some chicken breasts that I was going to cook. But we can go out if you want to."

"Yeah, let's go out tonight. Chicken sounds boring and I'm pretty hungry."

"Well, I definitely need to shower," she said, tugging at her saturated spandex tennis outfit. "I can get ready quick, though. Do you want to go over to the club?"

"No, I was thinking we'd go to the Italian place – Albano's."

"That sounds good. They're normally busy so why don't you call for a table and I'll get ready."

"I'll do that, dear."

She headed upstairs while he called the restaurant. He then fidgeted around downstairs until she reappeared ready to go.

***

Albano's was packed; however, they were seated in a secluded booth that allowed them to talk without having to speak too loud. She had been finishing her makeup in the car so it wasn't until after they ordered that they had time for a conversation. Dr. Anelo had been trying to think of interesting things to discuss, but had come up dry.

"How was tennis today, honey?"

"Okay, we won our doubles match. I didn't play particularly well. Chloe was on her game, though, and carried us. And how about your golf?"

"About the same. We had to rely on Grant to bear the team's burden."

"Oh, you played with Grant today?" she asked with more interest than Dr. Anelo would have expected.

"Yes," he said, looking at his wife more closely. "As you know, he's a good golfer."

"Definitely. And not too hard on the eyes to look at," she added.

Dr. Anelo watched her as she said this. She was looking away and seemed to be visualizing something – likely LoPario – while sipping her wine.

"I hadn't noticed," Dr. Anelo said, which was obviously a lie.

"Come on, Jonas," she countered. "You men check each other out just as much as the women do."

"I doubt that."

"If you say so," she said dismissively. "Even Jacob told me one time how cute he thought Grant was."

"Jacob? Do you mean Jacob the assistant pro?"

"Yes, that Jacob."

"Why would he tell you that?"

"We were just chatting one day during a lesson."

"About attractive men?"

"Sure. I think I asked him who from the club he would want as a sugar-daddy."

Dr. Anelo stared blankly at her for a moment.

"Really, Jonas? You didn't know that Jacob was gay?"

"Uh, no. I mean sure he dresses nice, but so do all of these other young guys these days."

"Boy, Jonas, we need to get you out more often. You're clueless. And you can't make your determination based on whether or not they wear a white belt with dark shoes. Although Jacob would never make that kind of fashion mistake."

Dr. Anelo tried to focus on the conversation, but instead found himself taking a mental inventory of his wardrobe. *What color was my belt today?*

"What exactly do you find attractive about him?" Dr. Anelo asked.

"He's one of those guys who has a really handsome face. It's in proportion – nothing too big or too small – but still has strong looking features. His body is well proportioned, too. He obviously takes good care of himself so he looks younger than he is. He can easily get women in their forties and fifties, which is what you usually see him with. It's probably because he wants someone more emotionally mature. But he could definitely land a good looking girl in her thirties and even a few in their twenties. Too young, though, and it would either be a gold digger or a girl with some kind of daddy issues."

"Do I help you with *your* daddy issues?"

"Jonas, please," she scoffed.

"It almost sounds like you've run this analysis on Grant before."

"Again, Jonas. Just girl talk. We can only talk so much about cooking and cleaning tips," she chided.

He decided not to push the topic any further and was relieved when the waiter brought them a focaccia loaf and olive oil so they could start talking about food. The rest of dinner was relatively quiet and Dr. Anelo paid little attention to what was said. He continually looked around and contemplated other couples in the restaurant. He wondered about their relationships and how many were engaged in extra-marital affairs. Of particular interest to Dr. Anelo were the respective ages of the partners in each pair. Many were close in age; however, he saw several that shared a gap similar to his. Dr. Anelo had always harbored some concern about having an attractive, younger wife. Tonight that mild unease was growing into acute anxiety.

***

On the way home, Lauren yawned several times and noted how tired she was. Dr. Anelo wondered if she was really worn out or if she was pre-positioning an excuse for when they returned home. He responded with his own body language – touching her knee and then running his hand slowly up her inner thigh.

"Sorry that you're so tired, dear," he said. "You should get right in bed when we get home."

She turned, smiled at him, and raised her eyebrows. Dr. Anelo felt a small flicker, but it was quickly extinguished. She picked up his hand and placed it back on the steering wheel.

"Focus on driving," she instructed.

"Yes, dear," he replied obediently.

By the time Dr. Anelo pulled into their garage his wife's eyes were getting heavy and her head was dipping down periodically. He quickly got out and raced around to open her door. She climbed out slowly and walked away. Dr. Anelo watched her legs the whole time. They were firm and well tanned from days spent on the tennis court. As her heels clicked across the garage floor, Dr. Anelo once again felt a spark of anticipation.

He followed her dutifully inside and stopped in the kitchen while she got a drink from the refrigerator. They continued through the hall and up the stairs to the master bedroom. She said nothing and didn't look back, acting almost as though he wasn't even there. Finally, in their room she set down her purse, stretched, and rolled her neck.

He set his hand on her shoulder and she looked askance at him.

"Alright, dear," she said begrudgingly. "That was a nice night out. I think I owe you something in exchange."

It took him a second to be sure she'd only spoken words because it felt like she might have slapped him. Her lack of enthusiasm was exasperating. His feelings swirled around and then finally settled – on guilt. He must have been asking for too much.

"I'm sorry, Lauren. You seem tired. We can just go to bed."

"No, that's okay. Just let me get changed."

"You're sure?"

"Yes."

"You must really be worn out from tennis. Here I thought I was the old one."

"Yeah, it was a long day out there," she said before walking heavily to the bathroom and closing the door.

He swiftly got undressed and climbed into bed. He knew, however, that there was no hurry. Her "changing" was going to be at least a twenty minute affair as she undid the outfit and makeup that she'd spent forty-five minutes getting together before they'd left.

After ten minutes alone he grabbed the remote and turned on the television. He clicked incessantly between channels for nearly fifteen minutes before the door slowly opened. She was wearing a simple, short nightie. A few years ago he would have considered it sexy, but it was a garment that she wore regularly so now it appeared more utilitarian. He was at least glad to see her give an approving smile as she lifted the covers and crawled in next to him. That was the extent of her foreplay as he was left to fondle and grope on his own. Despite her disinterest, the little blue pill was up to the task and soon so too was Dr. Anelo.

Aware of the growing presence between them, Lauren lifted up the sheets like a tent and pulled her knees up and back. The message was clear: come on in and get to work.

As he entered, all of the thoughts that had been cluttering his mind suddenly seemed to disappear. *My God*, he thought, *sex really can take your mind off anything*. The euphoria didn't last long of course. She put in minimal effort, occasionally mimicking some of his primal panting and grunting. It was almost absurd how hard he was working to make up for her shortcomings. Unfortunately he was positioned above her on his elbows when he saw her eyes dart involuntarily toward the clock on the night stand.

What the hell? he thought. Suddenly a new emotion took over – anger. He really wanted to stop and roll off of her, but nature's drive was simply too strong. Instead, he picked up his pace and slammed his way to climax.

She immediately dislodged him and wiped off on the sheets before sliding over to her side of the bed.

He was sweaty and exhausted. After a minute or two he caught his breath and edged toward her. He ran his hand down her arm carefully, almost apologetically. "Everything okay?" he asked.

"Sure, honey. Just a bit tired."

"Was it good for you?" he asked, immediately wishing he hadn't. *Could you have said anything more stupid?*

"Yeah, don't worry," she said, reaching up to turn off the lamp next to her – clearly a signal that discussion time was over. "Good night."

Don't worry? he thought. *Seriously?* She might as well have had the words DO WORRY tattooed across her forehead. He withdrew to his side and sat up in bed. He took a few deep breaths and tried to sort things out. He didn't know what to think. *Was it him? Was it her? Was she hiding something? Was there someone else? Was the marriage over already?*

He looked over at her lying in the bed next to him. He needed answers to questions he simply couldn't ask her directly. Dr. Anelo would have to find another way.

It was getting late and his body was spent. He peeked under the sheets at his flaccid member. The bright side was that he didn't need to contact his doctor immediately as it certainly hadn't lasted four hours. He dropped the covers and shifted around trying to get comfortable.

He should have been sound asleep, but his mind was wide awake and in overdrive. Dr. Anelo was replaying his wife's behavior from tonight and the last few months. Sorting through the random memories he tried to decipher any clues or patterns. There was a lot of time during the day while he was at the office when he had no idea what she was doing. She had her regular tennis games, but that still left a lot of free time. *Maybe I need to hire a private investigator?*

He also started tabulating the number of times they had had sex. He felt like it was pretty regular, however, now that he thought about it the number was lower than he would have expected. *Was she slowing down or maybe fulfilling her needs elsewhere?*

There was nothing he could do about it at this hour so he resolved to strategize in the morning. It seemed like he remained awake for several more hours, but at some point he finally drifted off.

***

What little sleep he had gotten was low quality. He woke up to his alarm and dragged himself into the bathroom to get ready. Lauren was still sleeping in bed by the time he got dressed and headed downstairs. He ate a light breakfast alone before heading out for the office.

Mornings for the couple had also changed. In the past Lauren would get up and eat with her husband even though she didn't have anywhere to be. Now, even if she was awake, she would stay in bed until after he left. He really didn't even know what she did until she headed out for a tennis match or lunch with her friends.

On his drive to work he continued his deliberations on how to figure out more about his wife's activities. Checking the mail was too old fashioned, besides, all they ever got now was junk. They shared an email account so there wasn't much to hide there – unless she had set up an outside one. She was always attached to her phone so it would be tough to snoop there without her knowing. He could, however, access their phone records online, which would give him a list of her calls for the month. Perhaps there was something around the house, but he wasn't sure what to even search for. That would be the easiest place to start and maybe he'd get lucky – if there was even anything to find. Dr. Anelo closed the office early on Fridays and Lauren played every Friday afternoon so he decided that would be a safe time to rummage around his own home.

The worry was festering inside him, but having devised a plan made him feel somewhat better. Now rather than being in a gray area of uncertainty he could hopefully head toward either black or white.

Dr. Anelo's first few patients provided a modest distraction, however, by mid-morning his thoughts had drifted back to Lauren. He wondered where she was and what she was doing. *Maybe she's sitting at home watching TV? Or maybe she's sneaking into her lover's house for an early rendezvous?* Although completely implausible, the second thought caused his whole body to tense up.

"Doctor?" a voice rang out. "Is that supposed to hurt like that?"

"Oh, sorry," Dr. Anelo stammered, not realizing how hard he was squeezing the patient's calf muscle.

"So what do you think?"

"Hmm," Dr. Anelo pondered, trying to regain his composure. "I think you need to stay off it for extended periods of time until we can perform both procedures. We can do the first one in the next week or two and then the second one in another two weeks. After about a week of recovery you'll be able to work back into your normal routine."

"Oh, shoot."

"What's wrong?" Dr. Anelo asked.

"It's just that we have a tournament at our club next week and I was hoping to squeeze it in before the surgery."

"I see. Well, as a golfer I can certainly understand your conundrum. However, as your doctor I think your best bet is to not take the chance. Your pain is going to get worse, which won't be conducive to good golf anyway."

"Alright, Doc, I'll skip it. Since you play maybe you could fill in for me?" the patient joked.

"I don't know if I'd advise that either..."

Dr. Anelo was relating everything to the situation with his wife and he wondered if someone was "filling in" for him right now. That thought rolled around inside his head for a moment and then transformed into an idea.

"Doctor?"

"What was that?" Dr. Anelo replied, realizing he once again wasn't paying attention.

"I was asking if you were alright. You looked a little out of it there."

"I'm fine. I'm a bit distracted today, but I think I just figured something out."

* * *

"Grant? Good morning, it's Jonas. How are you doing?"

"I'm doing fine, and you?"

"Excellent. I'm calling to see what you're doing next Saturday morning. We are going over to Windmill Bluff to play and we have a spot for you if you're available."

"I think I'm open. Hang on a second, let me check," LoPario replied.

Dr. Anelo waited anxiously for LoPario's answer. Now that he had a solid plan in mind he wanted to put it in motion as soon as possible. He tapped his pencil, wondering what was taking so long, even though it had only been about thirty seconds.

LoPario returned to the line. "Hey, Doc. I checked the calendar and that looks fine. I like that course so I'm looking forward to playing."

"Great. I'll drop you an email once I get our exact tee time."

"I'll watch for it. I was going to give you a call anyway. I need to talk to you about something on the medical side."

"Is it anything urgent?"

"No, no. I don't think so. Just a little issue in my leg. I trust you so I want to get your opinion first before I go to my general physician."

"No problem. I need to talk to you about something as well. I'll make sure we're in the same cart."

"Sounds good. Thanks for calling, Doc. I'll see you out there on Saturday.

* * *

Dr. Anelo was waiting fretfully by the bag drop at Windmill Bluff. He had already given the starter strict instructions about who was to be put on his cart. When LoPario pulled up, Dr. Anelo led the bag attendant to the car's trunk.

"Good morning, Grant," Dr. Anelo said, shaking hands.

"Morning, Doc."

"Be sure to put Mr. LoPario's clubs on my cart," Dr. Anelo directed to the attendant.

"LoPario? That's a great golfing name," remarked the attendant.

"Unfortunately I don't know how fitting it is right now. I've been feeling a bit more like high-Pario lately," LoPario said modestly.

"Sandbagger," groaned Dr. Anelo. "Don't be angling for extra strokes already. Come on let's check in and head over to the range."

***

The third hole was a difficult par three and, as was often the case, the groups ahead had already bogged down there. Dr. Anelo knew he'd have some time to speak with LoPario about matters outside of golf. He didn't want to seem too eager so he let LoPario go first.

"Alright, Grant, tell me what's going on with your leg," Dr. Anelo said.

LoPario threw his foot up onto the cart's dashboard and rolled back the cuff of his shorts.

"I've started to get some pain with these varicose veins and this one in particular," he said, pointing to the bulging, blue vessel on his upper leg. "I've been trying to ignore it and do the normal home stuff, like keeping it elevated, but it's getting worse. I don't want you to have to talk shop while you're golfing; I just want to know if I should schedule an appointment or give it some more time."

"No problem," Dr. Anelo replied. He instinctively grabbed LoPario's leg and began kneading and massaging it, watching how the vein reacted to different movements. "Unfortunately it's not likely to get any better. Your best hope is that it remains stable. We can try some minimally invasive procedures and see what kind of results we get first. If not, the surgery is pretty minor and I can definitely fix that critter," Dr. Anelo said and then slapped LoPario on the knee. "Give us a ring at the office on Monday and we'll get an appointment set up."

"Thanks, Doc," LoPario said. He checked the green and saw the group ahead still putting. "So what did you need to ask me?"

"Oh, that," Dr. Anelo blurted rather casually. He had rehearsed what he was going to say a hundred times, but was still uneasy. He looked around to be sure that the other groups were out of earshot and lowered his voice. "Kind of a strange request actually."

"Strange?" LoPario asked.

"You know my situation. I thought things were still good with Lauren, but suddenly I'm not so sure. Since our last round I've been really concerned that something is wrong. Maybe we've just hit a lull in the relationship. Or, maybe she's fooling around. I obviously can't ask her, so I have another idea."

"Why can't you ask her?" LoPario inquired matter-of-factly.

"I think it's a lose-lose proposition. If I ask her and she says no, either she's lying and I'll be even more worried, or if she's telling the truth then she's going to be suspicious of me. And what if she admits that she is having an affair!?"

"Yeah, I guess," LoPario said, not honestly grasping the logic. "It seems like you should try to take an honest approach, but based on my history I'm certainly not going to be your best moral compass. So what do you need me to do?"

"I know this is going to sound strange..." Dr. Anelo said before pausing.

"Okay, I'm sitting down, Doc. Lay it on me."

"I want you to hit on my wife."

"You want me to hit on Lauren? Seriously?"

"Yep," Dr. Anelo said, oddly pleased that LoPario was so stunned by the proposal. He'd rarely seen LoPario get flustered.

"And that's going to do what?"

"It'll let me find out if she is straying or not."

"Hmmm," LoPario mused, still digesting the request.

"Trust me. I've thought about this a lot, Grant. I think it's the perfect plan."

"That sounds like something they'd say on TV right before everything goes horribly wrong. What about getting a private investigator to follow her?"

"That makes me nervous, too. How do I get a good one that I know isn't some psychopath who wanted to be a police officer, but could never make it? What if he uses the assignment to start stalking her? I don't think I could trust someone I didn't know."

"Well, I suppose..."

"Let me ask you this, Grant. Would you sleep with my wife today if you had the chance?"

"Wow, Doc! This is not the conversation I thought we'd be having today."

"Come on, honestly?" Dr. Anelo badgered on. "Tell me."

"Of course not. She's a lovely woman, but I could never do that to you," LoPario said cautiously. He felt like he had given a good answer to a trick question.

"See! That's why it is perfect! I can trust you to make some advances while not having to worry about things going too far."

"But why me, Doc? Don't you have a pool guy or gardener that you trust?"

"God no! Hell, that could be who she's screwing right now. And don't let your head get too big now, but I know she – and a lot of the other ladies – and at least one guy – think you're a decent looking man."

"Just 'decent' looking? Hmmm, I would have hoped for a little more," LoPario said with faux seriousness. "I don't know, Doc. This is pretty heavy stuff. It's kind of nuts."

"It's not nuts, but I will be if you don't help me out. Please, you don't have to answer right now, just give it some thought today."

"Oh, that should help my golf game – weighing an offer from my friend who is pimping his wife."

"Alright, guys. The green's clear, let's hit," came the voice of one of their playing partners from up ahead.

"Okay, let's play," LoPario said, stepping out of the cart. At this point he really, really wanted to get back to golf.

On the walk up to the tee box Dr. Anelo felt the uncomfortable urge to lobby further. Dr. Anelo nudged LoPario and looked him in the eye. "Please give it some consideration."

LoPario held up both hands as if to plead with Dr. Anelo to stop.

"Okay, okay," Dr. Anelo said, backing away.

***

LoPario avoided the subject – and Dr. Anelo – as best as he could for the rest of the round. He was in the parking lot changing shoes at the back of his car hoping to make a quick escape when he noticed a presence behind him.

"Nice playing out there today, Grant. Always a good match."

"Not quite enough to beat you today though, Doc. I guess I was a little distracted,"

LoPario lamented.

"I know how that is. This business with Lauren has my mind all twisted in knots. I'm even worried that I might screw something up at the office," Dr. Anelo said, ignoring LoPario's tone and body language. "So can I count on you?"

LoPario took a deep breath. He intended to say no, but when he opened his mouth the words, "Alright, I'll do it," came out instead.

"Great!" Dr. Anelo said with startling enthusiasm.

"So what's the plan?" LoPario said with an equal lack of enthusiasm.

"I've got that all worked out. We're going to go for drinks at the club and 'accidentally' run into you there. Now I need you to come alone, though."

"Paula is out of town visiting family for two weeks."

"Oh, that's perfect. We'll spend some time chatting and then I'll get a message saying that one of my patients has gone to the hospital. It's nothing serious, but I better head down there just to be safe. I'll leave her in your capable hands and then you work a little of your magic and see what happens."

LoPario stared blankly at Dr. Anelo for a moment. "What if she's *into* it?"

"Then order her another drink and get her to give you some details about anything else she's been up to. After that put her off and say that it's too soon, she's too drunk, and that you can get together another time. Drop her off at the house – but don't you dare kiss her, lover boy."

"Believe me, I won't. And what if there's no interest?"

"Poke and prod a little bit. That's another reason I'm asking you. You know women better than anyone else I know. You'll be able to tell if she's lying or hiding something. My guess is that she'll be comfortable and willing to confide in you if the situation is right."

"And what if she's offended?"

"I thought about that, too. I really doubt that will be an issue. She knows your reputation and will probably be expecting some flirting. If anything, she might be more offended if you *don't* make some overtures. In the worst case she'll be a bit bent out of shape and you can call a cab to take her home."

LoPario again stared vacantly.

Dr. Anelo interpreted this as total agreement with his brilliant scheme. "See? We've got everything covered. How about we plan to meet at the end of this week?"

"That's fine, Doc. I'll call you about an appointment for my leg and we'll work out the other details."

"You bet, buddy," Dr. Anelo said, grabbing and shaking LoPario's hand. "And whatever needs to be done for your leg is on the house. I really appreciate you helping me out."

LoPario got in his car and left as fast as he could, making sure that Dr. Anelo didn't have a chance to ask anything else.

***

The bar at the club was moderately busy. Dr. Anelo had just excused himself for an "emergency". LoPario was now alone with Lauren. He rubbed his fingers along the smooth edge of the black granite slab and sized up his prey. He normally had the utmost confidence when he was alone with a beautiful woman, but tonight was different. LoPario felt like he was walking a tightrope and he was nervous. He was also uncomfortable that several patrons were sitting too close and might try to listen in on his upcoming conversation.

"It's kind of noisy up here," he said when another round of drinks appeared. "Let's go grab one of those tables," he added, picking up their drinks and motioning toward one of the two-seat high tops tucked in an alcove.

"Sure," Lauren replied.

Several sets of eyes followed their movement across the room; however, all of them had likely seen Dr. Anelo here with LoPario earlier. Hopefully that would offset some of the gossip that would otherwise arise.

LoPario continued with light conversation, trying to gauge Lauren's mood and level of inebriation. Luckily it didn't take long for her to shift the focus to relationships.

"Do you think you'll ever get married again?" Lauren asked.

"Never say never, but I can safely say *unlikely*."

"You don't seem like the settling type."

"Years ago, sure, but probably not anymore. So, is that what you've done? Settle?" he asked pointedly.

"I don't think marrying Jonas was *settling*. But things change as time goes on."

"Yeah, sometimes you need to find new things. Often you need to find them on your own, not with a partner."

She smiled with a gleam in her eye and leaned in a little closer. It was a look that LoPario knew well. Dr. Anelo had been right. This wasn't a green light to the bedroom, but she was clearly open to some flirting.

LoPario had been dreading the commitment that he'd made all week. Now he was actually starting to enjoy himself. He took several large swallows from his glass and returned the look. With the alcohol seeping into his system and the closeness of the table he was starting to see her differently. She was very attractive with flowing brown hair framing an inviting face. He looked down at her arms as she held her glass out in front of her. They were supple and golden brown. His eyes followed them back up to her shoulders that were modestly covered by her black cocktail dress. The next move was an unstoppable drift down toward her chest. Her tanned breasts were bulging upward from the wide opening. He noticed how nice and even her skin tone was; she didn't have a patch of sunspots like many women had already developed at that age. Just as his eyes arrived there she leaned farther forward and brought her arms closer together, which forced her cleavage to rise higher.

"So what about, Paula? Are things still good with her?" Lauren asked.

LoPario had thought about this topic beforehand. He didn't want to ruin what was a pretty good relationship, but he knew he could still cautiously use her to open the door with Lauren.

"It's been going well, but it's hard to tell where it will head. Like I said, trying new things is very important in life."

She smiled and nodded in agreement.

He sensed that the moment was right and scanned around the area. It was dark enough where they were sitting and the view of them below the table was obscured. LoPario looked back at Lauren and moved even closer. He gazed into her eyes and slowly slid his hand under the table. Instinctively he moved it far enough up before easing it down onto the soft, smooth skin on the inside of her thigh, just above her knee.

There was an immediate spark. He felt a sudden arousal, however, her body seemed to almost spasm and she jumped back into her chair.

The look on her face was instantly different and she was sitting straight upright. Her face was now serious as though his touch had dropped her blood alcohol level right off the scale. This too was a look that LoPario knew well – he'd just crossed the line.

"Sorry, Lauren," LoPario said, placing both hands on top of the table.

"Ahh, yeah, that's okay," she stuttered. "Probably my fault. Giving off a few too many wrong signals."

He smiled in a friendly manner and she did the same, like they were sharing a funny joke.

LoPario shifted the conversation directly in the opposite direction and they finished their drinks before he offered to take her home.

They were quiet on the ride to the house, both knowing that they were going to have to say something uncomfortable when they arrived. LoPario pulled into the Anelos' driveway, but left the car running.

"Thanks for a wonderful evening, Lauren. Sorry I got a little carried away. I hope you take it only as a compliment on your allure."

"No worries. I don't mind flirting a bit, but I am a married woman, Mr. LoPario," she said playfully.

"Really? Who is he?"

She once again offered her *friendly* smile.

"Seriously, though, I did enjoy our time together tonight. You're very easy to chat with. And if you do ever want to talk about anything, here's my number," he said, handing her one of his cards that listed his personal contact information. This was another one of Dr. Anelo's requests. He wanted her to have LoPario's number just in case she decided after the fact that she wanted to pursue something.

"Thanks, Grant," she said before sliding the card provocatively down into her bra. "Goodnight," she said and climbed out.

"Goodnight."

He watched her walk to the front door and go inside. He thought to himself, *damn, that was a strange night* and then drove home.

***

LoPario was eating breakfast and reading the paper when his phone rang. He was startled and concerned because rarely did anyone call in the morning.

"Hello?"

"Good morning, Grant. Well?"

"Jeez, Doc. You don't waste any time do you?"

"I need to know."

LoPario was aggravated and wanted to mess with Dr. Anelo a bit. He considered telling Dr. Anelo that after the club they stopped at a cheap motel where he thoroughly ravished Lauren. However, his friend was clearly becoming unstable about the whole situation so he decided otherwise.

"Doc, I'm sure you have a lot of patients that are worried out of their mind about some inconsequential spot or bump. I'll give you the same advice: don't worry about it. I don't think she's cheating. I just think she needs a little romancing."

"Really?" Dr. Anelo said, sounding surprised and relieved.

"Really. When was the last time you took her on a nice trip somewhere?"

"Well , the last year has been very busy at the practice and..."

"Doc, don't start making excuses. Suddenly a year will turn into two, and three, and then you'll be in trouble. Free up some time, book a trip, and see what happens. That's my prescription for you."

"Thanks, Grant. I can't tell you how much I appreciate you doing this. You're a true friend."

"No problem, Doc."

"And I'm going to take care of that leg of yours as soon as I get back from vacation," Dr. Anelo joked.

"Sounds good. I'll talk to you later." LoPario hung up, glad that his task was complete.

***

Three days later, LoPario's breakfast was once again interrupted by the telephone. It was a local call, but he didn't recognize the number.

"Hello?"

"Hi, Grant. Its' Lauren."

"Oh, hi. How are you doing? Is everything okay?" LoPario asked, worried that something had happened to Dr. Anelo.

"Well, yes and no. I need to figure something out and thought maybe you could help me."

"Ahh, why me?" LoPario said as he started to get a sinking feeling in his stomach.

"It's kind of what you said in the car the other night. And I feel like I can trust you."

LoPario shook his head and thought: *I've been getting that a lot lately*. He'd hoped that he'd freed himself from the whole Anelo family mess and now he was getting dragged back in. He looked at the clock and leaned back in his chair. "Alright, go ahead."

"Actually, I was hoping we could talk in person. I'm a little worried about speaking on the phone."

Wow! These two are both paranoid, LoPario surmised. "Do you want to come over here?"

"No, that's probably not a good spot. There are some other members who live near you and might see my car. I was thinking somewhere public. How about the coffee shop on Arlington Road? Would eleven o'clock work for you?"

Once again he wanted to say no, and once again he did the opposite. "Sure, I'll meet you there."

***

Entering the coffee shop, LoPario inspected the patrons. He was looking for Lauren while also trying to make sure there was no one else he knew there. He was starting to feel like some kind of secret agent and was afraid that the Anelos' paranoia was contagious.

Across the room, Lauren's waving hand caught his attention. He walked over and sat down without any other physical contact. She was wearing the standard tennis wife uniform: a tight blue skirt, a form-fitting sleeveless top, and a Nike visor that allowed for a pony tail in the back.

Wow, she looks hot. How is Doc not taking care of this woman? LoPario wondered.

It was loud inside and the cloak of white noise meant that they could converse comfortably.

"Good morning, Lauren."

"Thank you for coming, Grant."

"So what can I help you with?" LoPario asked, with no desire for small talk.

"It's complicated..."

"I'm listening."

"The other night you caught me off guard when you touched my leg."

"Again, sorry. That was wrong. A little too much alcohol. Sometimes married women are looking for a sideline activity. That was just me misbehaving."

"No, that's okay. I'm not offended at all. It just brought out something that I've been keeping a secret."

LoPario gave her a puzzled look and guessed at what she was talking about. "No, you shouldn't be thinking about having an affair, Lauren."

"Well, that's just it. I'm *already* having an affair."

Oh, shit! LoPario was stunned. Doc had been right all along. And now he'd told his friend that nothing was wrong. "I don't know what to say," LoPario said, telling the absolute truth.

"It's been going on a while and I've reached a crossroads. I have to decide which way to go. The last few days he's been ranting non-stop about us taking a grandiose vacation and asking me where I want to go. That's the last thing I want to do right now!"

LoPario's feelings of surprise took a sudden turn toward stupidity.

Lauren continued, "I think I'm going to leave Jonas, but I don't know how to tell him. I was thinking about ways that might make it easier. Perhaps if he were to *already* want to leave me? That might make him feel more masculine about how it ends."

"And how would you do that?"

"That's why I started revisiting our time together the other night. I wondered what Jonas might do if he thought the affair was with someone like you..."

"No! No! No!" LoPario burst out. He had no intention of digging any deeper into this pit that he was already stuck in.

"No, I didn't actually mean you, Grant. I think the two of you are too close. Maybe there was someone else you could think of that would fit the bill?"

"I have no idea," LoPario said with relief.

"I'm worried that if Jonas finds out about my lover's identity it will really hit him hard. I still love Jonas very much on some level and I don't want to hurt him. I have to weigh that against my own happiness though. Can I trust you with the secret?"

LoPario was burning with curiosity, but circuit breakers were kicking in full force. "No, I don't need to know and don't want to know."

He was now playing both sides and that could only lead to more problems for everyone involved. It was time for him to exit this Bermuda love triangle. "Listen, Lauren. If you invited me here for advice I'll give it to you happily. To do the right thing you should just come clean. Let it out there, deal with the inevitable explosion, and then sort out the pieces."

"Maybe you're right," Lauren said.

"That's my advice, Lauren. You obviously have a lot to figure out and I'd better be going. Good luck," LoPario said before standing and hurrying out. In his rush to exit he didn't even notice a member of their club standing in line as he zipped past.

***

The following week Dr. Anelo was starting to feel better. Things had been very busy at his office, providing a good distraction. He still hadn't pinned Lauren down on a vacation; however, he had a travel agent putting together several packages to choose from. His life seemed to be getting back to normal.

On Wednesday Dr. Anelo had a cancellation and was able to leave at noon. He was in the pro shop at the club checking in for his round. Several ladies who had finished their morning group were chatting near the entrance. Dr. Anelo hadn't been paying attention to them, but when he glanced in that direction he noticed that they were all looking at him. In unison they all directed their eyes elsewhere.

When he headed for the exit the pack had dispersed and he held the door for Mattie Hawkins, who was leaving.

"Oh, thank you, Jonas."

"My pleasure," Dr. Anelo replied, trying to make eye contact.

There was a moment of awkward silence as they walked down the gradually curving path outside.

"Everything going alright?" Dr. Anelo asked.

"Oh, sure," Mattie said dismissively.

"I saw your gang watching me inside. I was worried that my shirt was on backwards or something."

"No, no. Just us girls gossiping."

"About me?"

"No, nothing, Jonas."

He could tell that she was lying and at the same time desperately wanted to tell him something.

"Mattie, what about me?" Dr. Anelo insisted.

"Nothing," she repeated, trying to blow him off. Then she cracked. "We were just saying that you need to keep a close eye on that friend of yours, Mr. LoPario. He seems to like spending time with Mrs. Anelo."

"Oh, that. I know about them having a drink together."

"And you don't care?"

"Why would I? I was there with them that night at the bar before I got called away to an emergency."

"Yes, I saw you there. I was talking about the coffee shop."

"Coffee shop? When?" Dr. Anelo questioned.

"The other day. They were there together when I walked in and then he got up and left in a hurry. I'm sure it was nothing, though," she said, waiting to see his reaction.

"And this was after the night at the club?"

"Uh-huh. A few days later."

"You're sure it was them?"

"Quite sure."

"One hundred percent?"

"Yes, Jonas. Don't get all excited, I'm sure there's nothing for you to worry about. I'll see you later," she said before turning and walking off to the parking lot. The snide grin on her face showed how much she was savoring Dr. Anelo's reaction to her revelation.

Dr. Anelo remained frozen in place. His whole body was clenched tight. Every circuit in his brain was occupied with trying to process what he'd just heard. He had a round of golf to play, but his instinct was to get in his car and drive straight to LoPario's house.

A voice broke his trance, "Come on, Doc. We're on the tee in ten minutes. Get moving."

Although Dr. Anelo no longer had any interest in playing golf, he shuffled off toward his cart. He hoped that once he started playing it would take his mind off this new and problematic turn. That, however, proved to be wishful thinking. He played like crap, paid out his bets, and raced home.

At the house he found the garage empty as expected. Lauren also had a Wednesday afternoon routine and Dr. Anelo figured that he would have maybe an hour alone.

He went straight to their bedroom and began rifling through her drawers and closet. He caught a glimpse of himself in the mirror and saw a burglar breaking into his own home. Dr. Anelo tried not to leave things looking disheveled, however, that was difficult given his frenetic pace. He peeked under the bed, lifted the mattress, and rummaged in her nightstand. After twenty minutes of fruitless searching he began to feel silly. *Would she really be stupid enough to hide some physical piece of evidence in their room?* If there was anything to find it would likely be in electronic form. He hustled down the hall to their office.

Dr. Anelo was competent on the computer, but not savvy. He did a cursory check of all the email trash and spam folders. Again, nothing. When he tried to check the Google searches on their computer he could only seem to pull up a few days of history. As he scrolled down, he accidentally hit the "clear" button at the bottom and all of the data disappeared.

"Damn it!" he yelled, echoing through the empty house.

The next stop was their cell phone account. They were on a family contract so he could pull up both of their records. When he clicked on her number he was overwhelmed by the number of phone calls. He never realized how much she used her phone. He pulled out his own phone and looked up LoPario's number. He typed it in the filter box and hesitated for a moment. Dr. Anelo took a deep breath and then clicked "go".

The results hit him like a punch in the gut. There were numerous calls over the past few months, including the most recent one a few days ago – the day Mattie Hawkins must have seen them at the coffee shop.

Somewhere downstairs he heard a door close. He fumbled with the mouse, closed the browser, and shut the computer down before sneaking back to the bedroom. He wasn't sure why he reacted that way. *Am I the one with something to hide?*

Dr. Anelo picked up his work tablet from the dresser and opened his calendar. He checked his Friday morning appointments and saw the name: LoPario.

Perfect!

***

Dr. Anelo avoided his wife the best he could for the next two days. He would confront her soon enough. Right now he was solely focused on LoPario. His supposed friend had lied and made Dr. Anelo look like a fool.

On Friday morning Dr. Anelo woke up refreshed and well rested. He had slept better than he had for quite some time. Inside he was burning with rage; however, his outward demeanor was calm and collected.

Walking out of the bedroom, Dr. Anelo stopped and turned to look at his wife lying in bed. His feelings toward her had begun to shift. He couldn't decide whether or not he should be angry at her. Dr. Anelo felt that some of the blame was on him. Marrying a younger, attractive trophy wife was full of peril. Perhaps marrying her had been a mistake, but he saw no reason not to at least take corrective action. He closed the door and walked away confident in his game plan for today.

Driving in to the office Dr. Anelo listened to Vivaldi's Four Seasons. It was a piece that he played often on surgery days. The shifting tempo and depth reminded him of how surgery should be conducted: move with lively, quick tempo at certain points where the procedure allowed and with a slower, more measured pace when necessary.

He greeted everyone at the practice and then retired to his office to review his case notes on the various procedures that he would be performing today.

The first few cases had gone very well – Dr. Anelo knew he had absolutely nailed them. His assistant let Dr. Anelo know that Mr. LoPario had arrived and was being prepped for his operation. Dr. Anelo made one more run through the techniques he would be using on LoPario. He wanted to be one hundred percent sure he got it right.

Dr. Anelo was scrubbed and dressed when he entered the sterile, pale blue surgery room at his office. The lights were slightly dimmed. At full intensity they made the glossy tile walls gleam brightly and overwhelm Dr. Anelo's vision while he worked on minute structures within the human body.

"Good morning, Grant," Dr. Anelo said.

"Hey, Doc. All ready to go?"

"All set. We are going to get you all straightened out today," Dr. Anelo replied before going about his business of checking the tools and equipment.

Once everything appeared to be in order Dr. Anelo handed LoPario padded headphones and a pair of dark glasses with the sides covered.

"I'll be using some lasers periodically so we need to keep your eyes well covered. There's not a lot of noise, however, most patients prefer to listen to music. You can toggle the switch on the right side to change between selections. As I told you, we'll be using local anesthetic in a few spots along the leg. You'll feel a few pinches, but that should be it."

"Thanks, Doc. I appreciate your help on this."

"No problem. My pleasure, Grant."

Dr. Anelo worked quickly and efficiently through LoPario's varicose issues. As he was coming to the end, he requested that the nurse go out to summon the medical transport to take LoPario home and have his post-op items ready to go.

Dr. Anelo stared at LoPario who was sitting back contently listening to music with a happy look on his face. It reminded Dr. Anelo of something LoPario had said several weeks ago regarding Lauren. He had told Dr. Anelo that: "she looked very happy the last time I saw her." *I bet she did*, thought Dr. Anelo. He swiftly moved forward and completed his work on LoPario.

Afterward he gave LoPario his follow-up instructions and told him to call if he noticed any complications over the weekend. Dr. Anelo left the office feeling satisfied and at ease. He had accomplished everything he intended to do today. It was now mid-afternoon and the weather looked perfect. He headed straight to the golf course where he played nine holes of golf better than he had in quite some time.

***

On Friday evening Dr. Anelo was sitting in the living room casually sipping a glass of wine in a burgundy leather recliner. The humming of the garage door announced the arrival of Lauren. This time he was in no hurry to see her. He waited patiently for her to find him.

"Jonas?" she called finally.

"In here, Lauren."

"There you are," she said, entering from the hallway. "Are we going out to dinner tonight?"

"No, I don't feel like going out. Please have a seat, Lauren."

"Okay, is everything alright? Did somebody get hurt?" she asked, sensing his somber tone.

"No," Dr. Anelo said with a smile, thinking about LoPario on his operating table today. "Everyone is just fine. We do need to talk though."

"What's up, Jonas?"

"I'd always hoped that we'd never have this conversation, but here we are."

Lauren gave him an inquisitive expression, as though she had no idea what was coming.

"I know," he said dramatically.

"You know?" she replied innocently.

"About your affair."

She sat down across from him and said nothing. She waited, measuring what response she wanted to give, trying to determine what state of mind he was in. At this point there was no reason to deny it.

"How long have you known about it?" she ventured.

"Officially, only a short time. Now that I look back, however, probably a lot longer. I just didn't want to see it I suppose."

"So what do we do?" she asked.

"Good question," he answered in a very civil tone. "I've been thinking about that quite a bit as you can imagine. It's obviously not something simple. I don't think I can get past this so counseling isn't really an option."

"No, I don't see much benefit there either," she said, pleased that going their separate ways seemed to be on Dr. Anelo's mind as well.

Dr. Anelo chuckled deviously. He was so proud of himself. "I did go ahead and take an initial step this morning."

"And what was that?" Lauren inquired, expecting a stack of divorce papers to be thrown her way.

"I made sure that your lover won't be as able to satisfy married women going forward."

"What?" she said, wondering what he could have done. "How did you manage that?"

"Grant was in for his vein work today so I went ahead and made a few extra incisions while I was in that neighborhood."

"Grant? What does he have to do with this?"

The conversation had suddenly made an unexpected turn that Dr. Anelo was not prepared for. "So you're willing to admit your affair, but still trying to cover up who it is with?"

"I'm sleeping with someone else, but certainly not Grant. What the hell did you do?"

Dr. Anelo immediately saw that she was telling the truth and as the words were coming out of her mouth he wondered: *What have I done?* Now, somehow hoping for her help, he told her.

"I made several incisions to his erectile tissue. He'll no longer be able to get full erections...and maybe not any."

"Oh my God! Why in the hell did you do that?" she screamed.

"Because he was sleeping with my wife!" Dr. Anelo yelled back, now clinging to the hope that it was actually true.

"Why do you think it's Grant?"

"He lied to me about seeing you. And then there's this," he said, pulling several pieces of paper from next to the chair and shoving them toward her. "All of the phone calls you two have made."

She examined the papers quickly, noting the calls that Dr. Anelo had highlighted with an orange marker.

"I didn't make all of these calls," she said firmly.

"Then who did? It's your phone."

"You did!" she said, throwing the last page back at him. "Look at the bottom you idiot. You pulled up *both* of our numbers."

The small footnote was in tiny print, but he could still make out his number. She was right. Dr. Anelo's triumphant moment of revenge had morphed into the collapse of his world. His head was spiraling and his stomach was plummeting.

Lauren stood over him shaking her head in disbelief and disapproval. "Can you fix whatever you did to Grant?"

"I don't know," he lamented, staring at the floor.

"Well, I suggest you call him immediately and try. He's going to sue your ass off and you'll probably lose your medical license."

"Yes..."

"How could you have been so clueless and so reckless? This marriage is obviously over so I will go ahead and tell you the truth now. It was something I was planning to tell you anyway."

He looked up from the carpet at her face above. He really wasn't sure he could take any more right now.

"It's Gail Dayton. We've been together for over a year now."

Have I completely lost my mind? Dr. Anelo wondered after hearing the name. *Gail Dayton?* She was a young widow at the club whose husband had died a few years earlier. She was a regular in Lauren's tennis group.

"Yes, that Gail Dayton," she said, answering the obvious question for him. "We both sort of found each other at a tough time and something clicked. It started off as some simple physical play, but has evolved into something else. Certainly something more than you and I have."

She waited briefly for a response, however, he had none.

"Goodbye, Jonas. I'm leaving you. I'll start moving my belongings out next week. I'll have an attorney contact you and hopefully we can end things quickly. I'm not sure there'll be much to split up after Grant guts you," she said before turning and marching out.

Dr. Anelo sat for several moments in silence. He didn't know what to do next. He refilled his glass and sat back down in his chair in the living room – alone.

9. Final Round

"Come on, honey. Let's get going. We still have to pick up Grandpa on the way to the golf course."

"I'm coming, Dad."

"Don't forget to grab your shoes from the laundry room. I'll be loading the clubs in the garage."

"Okay."

On his way out Eric Donovan headed through the kitchen and was intercepted by his wife, Susan.

"Are you ready for your big round today, dear?" she asked.

"Yeah, it looks like it's going to be a nice day out there. Are you sure you don't want to come along? We've got room for another player."

"No, that's alright, Eric. I've spent more than enough time with your dad. Thanks for the offer, but you guys have fun," she replied, sitting down at the large kitchen table with the newspaper and a contented look on her face.

"Alright, we'll see you in a bit," he said, grabbing a couple of drinks from the fridge before going out the door to the garage.

Jenny had already popped the trunk and was loading her stuff into his car. Eric walked to the side of the garage to pick up his clubs. He stopped and looked at his father's golf bag, which was now residing here. It was a well worn, brown leather cart bag. Despite its age, the leather still had a slightly glossy sheen as his father used to clean it regularly with shoe soap. Hanging from one of the metal ringlets was a small pocket watch that his dad had inherited from his father. The watch kept perfect time and his dad was religious in using it to track the pace of play during his rounds. Even after spending years on the golf bag the recessed crystal didn't have a single scratch. Eric knew that he could transfer it to his own golf bag, but he wasn't ready to do it yet. Also, he traveled with his clubs frequently and was afraid that it might get lost, stolen, or damaged. He was content to leave it ticking right where it was for the time being.

Inside the bag were his father's well worn irons. He still carried two persimmon woods, but the driver was modern day. Last year Eric had taken his father to a demo day and had him fitted for a

460cc titanium driver. His dad had been skeptical, but after one shot he changed his tune and was sold. Then there was the putter. It was a hickory shafted mallet that had been with his father for decades. The grip was real leather that his father periodically had replaced at a local shoe repair store. The head was steel, but it had a piece of white marble inserted into the face. Because of the material, the ball made a distinctive click at impact. Other players would often ask his dad to try it out and would invariably cringe when they did. Compared to new technology that muted the connection of the ball and face, his dad's putter felt like hitting a rock with a hammer on a cold day. But that's what he liked so he stuck with it. His dad was always solid on the greens so it was hard to argue with the results.

Eric decided to take the putter with him so that they could hit a few putts with it. He only carried twelve clubs in his bag normally so there was room for a second putter. He carefully slid it into his own bag and then loaded the clubs into the trunk before closing it with a *thunk*.

Eric pulled out of the driveway and started heading across town. About halfway to their destination they passed the road that led to his father's home.

"I wish we could go to Grandpa's house," Jenny said sadly as she watched the green street sign pass by her window.

"Me too, honey. But he doesn't live there anymore."

"I know, Dad. I just miss it. We always had so much fun there. I really miss our summer picnics when Grandpa would cook out on the grill and Grandma would make all those great desserts."

"We all have fond memories there, but moving on is part of life, dear."

They rode in silence for the next few miles, acting interested in the sights although neither of them really was. Eventually Eric turned off and pulled into a long horseshoe shaped driveway. The middle of the horseshoe was carefully landscaped and featured a fountain at each end. There were several stone paths winding across it that led to a number of empty benches being guarded by statues. At the top of the drive was the large, solemn looking building where Grandpa Donovan now resided.

Eric pulled under the cavernous porte-cochere and parked at the outer edge.

"Alright, Jenny. Do you want to come in with me or wait here?"

"I'll stay here," she quickly replied.

"Okay. They know we're coming so it shouldn't be long. You can stay up in the front seat, I'll go ahead and put Grandpa in the back."

Eric turned and walked across to the main entrance where he entered through the imposing carved wooden doors. Inside the lobby it was very quiet, but he could hear voices coming from down the hallways. He went around a corner to the right and stopped at the first office where a heavy set gentleman with a large mustache sat working at his desk.

Eric tapped lightly on the door jam, "Hello, I'm Eric Donovan. I'm here to pick up my father today."

"Ah, yes, Mr. Donovan. I'm David Grigger, we spoke on the phone the other day," the man replied, getting up to shake hands with Eric.

"Nice to finally meet you, Mr. Grigger."

"Likewise, please just call me Dave. I'm sorry I was away previously, hopefully my staff handled everything appropriately in my absence."

"Yes, they've done a wonderful job," Eric said nodding.

"If you wouldn't mind, I just need you to print and sign your name here on this release form," Grigger said, pointing to a document sitting on the edge of his desk and handing Eric a pen.

Eric leaned over and signed.

"Thank you, Mr. Donovan. If you'd like to have a seat here I'll go and get your father."

"Thanks," Eric replied. "It won't take long, will it? I have my daughter waiting in the car."

"No, he's already downstairs here waiting."

Grigger disappeared down the hall while Eric sat down and looked around the office. He scanned the framed photos sitting on the desk. There were several shots of Grigger and his family enjoying vacations and other special occasions. His eyes then wandered along the wall examining the framed items that displayed Grigger's various certifications.

Eric heard footsteps returning down the hallway and he got up to meet Grigger as he approached.

"Here we are, Mr. Donovan," Grigger said.

"Thank you again for everything. My family and I really appreciate all you and your staff have done to help with our father. We're heading out to the golf course now."

"Oh, that should be nice. It's a lovely day out there."

"Well I don't want to keep my daughter waiting. Thanks again."

"My pleasure."

Eric took his father out front to the car. He opened the back door and carefully secured his dad with the seat belt to make sure he didn't fall over. Eric checked his watch and got back in quickly before driving away down the other side of the horseshoe. The course was only about ten minutes away, but Eric didn't want to be rushed to make their tee time.

Back in the car Jenny whispered, "Dad, do the people at Grandpa's club know about him?"

"Most of them do I would guess. You don't have to whisper, Jenny. He can't hear you, honey."

"Yeah, but I still feel weird talking about him when he's right there," she replied, still in a hushed tone.

Eric looked up at the rearview mirror and asked loudly, "Dad, is Jenny making you uncomfortable?" There was no response. "See, he can't hear you."

"Dad, that's really mean!"

Eric was just trying to add a little humor to the uncomfortable situation, but his daughter wasn't amused. "Okay, we'll be quiet the rest of the way. We're almost there."

A few minutes later they arrived at the Somerset Country Club. The turnoff was marked by a modest, gray granite monument stone with the club's name and logo. Eric drove up the tree lined entry road, but turned off before the clubhouse and pulled into a side parking lot that was adjacent to the club's cart barn. He found an open spot up front and parked.

"Alright, Jenny, let's check in and get a cart and we'll come back for the clubs and Grandpa."

"You're going to leave him here?"

"He'll be okay; it'll just take us a minute or two. Come on."

They walked around the back of the large, Spanish-style clubhouse and climbed the stairs that led to the pro shop. They passed several members and received hellos, smiles, and nods. The older members loved to see younger players out at the club. They always had clichéd comments about meeting a future pro or how bad she was going to beat her dad on the course.

Inside Eric and Jenny walked up to the wide, wooden counter and were greeted by one of the assistant pros.

"Good afternoon, can I help you?"

"Yes, we're here checking in for our round this afternoon. Two thirty-five under Donovan."

"Oh yes, Mr. Donovan. I didn't recognize you. I haven't seen you in a while. And is this your daughter?"

"Yes, this is Jenny."

"Hi," Jenny said meekly. She had always liked playing golf at the club with her grandpa, but she'd always dreaded being introduced to everyone. They either talked to her as if she was five years younger than she really was or they spoke about her as if she wasn't actually standing right there.

"My, you've really been doing some growing haven't you, young lady?"

Jenny just nodded politely and looked to her dad to move things along.

"Yes, she's like a weed – just keeps going," Eric replied, sensing his daughter's anxiety. Being the father of a teenage daughter had given Eric his own set of anxieties. She dressed like most of her golfing friends with an exceptionally short skirt and a tight fitting top that accentuated all of her recently formed curves. She wore her shoulder length, brown hair in a ponytail with a ribbon and fed it through the back of her cap. Eric tried to accept the fact that his daughter was growing up, but he still found himself scrutinizing the glances that she got from other male golfers when they were on the course together. "So we're all set?" He continued, handing the gentleman a credit card.

"Yep, let me just run this through. You should have pretty smooth sailing out there this afternoon, not too many other groups out on the course."

"That's good; we don't want to hold anyone up."

"We all miss having your dad out here in the mornings. Great guy."

"Thank you. It was tough for him to finally give it up. He spent a lot of good years out here at Somerset and made a lot of good friends. We have some fond memories as well," Eric said, nodding at Jenny.

"Well, you folks have fun out there this afternoon and come back and see us again soon," the man said, handing back Eric's credit card.

"Thanks again," Eric replied. "Let's go, Jenny."

Eric and his daughter quickly walked back down stairs and picked up a cart outside. They hopped in and zoomed over to the parking lot. Eric loaded up their clubs and moved the cart next to the car to transfer his dad.

Jenny walked over to sit down, but stopped. "Dad, is there enough room on the seat for the three of us?"

"Don't worry, you'll fit. Squeeze in here."

She still hesitated.

"Come on, Jenny. He certainly can't drive his own cart. Let's go."

She grudgingly wedged into the seat and they drove off toward the first tee.

There was no starter out this afternoon so they leisurely stretched out a little and warmed up before starting their round. Eric eventually walked onto the tee box and looked down the first fairway. "How many times did you start your day right here, Dad? Watching the sun break over those trees, smelling the cool morning air, sending your tee shot streaking down the dew covered fairway. I'm glad you had so many good years of retirement. You certainly deserved it."

Father and daughter teed it up and both hit solid drives that found the fairway. They were right where they wanted to be.

The weather was indeed perfect and the Donovan family was enjoying their round at Somerset together. Eric and Jenny were both playing great golf and they had fun reminiscing about different shots they'd once hit on the first few holes.

Midway through the front nine the course gradually started to change. As the holes got further from the clubhouse, the surroundings became more accentuated. Somerset was an older course and the interior holes were devoid of homes and condos. It was just golf and nature.

Number five was a challenging par four with a forced carry approach over water. Eric and Jenny had both once again found the fairway and were standing next to the cart surveying their second shots.

"Well, Jenny, I would never encourage you to intentionally take a dive in a normal round, but maybe we should put our shots into the lake to make Grandpa feel a little better?"

"I think we should go for the green, Dad. If yours happens to go in the lake then it was meant to be."

"I guess you're right. I just thought it would be a fitting tribute because Grandpa hit so many balls into that lake during his career here. He did a pretty good job of mastering the course, but this lake always gave him fits for some reason. This was just one of those holes that got stuck up in his attic and he could never seem to fully shake it. It's a beautiful lake, but it truly was your nemesis wasn't it, Dad?" he said, turning back toward the cart.

Jenny was away by a few yards so she hit first. She had conquered her fear of water on the golf course a long time ago so Grandpa's lake didn't intimidate her. When she addressed her ball and visualized the shot the lake wasn't even there in her mind. She focused on the flag and made a smooth swing. Her shot took off at a perfect trajectory and, although it faded slightly, found the right side of the green maybe twenty feet from the pin. Pleased with the shot, she leaned on her club and turned to her father, "You're up, Dad."

Eric normally didn't worry about the water either, but today's round was a little different. He felt a bit like a kid with his dad watching him over his shoulder to see how he did under pressure. Growing up his dad had always been very supportive in sports, but Eric knew that if he screwed up his dad would still give him one of those looks of mild disappointment.

Eric took a deep breath, relaxed his grip, and swung the club. He caught it a touch thin so the ball took off a little low. Jenny watched with anticipation and the ball screamed toward the shoreline at the back of the lake. Eric's ball cleared the edge comfortably, bit into the upslope, and then gracefully rolled onto the green.

"Nothing to it," Eric said smiling. "See, Dad, this hole is easy."

"Oh, so you planned to hit a line drive into the hill?" Jenny asked sarcastically.

"Yeah, that's how I drew it up."

"Please. If you hadn't snuffed that thing up front you'd be way over the green."

"Alright, smarty, last time I checked the card only has a box for my score, no spaces for style points. Let's go."

The next sentimental stop in their round was the large steep faced bunker that guarded the modest green on number eight.

"Ah, here we are at another one of you favorites, Dad," Eric said as they pulled up next to the green. "At least this is one that you finally made peace with."

Eric and Jenny walked up to the green with their putters, but Eric stopped at the edge to admire the gleaming white sand in the bunker. "Grandpa spent a lot of time in this little patch of beach. He used to curse it up and down for putting another dent in his front nine score. He always complained to the greens keeper that the sand was too soft. Then he finally got a new sand wedge and it turned out to be the magic wand that he needed to break the spell. I'm sure a lot of it was psychological, but once he got up and down a few times his confidence finally kicked in. From there on out he considered an approach in this trap to be a good miss."

After number eight, the next few holes started to rise gradually through some minor hills. The elevation changes gave the holes a different feel and the breeze picked up some strength.

The tee on number twelve marked the highest point on the course. This was a spot where members loved to pause to take in the sights and guests would routinely stop to snap a few photos.

Eric found his way to the middle of the tee box and took a deep breath. "Quite a view, isn't it, Dad? I know it's even more picturesque in the morning when you normally came through here with your group after the sun had risen over the hills. It's not quite the same today, but still pretty darn impressive."

"Are you going to hit, Dad?" Jenny asked a bit impatiently.

"In a second. I'm just trying to take in a little extra bit of everything today. Who knows when we'll be back out here again."

"Okay, I just want to make sure we finish and I don't want anyone coming up behind us."

Eric moved a few steps to his right while still looking off into the distance. "Go ahead and hit, Jenny."

She was more interested in the fairway than the scenery. She took advantage of the elevation and lofted a huge drive right down the pipe as her father looked on proudly. Last year Eric had been forced to finally break down and face reality: his drives were gradually getting shorter while his daughter's were getting progressively longer. Between her lessons, the equipment technology, and the growing strength in her young body she seemed to have taken giant strides in distance over the past few years. Jenny had gone from playing the senior tees with her grandparents, to the ladies' tees, to being able to manage the whites at shorter courses. Although the distance here at Somerset was a bit of a stretch, Jenny liked the challenge. Meanwhile, Eric still played many of his regular rounds from the blues with his friends, but didn't mind at all dropping down a set to hit alongside his daughter. It took some pressure off his game and provided a literal common ground for them to share.

When Eric finally teed up his ball, his mind was still elsewhere. He took a relaxed practice swing and then lined up behind the ball. He glanced one more time at the horizon and didn't even see the fairway. With an effortless swing he laced his ball right down the middle.

"Nice shot, Dad," Jenny said, somewhat surprised at the quality of his shot.

"Oh, thanks, sweetie," Eric responded, finally noticing his result. "It's amazing how easy the game can be when you don't over think what you're doing."

He reached down, grabbed his tee, and then took one last glimpse of the view. He snapped a final mental picture and then headed back to the cart.

By the time they reached number fourteen the sun had started to drop and the afternoon was cooling off to a perfect, mild temperature. Before they arrived at their tee shots in the fairway Eric steered the cart off to the side and headed across the rough to the edge of the tree line. He got out and walked over to a majestic pine. He looked it up and down as he approached and then slapped the trunk with his hand like he was patting an old friend on the back.

"Did you think we were going to play today without a stop here, Dad?" Eric asked, standing with his arm halfway around the girth of the wizened old tree. "This beauty has added a few inches over the years, but then so have we all. I'll never forget the time you pushed your drive over here and then tried to bite off a little too much to get to the green. Mom told you to just chip out to the fairway, but you assured her that you had plenty of room to work with. When your screamer ricocheted off this tree and smacked Mom in the arm I really thought this piece of lumber was going to send nearly five decades of marriage right down the tubes. I don't think I'd ever seen a look like that on her face before in my life. We were all worried that she was hurt, but somehow she didn't even flinch on impact. It was amazing; it was as though she knew beforehand it was coming and she'd mentally braced herself. She just shook her head and scowled, while you stood over here thinking really hard about what you could possibly say at that moment. I don't think your course strategy was ever the same after that shot."

Eric gave the tree one more slap and walked back to the cart with a smile. His dad's shot had been one of those strange family memories that would live on forever.

"I still can't believe he hit Grandma with his ball," Jenny said.

"It was one of those shots that you couldn't pull off if you tried. Hopefully he wasn't trying."

"I wonder what mom would do if you hit her with a shot?" Jenny pondered.

"Trust me, I'll do my best to never find out. Alright, back to our shots."

The sixteenth at Somerset started the final stretch of holes that were laid out in a straight line back to the clubhouse. Number sixteen was a moderate par three that played downhill to a large green. The generous landing area allowed for high shots to drop and stick, while low ball hitters could land shots short of the putting surface and let the topography take their ball safely aboard. Grandpa Donovan had always taken the low road and over the years he'd mastered this tee shot.

"Starting the homestretch, Dad. Here we are at the site of your one and only hole-in-one. Your punch six-iron always seemed to hit the right spot and send the ball on a smooth roll toward the hole. It's hard to believe you only got one ace out of all your rounds here. Countless times you scared the cup, but at least one time you got the line and speed exactly right. Alright, Jenny, step up there and do Grandpa proud."

"Thanks for putting on the pressure, Dad. I'll never get a hole-in-one that way."

"No pressure. That's a little ball and down there's a big hole. Nothing to it."

"If there's nothing to it why don't you have one yet?"

"It's a numbers game, Jenny. The more you play the more chances you have. I would have had more chances if I hadn't been working so hard to pay for my child's upbringing and save for her college education. Maybe I should change my strategy and let you pick up some more of the slack when you head off to school?"

"No, no, Dad. You're strategy is sound. Stick with it. You'll still get that hole-in-one eventually," Jenny said, grinning. She always appreciated her father's efforts and knew not to give him too much grief about his golf game.

"With the way you hit the ball, Jenny, you'll have one before you know it and I'll be able to enjoy it vicariously through you. I'm quite certain you won't have to wait until you are in your sixties like Grandpa. Hopefully I won't either."

On this day there were no additional aces for the Donovan family, just a couple of solid pars.

As they completed the last few holes, Eric began to feel more and more apprehension about arriving at the eighteenth green. He had been surprised and pleased when Jenny had agreed to join him for today's round. Her company had made the trip around Somerset far more enjoyable and relaxing. As they played, he could reflect on the past that was his father's while basking in the future that was his daughter's.

When they pulled up next to the final green, Eric stopped at the back of the cart and looked down at the clubs lining his bag. He knew he had to finally pull the one club that normally didn't reside there. Reaching down he carefully slid his dad's putter out of the bag. Jenny had already grabbed her putter and headed toward the green, but stopped when she noticed her dad's hesitation. She nodded understandingly and then swung her head toward the green motioning for her dad to head up. He smiled and joined her, walking up toward the hole with his arm firmly around his daughter.

Eric was away and went through the motions of lining up his putt. However, at this point his mind was no longer focused on golf. After taking his stance, he looked down and felt himself choking up when he saw his father's putter in his hands. Eric stood up and gathered his emotions before readdressing the ball and lagging his shot up to a few feet. He marked his ball and then watched as Jenny rolled her birdie attempt to just a few inches. She walked up and bumped her ball into the cup.

Eric replaced his ball and lined up the short putt. He made a confident stroke and noted the telltale sound of the ball clicking off of the marble face. He watched the ball roll slowly with the logo turning perfectly around the axis as it tracked toward the hole. The click of the impact was followed by the hollow clicking of the ball rattling around the bottom of the cup. He scooped his ball out as Jenny hoisted the flag and replaced it.

"Nice round, honey," Eric said, wrapping his daughter up in a hug.

"Thanks, Dad, you too."

"Thanks again for coming out today. I know it was pretty tough."

"I'm okay, Dad. It was just a little weird."

"I know, but it's what Grandpa wanted. Just remember this is our secret."

"Don't worry, Dad, I won't be telling anyone that we were out here spreading Grandpa's ashes across the sixteenth green."

They drove to the car and unloaded their clubs. Jenny stayed there and changed shoes while her dad headed off to return the cart.

As he walked back from the cart barn, Eric stopped and looked out over the course. The sun was sliding toward the horizon while the colors of the sky shifted toward the red end of the spectrum.

"Well, Dad," Eric said to the clouds. "You always loved to spend time here during your life and now you'll get to spend eternity at Somerset. The course will be forever graced with the spirit of Benjamin Donovan. Good bye, Dad. Enjoy your round."

***

Gryphen Reed, Somerset's head greens keeper, bent down and ran his fingers across the grass on the sixteenth green. All of the putting surfaces were growing nicely; however, this one was doing freakishly well. The blades were completely uniform and after pacing back and forth he couldn't find a single weed. He'd never seen a green this perfect before.

As he examined the agronomic wonder, he kept replaying a memory in his head from several weeks earlier. Gryphen had been working on a sprinkler on the fourth hole, which afforded him a view of the sixteenth. He'd seen a man and a girl playing alone. After they'd finished putting, the man had taken a small container and scattered something powdery across the green. Gryphen had intended to go check it out at the time, but was distracted doing other things and had forgotten all about it that day.

There were no longer traces of anything on the green itself. In the fringe along the edge of the green he did find several grainy chunks of whitish material, but they weren't rocks. He realized that they were pieces of bone.

Hmm, I wonder...

About the author

Tate Volino lives with his wonderful family in Osprey, Florida. This is his fourth novel. He enjoys playing golf, watching golf, and reading about golf.

After escaping from Corporate America at a reasonably young age he now spends his time writing, reading, and raising kids.

Made in the USA
Charleston, SC
22 February 2014